SWAN AND SHADOW
ORDINARY SORCERY
BOOK I

ALEA HENLE

ISBNS: 978-1-952735-01-1 (e-book), 978-1-952735-22-6 (print, as by Alea Henle), 978-1-952735-03-5 (inactive print, as by A.R. Henle)

Published by Crabgrass Publishing

Editing by Rare Bird Editing

Cover design by Augusta Scarlett

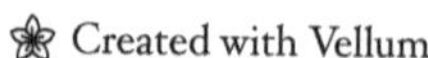 Created with Vellum

The swan on still St. Mary's Lake
Float double, swan and shadow!
William Wordsworth

A swan turned into a man on the best worst day of my life. Everything sucked big lemons until that moment.

My sneakers pounded against the path around the lake, kicking up bits of gravel that skittered in my wake. Crushed pine needles scented the air and made me long for fall and cups of hot chocolate. The air lay still and warm, but I worked up a nice layer of sweat. My Arden College T-shirt and matching green shorts stuck to my skin, although my hair streamed back from my pony tail. Even my fingers pinked up where I held tight to my cell phone, making my skin rosy against the black case instead of the usual beige. Alas, every twenty steps or so my wire-framed glasses slipped down my nose no matter how many times I shoved them back up.

Varied trees grew along the path. Pine and maple, oak and sycamore. A few leaves showed signs of turning orange and gold, but most remained green. I ran through a world of deep shadows and flickering lights. Lampposts cast ovals of light on the path at regular intervals. Here and there blue lights gleamed from emergency phone towers.

Mom would have a litter of kittens if she knew I'd gone off on a post-twilight run. She'd yell about danger lurking behind every bush and tree. To which my older sister would retort that at least I was wearing shoes and clothes I could run in, and they'd be off on their usual argument about how safe women were or could be in the world. Memories of their arguments rolled through me as I pelted on, the next-best thing to calling them.

Starlight reflected off the lake to my left, along with bits of moonlight from the waning crescent high in the sky. When the path moved farther from the water, the reflected light dwindled to firefly-flashes between thick foliage.

Across the lake, warmer yellow streetlights and lamps affixed to houses glimmered as though not-so remote stars flickered between branches. They grew closer and bigger as the path wound around to where the college's property ended and the suburb began.

The house at the edge of the development had a six-foot wrought-iron fence lining the path. Someone had cleared the ground between fence and lake. Or maybe it was like that to begin with: a rocky stretch with a clear view of the water and the bright lights of the college across the way.

Nothing burned so bright as an immense star blazing across the dark sky.

My legs ached, reminding me I hadn't run for a while. I backed up against the fence, skin cooling as my sweat dried.

By then, the arcing light hove into closer view. Not a star but a swan, bright and radiant as it danced in the air. Drew near, moved far, and back and forth. It circled and sank down toward the surface. White wings widespread and neck arched in the air reduced to a blurry blob in the reflection mirroring the flight from below.

Then the swan landed close by and swam nearer. Ended up half-turned away from me a bare five feet from the beach.

So beautiful, the sight stole my breath. The classic image of bright white plumage floating on an almost mirror-perfect surface. A few faint ripples marred the swan's reflection. An almost irresistible urge to pet it, should it come near enough, had me twisting my hands.

The swan reared up. Feet paddled hard, churning the waters, as it spread its wings wide. Wider. At least as broad as I stood tall. I hadn't realized swans grew that big. The gold-tinged beak sharpened, and I lost any idea of petting it, though I still wanted to touch the feathers.

A silvery aura outlined the bird against the dark waters and the distant shore.

In that moment, everything changed.

Wings shrank into human arms. The oblong body narrowed and lengthened to a broad torso. The beak dwindled into a nose, and the small white head expanded and grew brown hair. White feathers darkened to gold-tinged skin and shimmering lake waters lapped at a well-shaped backside.

The swan became a naked man.

Arms, legs—every part of *my* body froze in mid-breath. Mouth hung open. Body swayed. My hands gripped the iron fence posts tight.

One blink, two, three. The bird didn't re-materialize. The man remained there, naked as the day he was born and in the spot I'd seen the swan a moment earlier.

I'd never seen people in the water around here. Most of the shore was choked with thick weeds, so townies and college kids swam at the public beach on the far side. Or jumped off docks, of which none stood nearer than eight houses over. Even the most drunken or take-any-bet students didn't wade into the lake except for the Midnight Ice Plunge, and that took place in January not September.

Several feathers floated on the water around his thighs. Another rested atop his head as he stared down at the lake surface. Part of the feather's down tangled in the man's hair, but the shaft stuck out. It bobbled. Ridiculous, yet a sudden desire to hold the feather rose within me.

An instant later, a gust of wind blew it loose to dance on the breeze, wafting my way until it hovered above me. Letting go of the fence, I stretched out a hand. The wind died away, letting the broad, white feather float down into my palm—still warm from his body.

My legs weakened with this physical proof a swan had flown in, that I hadn't imagined it. I swayed for a moment, then slid down against the fence poles into a heap at the bottom. Wrapped my arms around my legs and hugged them to my chest. My lungs ached with every breath, as though the air turned to liquid ice.

The swan-turned-man failed to notice the feather's flight. Instead, he slapped the water, raising a great splash. Drops arced through the air, glittering as they fell back into the lake.

A moment later, he beat the surface of the lake full throttle. Shoulders flexed and arms lashed out. He fought the water as though an enemy bent on destroying him. Smacked the surface hard, each blow resulting in great waves and gouts. A few drops reached me despite the distance.

How did he resist crying out in pain? His hands must've hurt from the blows, yet he only huffed.

After a few minutes he ended as he'd begun—staring down. Head low and shoulders heaving.

My fingers stroked the soft feather over and over.

Then he turned and trudged out of the water.

Fine muscled legs, strong chest with a dusting of dark hairs, and . . . oh . . . even in the sharp contrast between light and shadow, he had an unmistakable face. An oval dominated by deep-set eyes and thick eyebrows. Angled cheekbones and stubble on his cheeks and upper lip. Starlight leached color from his skin, turning it silver-white against dark hair cut short.

Evan Roth.

Twice a week since the semester started—and all of last year before that—I had an excellent view of his face bent over a violin during orchestra rehearsal. One of the heart throbs of the orchestra, after the lead percussionist and the concert mistress.

Evan—a swan.

My fingers tightened around the feather.

Standing on dry land, he clapped his hands and a towel—white with red stripes—appeared out of nowhere.

He dried himself off with efficient snaps of the cloth against arms, legs, and torso.

Another clap, and the towel vanished.

More claps summoned clothes piece by piece. Dark brown shorts. Battered sneakers which he slipped on without socks. An Arden T-shirt matching mine only his had the Tree of Knowledge sprouting from a scroll of music instead of a book. Then a comb to run through his hair. He bent over the water once to check his reflection before he sent it back from wherever he'd summoned it.

Each spell made my hair stand on end as though I'd taken a too-big bite of mint ice cream.

Magic, magic, magic.

He still hadn't seen me.

I couldn't let him run off without talking to him, asking about it all, no matter that I'd meet up with him at the next rehearsal.

A fog seemed to have settled in around us. Not seen but felt. Certainty thrummed in my bones that I had this moment, this chance—if he went off, I'd forget.

I set my jaw and vowed it wouldn't happen.

"Hey, Evan!" Springing to my feet, I grabbed hold of the fence for steadiness.

He startled, arms pulling tight against his sides and hands rising in fists. Then he got a look at me and relaxed. He gave me a polite smile, the kind meant to keep people at a distance.

"Hi, uh, Viola, right? Clarinet."

In other words, he found me familiar but not memorable. I gave him points for getting my name right—*Vi*-ola, like violet, because no way am I a stringed instrument. But while he got the general category of instrument I played right, he guessed the actual one wrong. Unsurprising because he ranked as one of the orchestra's good lookers with instrument or without. Not me, in part because no one looks good close up when blowing through an oboe, or other wind or brass instrument for that matter. Indeed, oboists often joked the instrument was an ill wind that nobody blows good.

He nodded, then turned to walk off.

I lunged after him and grabbed his arm.

"How'd you turn into a swan? From a swan into a man, I mean, but you must've turned into a swan first to turn back."

He stiffened, eyes staring right into on me—close enough to show thin, spiky yellow rings spread through the green.

"Are you a sorcerer?"

"What?" My turn to draw back. "A sorcerer? Is that what you call yourself?"

"You are, aren't you?" His hand wrapped around my wrist, holding tight enough the sinews made a crackling sound. He stopped the instant I winced. "Tell me you are."

I shook my head, glasses slipping down my nose until I pushed them up with my free hand.

He grimaced and cursed. Not magical curses, or even creative. A lot of f-bombs. After which he stared right at me again—still holding my wrist, though not so tight.

"There's still time. Forget. You saw a swan. Fine. You saw me. Fine. You didn't see me change shape, or anything else sorcerous. Forget before it's too late. You're only safe if you don't believe."

He pulled free, waved a hand, and ran off.

I gaped, then snapped my jaw shut and pelted after him . . . but everything that could go wrong did. I tripped on the second step and lost seconds righting myself. A sudden wind whooshed up fallen leaves from the underbrush and blew them across the path ahead of me, making me slow and bring up my hands to shield my face. Somehow I knocked off my glasses off. They fell into the bushes with a clatter.

After several minutes of searching, I found them—without a scratch.

Too late to catch him, so I gave up.

He told me to forget sorcery, but he shouldn't have used it to slow me down and keep me from following him. That made me believe all the more, though his warning rang in my ears as I headed back to campus.

You're only safe if you don't believe.

❧   2   ❧

I forgot in under an hour the first time, starting the instant I set foot back on campus.

Sweaty and huffing, I emerged where the trail around the lake met the academic quad. The gravel path gave way to pavement. The pine-scented woods had already dwindled to bushes, but ended there. To my right lay the octagonal bandstand projecting out into the lake. Starlight reflected off the tin roof while I stood in comparative shadow despite a nearby lamp post.

Straight ahead lay another blaze of light: the library. One of Arden College's landmarks, it was architecturally insane: a multi-towered castle along the lines of Neuschwanstein by way of Disney's Cinderella—but rendered in glass, steel, and some kind of pink stone that stained skin if touched for long when wet. Drunk climbing the front facade during the first and last rainstorms of the academic year ranked as a popular pastime with certain groups of students.

Most students loved it because it held so many study rooms and quiet places for solo study. They even got used for that purpose at least half the time.

My favorite study room lay at the top of the tower. Few students realized it existed and was available for reservation, but I made friends with a faculty brat at the start of my freshman year. He knew all the best places.

Including the tower room, now dark as it loomed against the sky.

Earlier that evening, lights had blazed from every window. I'd gotten a clear view while wandering around campus talking to my younger sister. It was those two things combined, or what they represented, that sent me off into the woods.

In some ways, it started with my sister. Bea didn't make or receive calls as a general rule. Preferred texting or testing any new messaging software where she could write instead of speak. So when my phone had rung and her name popped up as caller, I answered.

"They're at it again." She didn't even wait for me to say hello.

"I'm sorry."

No need to ask the who and what. She knew I knew: our parents, arguing for the umpteen millionth time. They tried not to do so in front of us—me, Bea, and Rose, our older sister. Mom tended to wait until she and Dad were in their bedroom when they shared one, or stayed down in the living room with him after my sisters and I retreated to our bedrooms to get away from the tension in the air. Dad would head off for a walk or something and then return saying he wanted to show Mom something out in the yard.

They never seemed to realize how much we heard. Maybe not the actual words, but the sound of loud voices drifting out of the room or up the stairs. The way they stood, gestured, and looked at each other.

Mom had the three of us bim-bam-boom: Rose, then me two years later, and Bea two after that, so Bea got the worst of their increasing arguing. She stuttered, part of the reason she was the shyest of us to the point she always wore her dark brown hair with no bangs so she could hide behind and peep through. Although she had speech therapy and did regular exercises, when she got stressed or over-tired her stutter came back.

"What's different this time?"

"I d-d-dunno, but Mom's spitting b-bricks. Slammed the d-door."

Unusual. Both had tempers and quick tongues, but never did much more than exchange angry looks and snide digs in front of us, plus the intermittent never ceasing arguing behind closed doors. We'd got used to it.

"Are you okay?"

She gave a heavy sniff, and the sounds of static or something crumpling came through. "Yeah."

The mere fact she'd called instead of texting meant she didn't feel comfortable at home. Her room lay at the other end of the second floor, but if our parents started shouting she had no place in the house to get away from their voices.

"Is Mikey home? Maybe you can stay with her tonight." One of Bea's best friends lived two houses over.

"She's at her other mom's."

"How about Nissa? You could take a ride over. I'll pay if you don't have the money."

Bea had a better time in high school than me thanks to Mikey and Nissa. I started with two friends, one of whom moved away the middle of the first year, and the other got sucked into the top clique. Bea's friends stayed solid, and they signed up for a lot of the same courses so they could stick together.

"Mom will freak if I leave and she c-can't find me." Even though she hadn't lost the stutter, she sounded less tense.

"Text her and Dad that you need to work on a study

project you forgot to tell them about. And leave a note on the kitchen table. They'll survive." If they even noticed. No, they would. No matter how they felt about each other, they made it clear they loved all three of us. They just got lost in anger. Or something of that nature. I kept taking psychology classes every semester in hopes I'd figure them out. Hadn't worked out yet, and I was losing faith it ever would.

"Will it b-be okay?"

"Maybe they'll notice and wake up and do something. They're going to split sooner or later, if nothing else changes. Probably after you start college next fall." We could hope. The break would hurt, but less than the push-me-pull-you.

"I hate when they d-do this."

"I know. I hate you have to go through this. Text or call Nissa and see if she's okay with it, all right? Ask her to give you a hug for me."

"Miss you."

I couldn't study or focus on anything until I knew she'd settled. Ways I wasn't able to help ran through my brain. Making arrangements for her risked undermining her. Calling our parents and demanding they stop arguing was fruitless as neither would pick up the phone until the argument ended, at the earliest.

If things didn't improve, I'd sit them down when I went home for fall break and tell them to split up already. Maybe.

In the meantime, my legs twitched with restless energy. I texted Rose to update her on the situation, then wandered campus. I started by going around the residential quad, moved on to the academic quad, and ended up at the library. By which time Bea had texted her safe arrival at Nissa's.

As a result, I wound up taking the path between the theater and the library. There weren't any bushes, but several tall trees offered shade in the daytime and shadows at night.

From that angle, I had a fine view of the well-lit library entrance but folks there couldn't see much of me.

Including people I would have sworn I knew well, all headed into the library together.

First and foremost, my roommate Gloria stood out. The neon-yellow streak in her black hair glowed in the dark. She still wore the blue-and-purple patchwork top she'd paired with jeans that morning after asking me three times if I thought it clashed with her streak. We were in our second year as roommates, but still got along even though we came from very different backgrounds: me a white musician from a splintering nuclear family in a suburb of Philadelphia and her the Latinx folklorist scion of an old San Diego family known for profitable patents on audio tech inventions. We had a suite with two tiny bedrooms, separate bathrooms and a shared living area, but talked all the time and had a class together.

Yet somehow she'd skipped mentioning heading to the library tonight with our mutual friends Emilio and Ruth. Gloria and Ruth off on their own I could understand. A hook-up last year had turned into an ongoing affair, even if neither of them would admit to going steady. Why would the two of them head out with Emilio, and not me or our other friends Alex and Gordon?

The three didn't have any classes in common. I'd never seen them hanging around without at least one of the rest of us; usually Alex who was the center of our small group.

Nevertheless, there they went along with two others we'd palled around with last year on several occasions.

My older sister, Rose, would push me to go over and join them if I wanted to. "Nobody reads minds," she'd told me over and over. "They didn't think to ask, but so what? Assume they want you to go along and you'll be right more than half the time."

Or wrong. She never understood how hard I found even thinking about asking. Maybe she didn't mind if they told her she wasn't invited. Not me. Asking meant risking a no and getting told outright to go away no matter how politely—or allowed to accompany them on sufferance, which was as bad or worse.

Nobody texted me to see if I wanted to join them—and I checked a dozen times at least. Even dared text Gloria asking about her plans and did she want to get together and chat over the stupid assignment due the next day. To which she replied no, too busy, but how about tomorrow after breakfast.

The lights went on in the tower room. I couldn't see details from a distance, but Ruth's bright pink shirt shone through the windows.

Half of my friends got together without me.

That sent me off running around the lake.

Because having friends in college meant the world to me.

There wasn't enough money in the world to pay me to go back and relive high school.

I'd had no friends. None. Zip. Some of the other musicians in orchestra hung out with me on occasion, on the down-low, but nobody ever got close to me. When I walked through the halls, other students drew back and made faces. Whisper campaigns accused me of unnatural acts, although I never figured out why the top clique chose me to pick on. What had I done? Nothing! Nevertheless, they faked photos putting my face on porn stars. Someone filmed me in the school restroom one of the few times I was stupid enough to use it and edited the video to add animal parts and blood, then shared it on social media. No got caught or punished. By the end, some of the teachers even seemed to believe the stories about me.

When I arrived at Arden, I landed in a honey-sweet position of making actual friends. People who wanted to do things with me other than assault or threats or nasty tricks and touches and gaslighting. As in getting texts saying hey we're heading over to dinner or a movie or a party and do you want to go along?

It started with a frisbee disc landing on the sidewalk in front of me, less than an hour after my parents left campus. I looked around and saw a man headed towards the disc. Before I could think twice I grabbed it and tossed it at him.

Any time I closed my eyes, I could summon the memory of him stretching to catch the disc. Long and lean, with shoulder-length hair dark hair, gorgeous dark-brown eyes, and bronze skin with amber highlights.

He hadn't expected me to snap it hard and fast, and gave a full belly laugh. As attractive as I'd found him in motion, the amusement got me. Because he laughed at himself for under-estimating me; not at me.

"I'm Alex Noches." He stretched out a hand and I took it, trying to ignore my nerves jingling in excitement. A moment later he introduced me to the other players. Emilio and Alex were cousins, both Filipino-American but Alex was local while Emilio came from LA. He stood a head taller than Alex, but had the same general build and coloring. Emilio and Gloria, from San Diego, had a mock-quarrel going over the comparative merits of their hometowns, which they punctu-ated with graceful tosses to anyone except each other. Also playing were Gordon and Ruth, both whites from New England who sided with Gloria and fancied her.

Next thing I knew, we headed to dinner together and made plans for another game the next day. Picked up other folks at that point when several of us turned out to be in the same intro course.

From that first day, we spent a good chunk of our time together. Met up at least once a day, for lunch or dinner or frisbee or all three—and we lasted the whole of our first year.

We all had interests others didn't share—for instance, I was the only musician in the lot. So we had other friends we hung out with on occasion. Two dropped out by the end. One got sucked in by the baseball team in the spring, stopped hanging out with us. Another decided to transfer for some unknown reason. Nevertheless, the rest of us stayed tight.

Things dwindled over the summer to a couple of texts a week, but by arrangement we were all coming back to live in the same dorm—except for Alex and Emilio. They lived off-campus one street over, at home with Alex's father, a professor at the college. Emilio's parents preferred him living with family over staying in a dorm.

Last week we laughed and joked together, as though nothing had ever parted us. Met up for lunch or dinner once a day, partying together, and studying in our favorite tower room.

Best time of my life.

Only something, somehow, had changed.

I didn't know when or how—only when I realized it: the night I saw the swan turn into Evan.

At least it was Evan and not someone I knew well. If I'd seen a swan turn into someone I considered a friend, I'm sure I'd have turned around run so far and so fast I'd beat the wind.

Instead, I wound up back on campus in time to see my friends exiting the library with an addition: Alex. All my hope of having misunderstood, of there being a good reason for their not including me, dissolved.

Alex hadn't gone in with them, but he strolled along with the rest as they left. Fine and dandy in a white T-shirt and shorts. My first college friend, crush, and kiss. We'd fooled around some during finals last spring. Nothing since, though we'd texted a couple times a week over the summer, then hung out and laughed and flirted like crazy when we got back to campus.

All of which turned to ashes when I watched them laughing together—without me.

I didn't move, much. Shades of the past and all that jazz. Maybe I pulled out my phone—fingers fumbling as a thin layer of sweat covered them—and scrolled through the calls and texts and even emails to see if any came from any of them.

Nope. None.

All of my best friends, the people I cared most about in the world other than my family, got together without me. Had fun together without me. Didn't seem to miss me at all.

Their laughter shifted in my head into the mockery I'd faced in high school. I froze, knees and ankles locking, as I waited in the shadows. Watched. My phone dulled and dark in one hand. The other holding a feather.

My fingers rubbed against the fluff, the barbs.

I remembered.

If I hadn't seen them leaving together, I might not have.

My friends had a secret meeting without me.

So I kept my own secret from them. Twisted logic, but it made me feel better.

$$\text{❀} \quad 3 \quad \text{❀}$$

I still managed to forget sorcery that night.

Woke up as though nothing strange had happened the night before. Late, for that matter, on my side under a single sheet while my third back-up alarm blared a warning that if I didn't get my act together I'd be late to Professor Noches's class. Not acceptable, no way no how. He was nobody anybody wanted on their bad side and he started class right on time rain or shine.

He also happened to be Alex's father, so I'd seen him here and there over the past year, but he didn't cut me or anyone any slack for anything. The man had a spine straighter than a plumb line, though he looked like Alex aged up about three decades. Some wrinkles and gray hairs at the temple, and hair thinning just a tad on top. Slightly thicker waist with a bit of a pooch. He preferred polo shirts, slacks, and sneakers. He told me and Alex's other friends we could call him Sebastian, but I never managed it except when pushed, and the same held true for the others.

Alex had the cheerier and more outgoing disposition, but no one ever mistook him for anything but his father's son—

but with a more bendy spine. Plus dimples when he smiled. And less gravitas. Nevertheless, when he wanted to, he got as intimidating as his old man.

Noches wasn't someone I wanted to piss off by being late to class.

Shoving my glasses atop my nose, I jumped out of bed. Leapt across the clothes I'd left scattered on the floor and grabbed clean clothes from the closet. Whatever came to hand, which wound up being pink shorts and a bright purple T-shirt with a dragon curling over the shoulder. Slipped my feet into sneakers. Ran a comb through my hair. Snatched an energy bar from my stash.

I paused long enough to text Bea and check on her.

Then went for my backpack and stopped cold.

A white feather rested atop it. A wing feather. Long as my hand with a thick shaft and hundreds or thousands of soft, tiny barbs forming the vane.

Touching it brought everything back.

Everything.

At that moment Gloria yelled at me from the other bedroom in the suite.

"Pick up your feet or you'll be late. I'm off." Noches taught the interdisciplinary class she and I were in together. On symbolism of all things.

A choice between luxuriating in remembering the swan and Evan—or getting myself in gear to reach class before the professor did. Easy peasy. There'd be time to fondle the feather later.

I tucked it in the front pouch of my backpack, all the same.

Then forgot again within an hour.

Noches started discussion off with the image of a stop sign with big white letters on a red background—in the form of a triangle rather than six-sided—and got us arguing about whether or not this counted a legitimate road sign. Those students who liked the triangular version made up for their fewness with their volume.

After class, I slung my backpack over a shoulder and headed over to the archives to work a couple of hours at my campus job.

Leaving the classroom building had the effect of moving me into a different kind of world. Inside smelled of dust and sweat and lemon polish. Outside a fresh breeze tossed the first falling leaves in the air to make patterns on the lawns. Sunlight gave everything a gold tinge, in contrast to the hard, white-edged florescent lighting.

I quick-stepped along the path, then a warm, resonant voice called me.

"Heads up, Viola."

Even as I glanced around, I threw my hands up ready to catch the bright green disk spiraling toward me. Two steps to the side and I snatched it out of the air before it could curve around my back. Alex had given me a gentle toss, so of course I snapped my wrist as I sent it back on a wicked fast tangent.

He had to stretch to catch it, which meant I got to see him in action. Dark hair flying. Legs moving. Torso lengthening to the point his T-shirt rose above the waistline of his shorts. Arms out as though dancing across the green. An instant after the disc reached his hand, he whipped around and returned it.

My fingers smarted after I caught the rim on the return. Instead of tossing it, I held it hostage. Rolled it around my pointer finger as I tilted my head to one side and watched him.

Didn't take long for him to laugh, a full belly chuckle that always made me smile, and trot over to my side. He had a few inches on me, and he edged in close enough I cricked my neck a little to meet his warm gaze.

He wrapped his fingers around the frisbee rim, but I held on.

"Do I get my disc back?"

"Yours? Last catch keeps it, isn't that the rule we play by?" I held on as we both tugged, neither hard so it inched back and forth between us. "Don't you have class now or something?"

"I was on my way." He bopped the tip of my nose with a finger. "Then I saw you."

"How sweet." He'd thrown a disc at me with a moment's warning. I let go and he stumbled back a few steps, but righted himself fast. "What do you want?"

His eyes sparkled and his lips curved in a teasing smile. Disc still in hand, he crossed his arms over his chest and leaned back. A familiar pose, often the start to a very particular game: who'll break first?

Not me. I matched his posture and position, tapping one foot against the ground. He wanted the favor after all.

The seconds ticked by. His smile grew wider. I tilted my chin up and licked my lips. At length, he shook his head and laughed.

"If I wanted something, I could've texted you." Another bop on my nose.

"Uh-huh." I lowered my arms, grinning in victory. "So, what is it you want that you don't think texting would get you?"

"There's tilapia for lunch today, and it always goes fast." He tucked the disc in his backpack. "Grab me a fillet, will you? I'll probably get there too late for anything more than flakes."

"What's it worth to you?"

He mulled it over for a few moments, stretching. I kept my gaze fixed on his face, though I might've glanced out of the corner of my eye.

"Favor for favor." He hoisted his backpack over his shoulder.

"Fine. Where were you last night?" I kept my voice as light as I could, watching him close.

"Why?" Turning his wrist, he checked the time on his smartwatch. "Were you looking for me? I didn't get any texts."

"I went out for a run last night and thought I saw you over by the lake." By the library, though I wasn't quite brave enough to say as much. Or ask outright. Too many bad possibilities.

"The lake." He reared back, rubbing his chin with one hand. He shook his head. "I went for a jog. Happens now and then. I'm sorry I didn't see you, we could've run together. But I'm late now. Don't forget the tilapia."

"I won't." I heaved a sigh and pulled my backpack around to get my phone and set a reminder. Not that I'd forget, but it never hurt. Maybe he'd think to include me next time. Or at least not exclude me. Not drop me. All manner of possibilities floated in my head, paranoid or real.

Alex turned before he'd gone more than a couple steps, and waved at me.

"I owe you!" He pressed two hands to his mouth and blew me a kiss. Then ran off.

A moment later, an invisible kiss landed on my lips. I jumped at the unexpected caress. As though he hadn't run away so fast, but taken the time to give me a proper kiss.

I saved the reminder and slipped the phone back in, brushing the feather.

One touch brought back everything. The swan, Evan, sorcery.

Rather than risk forgetting yet again, I fastened the swan feather in my hair so it brushed my skin, reminding me. A trickier proposition then it sounds, because none of my barrettes held the quill for long, plus it kept banging against my glasses. I wound up jury-rigging a solution with a rubber band because I didn't have any ponytail holders at hand.

Some people noticed. Most didn't do much—rolled their eyes or got a chuckle out of it.

Professor Noches, on the other hand . . . We should've passed like the proverbial ships in the night through the second-floor corridor in Guardian Hall. That's what happened the previous week when I got out of Psych and he wrapped up teaching some other course at the far end of the hall. I headed out one way, he headed back to his office the other, and nothing more major than a nod happened.

This time, he stopped in the middle of a corridor. His gaze fixed on the feather, or so I figured out when his eyes tracked me as I walked toward him.

I had no interest in sticking around the hallway any longer than I had to. The college—or someone somewhere—had turned off the air conditioning already. Classrooms had windows and a chance at a breeze or cross-vent, but most of the hall went stuffy and smelled of sweat and dust and other things I didn't want to analyze.

"Interesting decoration." He lifted an eyebrow and pointed a finger at the feather. "Your choice for Thursday's presentation, perhaps?"

Way to put me on the spot. He'd gone over the assignment earlier—pick something and discuss some of the ways it either served as a symbol or incorporated them.

I didn't know what showed on my face, but he laughed. Not a bad sound, but after four years of high school torment, I recognized when someone was laughing *at* me.

"What, haven't you been thinking about this ever since class? It's in the syllabus." Another laugh, though this one seemed more general.

"Maybe I will use the feather. I hadn't decided on

anything else." Hadn't thought about it much, either. "I just found it yesterday."

"Found it." He went so straight his spine cracked, then gestured at the feather. "May I?"

"Okay." I declined to pull it out, after the trouble I'd had getting it fixed in my hair to begin with. But saying no didn't seem right, either. He hadn't asked that much. "I guess."

Noches didn't move any closer. He stretched out an arm and ran a finger down the quill. A chill rippled through me, sort of like a cold version of static electricity. I shivered as goose bumps lined my arms, although they faded before long.

When he pulled back, he rubbed his fingers. The pointer had a dull, waxy look, as though blood drained from it. Within a few moments, the color came back and his whole hand had a ruddy bloom under the bronze skin.

"That's a swan feather."

"Yeah, there was one on the lake the other day." I ran a hand over my hair and the feather. My hair seemed smooth, but touching the feather vanes resulted in a residual shock and a few goose bumps on my arm, much less than before.

"It's back, then." He shook his head. "I thought it had left."

"You've seen it?" Had he seen anything else, such as it turning into Evan? We might not even be talking about the same swan.

"From a distance. There used to be a mated pair of swans in the lake, long ago, but no one's seen more than one for a while. They can live a long time." His lips tightened and eyes narrowed, then he shook his head and wagged that same finger at me. "In case anyone hasn't warned you, swans are mean and fight nasty. Best stay away."

"Got it."

He nodded. Pulling a phone from his pocket, he started texting away as he walked down the corridor. I turned to watch him—he didn't bump into anything. Students rushing for classes made way just as they did for me, although I got an elbow or two knocked against me in recompense for standing in the middle of the hall while they made a wide circle around him.

Gloria noticed the feather, too, when I stopped off in our suite after dinner to grab my oboe.

She sat sideways on the blue cushy chair by the window, bare feet dangling over the arm. At some point after lunch, she'd pulled her hair back in a messy knot. One hand held a battery-powered fan directed at her head and upper body. She wore a blue boat-neck top and lightweight blue capris, and breeze blew in through the open window, but all the same her skin shone with a layer of sweat.

"Hey, what's this?" She made a gesture for me to turn around.

I rolled my eyes, since I hadn't changed clothes and she'd seen it all at class and lunch, but obeyed.

She had much better fashion sense than I did. I was better at colors, but whatever I wore was just clothes except for rare, special circumstances requiring hours of preparation. She put clothes on and they became an outfit. Day-in-day-out she ranked one of the best dressed people around, if not *the* best dressed. And nice and smart, on top.

"I like the feather. It suits you. Would work better if your shirt had some white in it—aren't you supposed to be good with colors?"

"Yeah, well, it was an impulse." I stroked a hand over the soft down.

"Go with it." She turned both thumbs up, even though it meant tilting the personal fan down so it made the loose hem of her shirt flutter. "Where'd you get it?"

"Saw a swan out on the lake last night, over by the library."

Gloria nodded, giving no indication this meant anything to her. No wince or start or any sign of awareness that I might have seen her with the others. Instead, she went back to fanning herself and gave a big yawn.

She didn't come clean about getting together with our other friends the night before. No more than Alex had, or Emilio or Ruth. Not in class or at lunch.

Every single one acted all day as though nothing had changed.

❊ 4 ❊

alking into the music building made me shiver in a good way, as anticipation built along with welcome air conditioning. In a few moments, I'd enjoy the company of people who understood the difference between F and F sharp plus the pleasure of the music itself. This early in the semester I hadn't heard the pieces we'd play umpteen hundred times so they still counted as new and fresh. Later in the semester, I'd sometimes get bored while waiting on the violins or violas or brass section to polish some part to the conductor's satisfaction—second oboists didn't get interesting parts. Some other musicians joked no one could tell the difference between a good oboist and a bad one. All the same, I almost always enjoyed listening and participating as many different instruments combined to form a single piece of music.

Evan distracted me this time.

Then again, the reverse seemed also true.

I slid into the rehearsal room a couple of beats ahead of the conductor: tall, broad, white-haired Professor Rodriguez. Turned my phone to silent and tucked it in my shorts pocket, then set to work assembling my instrument and fastening the reed in the mouthpiece. Nothing I hadn't done a thousand times before while all around me folks started tuning up. Strings, brass, other wind instruments—a few strains here and blasts there.

My blood started pumping, warming me up despite the heavy air conditioning.

Until little prickles of cool ran over my head and neck. Not all of me, just the right, which happened to be where the feather hung in my hair. As though a small, personal rain cloud hovered over me and let loose drops on that side.

The prickles were intermittent—stronger, then weaker, then strong, then gone. I caught Evan staring at me from his seat among the second violins and put the clues together quick enough even though he glanced away as soon as I caught his eye.

We wound up playing a game of peekaboo the whole rehearsal. I did more peeking than him—the pieces we worked on had more work for violins, as usual, than oboes, at least second oboes. Though I tried to keep my perusal discreet, as musicians tended to gossip.

Evan put his violin and bow in the case and snapped it shut while I had to disassemble my oboe, pull a cloth through to cleanse spit from the body, and place the pieces in their proper place in my case. I moved fast. All the same, by the time I finished Evan had booked it out the door.

Grabbing my case, I jogged after him, shoe soles squeaking against the tiled floors. Left the practice room at the same moment he exited the building—and glanced back at me.

"Hey, Evan—"

He flicked his fingers, and the rubber band holding the feather in my hair broke with a twang. The ends snapped against my skin, raising welts.

He shouldn't have done that.

I stopped long enough to snatch the feather from the floor, but left the broken band behind. Holding my instrument case in front of me, the feather clutched in one hand, I burst outside.

Evan had jogged halfway down the path. His green T-shirt and shorts faded into the growing gloom of twilight, making tracking him hard—but not impossible.

"All I want is to talk!"

He didn't stop. If anything, he started moving fast.

I ran faster. Huffing and puffing, with my instrument case banging away at my thigh and my right hand cradling the feather.

He carried his violin case in both hands, until he managed to make it vanish somehow. His hands hung free at his sides as he sped up. His shoes kicked up grass clippings from the day's mowing. These blew into a cloud, obscuring his passage.

Taking a deep breath, I lifted my case high enough to cover my eyes for a few minutes and darted through. Held my breath. Gritted my teeth.

No way would I lose him.

On the other side, the sun had set and the world filled with shadows. Evan managed to become almost one with the shadows.

Faint, glowing green footprints continued a diagonal path towards the lakeside.

I followed the glimmering path, footprint for footprint. Sweat slicked my hair against my head. A few pieces of grass stuck to my face and arms, and worst of all my glasses fogged, but I persisted. Time enough to wipe them off when I'd tracked Evan down.

The footprints led me to the same lakeside path I'd run along the night before. If anything, they showed brighter when pavement gave way to gravel. Flecks in the stones caught light and magnified it.

My legs ached, not least my bruises, and I started to tire. Maybe I slowed down the last length, but it didn't make much difference.

Evan bought himself too much of a lead.

By the time I reached where the path veered closest to the lakeshore—in front of the house with the wrought-iron fence—a few pieces of clothes remained to indicate Evan had paused there.

A T-shirt flung to one side. Shorts and undies in an untidy pile atop battered sneakers.

There on the water, about ten feet from shore, floated a white swan.

Beautiful as the night before, if not more. Creamy white plumage, ruddy beak, black around the edge of beak and eyes.

My chest heaved from my exertions. Legs shook a little, muscles sore and wobbling.

The swan stretched his neck and gave a mocking honk.

A moment later the clothes vanished.

"Wretch! You knew I wanted to talk to you." My hand spasmed and I dropped my oboe case, which hit the gravel with a thud. "What's so bad about talking? All I need is a little information, that's it. Stupid bird."

The swan gazed at me for a long moment, then turned away. He paddled a diagonal line across the lake, gathering speed. Stretching out his neck and wings, he took flight.

Gorgeous—white down against the midnight-blue sky— and frustrating as all get out.

"Evan!" Futile, but the name burst from me all the same. I didn't move just in case he turned back. No such luck. Instead I tracked his flight across the sky, left alone and without answers. "Damn it."

Something creaked behind me. I whipped around,

fumbling for the phone I'd tucked into my pocket what seemed like aeons ago.

The gate in the iron fence swung open, hinges protesting. A woman stepped through then stopped an arm's length away. Pure white hair glittered in the light of a nearby lamppost, silvering her smooth features and pale skin. She stood an inch shorter than me, but her straight posture gave her extra stature. Sandals graced her feet, and she wore a crisp tailored blouse with slacks.

"How do you know my son?"

"Your son?"

She took a step closer. The shadows made it hard to see details, but I couldn't miss the likeness—an older, female version of Evan.

"You called him, even if he ignored you." A small huff escaped the older woman. "He does that to me. Often."

So she hadn't seen me with Evan, just the swan. "You mean the swan?"

"I mean my son when he is himself. The swan . . ." she shook her head and gave a low, whistling sigh. "I have no hold on him when he is not himself. But you have not answered my question. How do you know him?"

"We're both in the orchestra." I picked the oboe case off the ground and brushed dirt off the soft fabric top-layer.

"Ah, that would explain why you look familiar. Did you play in the concert last May?"

"Yeah."

"Well done. I enjoyed it quite a bit." The woman pointed toward the white feather still tucked between my fingers. "Yet playing in the orchestra does not explain how you recognized him as the swan."

I busied myself dusting every speck of dirt off the case—and watched her out of the corner of my eyes. She stood, still and calm, waiting. I broke first.

"I saw him change, last night."

"*Last* night?"

"Yes. Swan to human. It had to be sorcery, he said as much but he wouldn't explain. He told me to forget." The suggestion still stung.

"But you remember." Evan's mother nodded.

"Sort of." I stroked the white down of the feather. "I keep almost forgetting, but I don't . . . I don't want to."

"He should have done more for you." The woman blinked hard and shook her head. "Forgive him. He does not control all his actions. So that I am clear on all details: you saw him change form last night . . . I take it you were not a sorcerer, a practitioner of magic, before that moment?"

"No."

"Then you have a great decision before you, and little time left in which to make it." A quick breeze whipped the feather from my clutches, wafting it to rest on her hand. "I am Regina Roth. What my son did not do for you, I will—to ensure you have sufficient information to make an informed choice."

❈   5   ❈

Getting information involved drinking tea. Regina's choice, not mine. Peppermint, which meant the house—or what I could see of it from the breakfast nook—smelled lovely as it mixed with the scents of flowers and balsam.

The nook itself took the form of a glass enclosure jutting out from what seemed to be a family room with a big television, fireplace, and soft couches. Almost a greenhouse, with climbing plants hung over elaborate trellises and small trees in big clay pots. The glass windows offered a full view of the backyard sloping down to the fence and lake. The dark wood table gleamed beneath bright yellow placemats with ironed napkins. Matching yellow cushions covered the chair seats.

I sat as straight as when I played the oboe. My back didn't touch wood. My feet lay flat on the floor with my instrument case tucked between them—not for fear of theft but so as not to knock even a leaf off one of the plants.

Regina didn't return the feather. Instead she placed it on the brick mantel over the fireplace—where it joined several dozen others.

She offered a gracious welcome without any hint of annoyance as she bustled about heating water for the tea and setting out cups, saucers, sugar bowl, and creamer.

This part of the house spoke of wealth such as I'd seen only on TV or films. The bone-white china alone had a dainty, gilt-edged pattern I hardly dared breathe on lest I break something. At home, we never used the good china. Both my parents worked decent jobs, but we were far from rich. I attended Arden thanks to a very generous scholarship that covered all my tuition and half room and board with a guaranteed work-study position on campus.

Regina told me to call her by her first name. After filling both our cups with hot, minty liquid, she settled into the chair opposite me. I mirrored her, adding a little cream and few specks of sugar. Steam rose from the surface, so I wrapped cool fingers around, to keep from drumming them against the table.

Bending over her cup, Regina blew on it. The liquid rippled, and all at once the amount of steam on both cups reduced. She lifted the cup and sipped.

The tea was tasty and just the right temperature, though I took a no more than few sips, to be cordial before setting the cup down with utmost care. I wasn't thirsty for anything but answers. But as a guest in someone else's house, I waited with as little fidgeting as I could manage.

She drank at least half her tea before settling the cup back in the saucer with a soft chime.

"Now, when did you see my son change form?"

"Last night." I drew in a deep breath and exhaled as though sustaining a crescendo.

"At what time?"

"About nine. I think."

"House, what is the time?" Regina tilted her head to the side.

"The time is now 9.05 P.M." A mellow woman's voice said.

"Then you have tonight left." Regina took another sip of tea.

"For what?"

"To accept the truth of sorcery. If you don't, then your mind will rewrite the events of the last days in keeping with whatever you believed before."

"But I've already accepted that sorcery exists." I shook my head, blood pulsing at my temples. "Why else would you have caught me talking to a swan?"

"You said you keep almost forgetting seeing my son change form."

I nodded.

"Then you have not accepted the truth of sorcery. If you had, you wouldn't forget."

"Okay." I snapped my mouth shut and took a deep breath to keep my tone polite. "Then what do I need to accept?"

"With sorcery *anything* is possible."

"Isn't that the definition of magic?" I lost my cool and rolled my eyes. "That you can do things that aren't otherwise possible? Break all the rules?"

"The rule of sorcery is that there are no rules." She sipped her tea—maybe to hide a smile.

"Very funny."

"I am quite serious." She put her hands together and held them over the table, then let them fall open as though cupping something—or imitating a book. "Imagine, if you will, that somewhere, somehow, there exists a great book of nature which contains all the laws of nature: gravity, motion, supply and demand. People who do not accept the truth of sorcery may seek to discover these laws. Sometimes people talk of breaking the laws of nature, but what they mean is discover any corollaries or ways around a given law. They're not breaking the laws. Sorcerers, on the other hand, know that under the right circumstances any law in the book of nature can be revised and rewritten." She slapped her hands together, and the crack echoed around the room. "Because *anything* is possible."

"Okay." I played along. "So, if anything is possible, why doesn't it happen?"

"Anything being possible does not mean that anything is probable, nor that rewriting the book of nature is easy. It is not. Disbelief has a power all its own. Indeed, one of the laws of nature, at least according to Western practices, dictates that under most circumstances disbelief rules over belief. Therefore, performing any spell in front of a person who doesn't believe it is possible is exponentially more difficult than doing so before a person who believes. To the point of impossibility, which is why most of us don't bother."

I took a deep draft of tea while trying to work through the ramifications.

"So, Evan couldn't have turned from a swan into a human if I didn't somehow believe it was possible?"

"If you didn't believe it possible *and* he knew you watched, then he might not have been able to change." She tilted her head to one side. "If he didn't know you were there, it might have been a little harder for him, although not so much so that he didn't change."

"This is making my head hurt." I rubbed my temples. Took another sip of peppermint tea, which soothed mind and body as it went down.

"Magic does that a lot." For the first time, she gave me a wide smile. A real one, wide and welcoming.

"So what happens now?"

"We wait." She shook her head and extended her hands, palms out. "You'll either accept or you won't."

"And then?"

"If you do accept the truth of sorcery, you need lessons. I

know of people who turned into sorcerers and learned things the hard way. I'm one myself and none of us recommend it. It's hard enough being turned, when the sorcerous worlds is dominated by born sorcerers who drink the rules of sorcery with their mother's milk." Her eyes grew distant for a moment, then fixed on me as her lips twisted in a lop-sided smile. "I would be happy to teach you."

"What would that involve?" Having someone help me figure things out sounded wonderful, but I refused to leap at her offer.

"Covering the basics, showing you some spells I know and use on a regular basis and how I work them, and giving you a safe space in which to practice." Regina ticked them off on her fingers. "And, of course, helping you find other teachers. It's a good idea to learn from as many and as different sorcerers as possible, since everyone has different ideas of what is possible with magic."

I accepted her offer after as much thought as I could manage. We settled that I'd come for my first lesson in two nights. If I didn't show up, she'd assume I didn't accept sorcery and forgot. All very simple, in comparison to the task ahead of me: accepting or not.

Before I left the house, or even the table, she took care to offer one last piece of advice.

Or, more specifically, a warning.

"Assuming you do accept sorcery, do not drink any alcohol or take any mood-altering drugs, nothing hallucinogenic." She set the cups and saucers in the kitchen sink; the china chimed as it met stainless steel. "Caffeine is acceptable, but don't consume any more coffee or tea or soda than you're used to. At least, not until you've mastered the basics of magic."

"Why not?" I picked up my instrument case, wincing as my muscles ached at the weight after carrying it while I ran. The prohibition didn't sound too difficult to follow. Irritating, yes, but I almost never consumed more than one or two drinks at parties.

"If you believe anything is possible, then you could work spells under the influence that you wouldn't dream of sober." She actually wagged a finger at me. "I realize you're a college student and this is asking a lot, but trust me on this. It's not worth it."

❦ 6 ❦

The temperature had dropped quite a few degrees by the time I left the house. A cool breeze blew up from the lake, carrying the croak of frogs and the haunting cries of loons. A few stray leaves, half green and half brown, flew by. Not quite fall, but no longer full summer. Stray goose bumps formed along my arms and legs. My T-shirt and shorts didn't keep me warm without more active movement, but this wasn't the place to jump into action.

Light spilled from bright floodlights nestled high among the eaves and set to detect motion. I cast a sharp shadow against the grass and the stones paving a path down to the gate to the lake. Twice I stepped half-off a paving stone and had to correct before I tripped and fell. It made me wary and slower than usual.

Regina accompanied me. At first she lagged, her sandals slapping against the stones. The back of my neck prickled. I couldn't put my finger on anything, but I preferred seeing her to having her right behind.

After the second near-trip, she slipped around me.

"Follow me."

Although having her before me doubled the shadows, it did help. I stayed a few steps back, close enough to plant my sneakers on every stone paver a breath or two after she'd left it.

At the bottom of the slope, the gate swung open with a minor creak. Regina ushered me out, then stood frowning up at the lamppost casting a circle of light over this part of the path. Others formed a line of beacons leading to campus, but dark gaps lay between them.

"Are you sure you don't want a ride?"

I'd declined when she first offered, back up at the house. Unease rippled through me. Odds were I'd be fine. I could run pretty fast, although the oboe case would slow me down, but my muscles ached after last night's run plus the dash earlier this evening. All the same, the notion of riding in a car with her the long way around—since the subdivision didn't have a direct road connecting it to campus—didn't appeal.

Before I made a decision, a crunching sound had both of us whirling around.

"I'll walk her back." Evan moved out of the shadows into the pool of lamplight. Golden highlights glinted in his brown hair as he toweled it dry, snapping the fabric back and forth. He wore the same clothes as earlier, down to his scuffed white sneakers, and seemed dry except for his hair.

He tossed the towel into the air with a flick of his fingers, and it vanished before it could hit the ground.

"I'm so glad you're back safe." Regina wrapped her arms around him in a quick, tight hug.

She moved fast. I barely took a breath before she blew by. The action startled me, as she hadn't seemed a major-hugger type.

Evan patted her back. They stood at the edge of the light, sideways to me. He glanced at me over her shoulder, his mouth twisted to the side. "I see you're still here."

"I've told her the truth of sorcery, since you didn't." Regina pulled back and wagged a finger at him, although she had an indulgent look on her face.

"I thought as much." His green eyes remained fixed on me. "But I'm the one who may have turned her. I know the duty."

"I've offered to teach her, if she makes the final leap," she said. "You've got more than enough to do already."

"And little enough time."

Regina flinched. Her back straightened with a snap.

"That's uncalled for. You owe both of us an apology."

"Sorry, Mom." He ducked his head, running a hand across the back of his neck. "I know you're doing your best."

"Acknowledged." Regina raised one eyebrow. "And for Viola?"

"Please allow me to make up for my rudeness by escorting you to your dorm." He offered a bow, although his mouth had a sardonic twist.

"You may."

A second's silence, then he burst out laughing. The sound rang out across the water, a faint echo returning. His expression changed, turning bright and almost cheerful. "I may do what? Make up for my rudeness or escort you to your dorm?"

"We'll see." The laughing Evan would make for decent company, the sulky one not so much. But I wasn't stupid enough to decline. "I'll at least accept your company as far as campus."

After an exchange of glances between mother and son, and a final smile from Regina, we got underway. Evan set a swift pace. Although he didn't grab my hand and drag me along behind, I felt a distinct breeze impelling me along in his wake. Maybe a literal wind whipped me along—or just the power of his determination.

The speed did get my blood moving and thus warmed me up.

Yet it also meant I moved fast for the second time that night with my oboe case banging against my side. I switched it back-and-forth between hands until both arms and legs ached. The case wasn't made for quick hikes. My parents hadn't bought a light, bells-and-whistles case with extra padded sides and a shoulder strap. Instead, I had a cheaper and tougher to destroy version that resembled a hard-sided briefcase and weighed several pounds.

I carried it, risking sores on my hands and bruises on my thighs, but Evan found it more irritating. He kept glancing back at me and frowning at the case until he halted and held out his hands.

"Here, give it to me."

I took all of a moment to consider before handing it over. Underestimating the weight, he lurched to one side. Glared at it.

"I've done enough little things tonight, what's one more?" He clapped a hand against the side.

It vanished.

His clothes disappearing I could accept. I didn't care about them, and enjoyed looking at him without them. Same deal with the towel.

But those were his. The oboe and case belonged to me.

"Wait, where did you send it?" I resisted looking for it to appear behind a tree. Nothing else had, after all. Plus, we stood at the edge of a pool of lamplight with pine trees all around.

"Wherever you usually keep it." Evan shrugged. "I sent it to its home."

"As long as home is my dorm and not home home." What a mess that would be, having it manifest in my bedroom at home. At least at this time of night no one would be—should be—in there. Unless Dad had moved out of the master bedroom and took over mine, which had happened twice last year.

"Nah, it didn't drain me much so it probably stayed local."

"Probably?" All sorts of unpleasant possibilities flashed before my eyes.

"If it didn't, let me know and I'll summon it back."

"Let you know how?" I braced both hands on my hips and glared at him.

He sighed—long and dramatic, although he didn't roll his eyes—then snapped his fingers and his phone appeared in his hand. The surface sprang to light as his fingers flew and entered the password. He tilted his head, an expectant look covering his face. "Your number?"

I gave it to him, then my phone rang. Stopped a moment later.

He snapped his fingers again and his phone vanished.

"Happy now?"

Happier, though I refused to admit it. "How am I supposed to reach you if you don't keep your phone around?"

"I check my calls at least a couple of times a day."

"That's all?" Visions of missing my oboe and paging him constantly in search of it with him not answering had me clenching my teeth.

"I promise you'll have your oboe case tomorrow, if you don't find it waiting in your closet or under your bed tonight."

We stared at each other for a long moment. I bent first. "Okay."

Whirling around, this time I led the way. He followed hot on my heels. His breath warmed the back of my neck, although he didn't say anything.

And didn't say anything.

Still nothing.

"Well, aren't you going to warn me or anything?"

"Not here." Evan shifted to walk alongside me. Although he appeared calm and cool, a few drops of sweat beaded his forehead. A woodsy musk emanated from his body. "We need more distance."

He refused to explain distance from what. Once we reached the campus, his stance changed. His shoulders and arms loosened, neck cracking as he rolled his head around.

Instead of taking a path across campus to the residential quad, he kept to the lakeside. I followed, in hopes acquiescence now would gain me answers soon.

We ended up in the bandstand. An octagonal tin roof covered a wide space at one end of a very long concrete jetty. It lay open on five sides, with wooden railings painted green along the edges facing the water. The orchestra accompanied a musical here late last spring, with our conductor grousing the whole time about the lousy acoustics.

The jetty and bandstand were better known as the stage for Shakespearean plays. Every year the theater department performed one out of doors. Never rained out, according to the count kept by the student newspaper, and always with elaborate special effects. Last fall they did *The Tempest* for parents' weekend, which filled my Shakespeare-nut father with delight. I'd sat in the audience with him and Mom and Bea as we all oohed and ahhed at the shipwreck staged ten feet off the jetty.

A few students studied on the veranda outside the library, close against the well-lit glass walls, but no one lurked anywhere near. Although voices did sometimes carry across water. At any rate, Evan whirled around with a finger pointing out and then nodded his head.

"Now we can't be heard." He leaned against the railing, arms crossed. "What did my mother tell you?"

"That I have to accept anything is possible with magic, or

I'll forget." I rubbed my hands along my arms and kept my legs moving so as not to cool down too fast.

"You'll be lucky to forget."A somber expression crossed his face, but he shook it off. "Nothing more?"

"Not to drink alcohol or take drugs."

"Nothing about accidental sorcery?"

"No."

He made a disgusted sound and hit the railing with a clenched hand.

"It's reason number one not to accept sorcery, not to believe." Rising from the railing, he walked over in front of me and laid warm hands on my shoulders. "You're only safe if you don't believe."

The same refrain as last night.

"Okay, so what should she have told me?"

"When you accept sorcery, it fills you. You can do spells, yeah, but not just consciously. You're also at risk of doing magic by accident." He frowned, gaze turning distant for a moment. "You know the tale of Circe?"

"Wha . . ." I reared back, frowning at his sudden shift of topic. "The ancient Greek sorceress who turned men into pigs?"

"She might not have meant to do the first one. But if she'd accepted the truth of magic, then being mad and pointing a finger at a guy and saying 'you're a pig' could be enough." He lifted one hand long enough to point out at the lake. A cloudy shape formed there for a moment, wisps of smoke and fog coalescing into an unmistakable pig shape complete with bristles, ears, and snout—then dissipated. "Maybe she was sorry after, maybe not, but the guy was still a pig."

"So, I might turn guys into pigs?" The possibility did give me pause, although not the way he intended. If I listed the people I'd like to turn into pigs, it'd run as long as my arm at least. Especially if I could change women as well as men into pigs. I might even be tempted to attend a high school reunion in that case.

"Or worse."

It still didn't sound all that bad.

"You could be cursed. I'm a case in point,"—he patted his chest—"cursed since forever. I live half a life and count myself lucky if I spend twelve hours out of twenty-four as myself."

"You mean you don't change into a bird because you want to?"

"On occasion." He let out a whistling sigh. "It's a release, of sorts. Flying. Away. But most of the time changing isn't a choice. It's because I have to. Because I'm cursed. So don't accept sorcery. Disbelieve. Stay safe."

My head ached as I tried to parse the meaning out. Tried, not succeeded, because it didn't make sense. "But if magic means anything is possible, then can't you break the curse by disbelieving yourself?"

"If it were that easy, don't you think I'd have done it? Some people born to sorcerous families disbelieve and stop being sorcerers, but it's hard even when they're not cursed." He dropped his hands from my shoulders and grabbed my hands instead. "To go from believing to not believing, you have to let your life be rewritten without any magic you wouldn't otherwise have believed. When it happens, if it happens, it's usually between ages five and fifteen, you know, when normal kids stop believing in Santa Claus and the tooth fairy and start to consider themselves grown-up. Problem is, I was cursed before that. Even if I'm willing to pay the price, I haven't found the way. Sorcery doesn't make lives any better, it just means you fuck things up more ways. So don't believe."

Magic messed things up because anything was possible.

Anything.

Evan must've read something on my face, for he leapt

towards me and grabbed my arms. His fingers pinched tight as he clutched me, shaking his head.

Or I shook mine.

The world remade itself in the space of a moment.

I believed and accepted.

7

My first day as a turned sorcerer stank. Believing and accepting sorcery opened my eyes, ears, and every sensory organ to a changed world.

So distracting.

And irritating.

Everywhere I turned, new evidence of sorcery manifested —all of which I'd managed to spend the whole of my life ignoring.

The following afternoon, I got hijacked into playing frisbee with Alex, Ruth, and Emilio. Not a game, more hacking around.

Last night's cool snap had settled in, but none of us adapted yet. We all wore shorts and T-shirts with various slogans, and sneakers or sandals. I had my hair back in a pony tail the breeze kept swishing against my neck.

Ruth sent a long, arcing toss Alex's way. He batted it over to Emilio with a quick flip rolled high before falling almost into his lap. In turn, he sent a swooping curve right back to Alex that made him run and stretch.

Under normal circumstances, I'd have watched Alex in motion.

Except, in the background, one of the groundskeepers used wind to clear the first batch of fallen leaves from the lawn. Arden made a point of being virtuous stewards of land, environment, and climate—and the marketing team never let anyone forget it. No one ever used a leaf blower. The groundskeepers cleared the fields the old-fashioned way: rakes and tarps.

Yet there stood a woman in a green and golden-brown uniform directing miniature whirlwinds to pick up leaves and plop them atop a growing pile on the dull brown canvas.

Magic.

Nothing else offered a satisfactory explanation for that or the dozen other impossible acts I saw over the day. The kinds of things no one could ignore, except everyone did. Ignore them, I mean.

Books whooshing through the air, smooth as a disc, to pile themselves on a library cart.

A janitor sweeping up broken bits of pottery in the cafeteria at lunchtime, then the bits reforming into an unbroken plate that the man deposited on the rack for dirty dishes.

A student I didn't recognize snapped their fingers and changed the color of their backpack from blue to blue with big purple flowers in the blink of an eye.

I, on the other hand, didn't manage a single conscious spell the whole day. Snapping my fingers and clapping my hands made my skin redden and ache. Pointing at things made no difference either. I didn't quite dare try people, after Evan's warning. The farthest I went was to say "you're a pig" in the privacy of my own room, with my voice soft, and even so felt a fool and gave up after the second attempt.

Contrary to what Evan had said, believing in sorcery did not lead to doing it in my case, at least.

I spent the day marveling over all these evidences of sorcery I'd ignored and not seen before now.

And avoiding my friends.

Or trying to, because my secret had changed. Before it served as consolation, something to hug to myself and plot ways to hint or tease them. Lure them back to me, one way or another.

Then it became something to withhold. A new way of viewing the world that I couldn't share, because they wouldn't understand, wouldn't believe, and might even laugh at me for trying. Been there, done that, albeit without sorcery, and still have the scars.

Not fun.

By dinner, I longed for a warm bed to crawl into and pull the covers over my head. Instead, I sat down at a table with my friends. The noisy hall, with its hard flooring and people walking every which way, made it hard to concentrate on conversation.

Between the lot of us at the table, we had plates of pizza, sushi, pot roast, a weird salad of nuts and sprouts and stuff, and bowls of cereal. I wound up with chicken flambé and asparagus. One of my favorite dishes. Savory, with green crunch when the asparagus wasn't cooked within an inch of its life. I could eat it every day, but it only showed on the menu once a month so I should've been in food heaven digging in with my fork and knife.

I started out that way, but the first bite revealed a slanted line across the plate.

Theoretically, all the dining hall plates looked the same: thick, off-white porcelain. In practice, some accreted stains or cracks from knife scrapes or things like that. There had to be hundreds, if not the thousands of them.

All the same, every bite I consumed revealed more crack

lines on my plate and made me wonder if it could be the same one broken and reformed at lunch.

Odds were—no.

But the possibility made eating less important than pushing my food around on the plate to try and match the cracks against my memory of how the plate had splintered. Stupid, maybe, yet it became almost an obsession.

It also attracted notice. All six of us there that night. Alex and Emilio didn't live in on-campus but Alex's father didn't mind them eating with us half the time so they could have what the Prof once described as "a more authentic college experience."

I'd learned in high school to pay attention to what I could see out of the corners of my eyes—and they kept glancing at me until they made the decision to do an intervention of some kind. Undercut because they telegraphed this in advance by playing a quick game of glancing at each other and gesturing. They might've shared one or two grimaces as well.

At length, Alex, despite sitting across the table, leaned over to study my face.

"You don't look so good." He shook his head.

"Distracted, not eating your favorite meal," Emilio ticked off reasons on his fingers, shaking his head. "Not to mention lines under your eyes suggesting you're not sleeping, plus you're even paler than usual."

"You don't go telling a woman she doesn't look good." Ruth rolled her eyes at Emilio and Alex, then turned to me and gave a decided head shake. "Though it's true you're not your usual self today."

"Then what do you do?" Emilio leaned back and crossed his arms over his chest.

"Watch this." Ruth leveled a stare not at Evan but Alex, then turned to Gloria. The two of them hooked up within a month of meeting and lasted all year even though they refused to be roommates, claiming it would kill their romance. "You game?"

"Honey, is there something wrong?" Gloria smiled back at her. "You need a little TLC?"

Ruth laid her head on Gloria's shoulder, pretending to sob, and the next thing the two of them were kissing. Again.

Emilio and Gordon laughed. Unique sounds, easily attributable to them. Emilio's low and rolling, with a bit of a growl in it. Gordon's in the middle-range and syncopated.

The sounds flashed me back to the other night, when all of them except Gordon left the library after gathering without me. This, in turn, reminded me of my secret from them. Which made my stomach roil so that I couldn't eat.

"Maybe you're coming down with something." Alex had left the table and returned with a glass of orange juice which he set before me. "Don't forget to get your vitamin C."

Their care made me feel worse. Secrets bred secrets bred secrets.

I needed someone to talk to, but had no one. I'd tried texting Evan earlier, but got no answer then, not even contact information for his mother to see if maybe, somehow I could move up my first lesson to tonight instead of after rehearsal tomorrow.

Just in case he'd got back to me, I pulled out my phone. The front panel showed a series of unread texts, but nothing new from Evan.

One from the first violinist about orchestra business.

A classmate in psych wanted a copy of my notes asap.

A wind instrument player suggested meeting up before rehearsal tomorrow to talk reeds and stuff.

I logged into my phone to reply when I noticed a text to me and my older sister I'd somehow missed . . .

From Bea.

<<What's up with Dad?>>

Clicking on it unfurled a long list of texts, all of which had escaped me—and any of which would've had me getting back to her under normal circumstances.

<<Where's Dad?>>

<<Have you heard from him?>>

<<From Mom?>>

<<Has anyone told you anything?>>

<<No one's telling me. But something's wrong.>>

<<Mom's tripling the garlic in the spaghetti sauce!>>

The garlic multiplication was a very bad sign because Mom did that when spitting mad at Dad. They both had all these passive-aggressive tactics that they mirrored back at each other except for those occasions either of them remembered me and Bea and Rose were stuck in the middle.

<<What's up? Do you need to talk?>> I texted Bea.

Even as a new text arrived.

<<Vi, you there? Call me!!!!>>

"Sorry, text from Bea, gotta go." I grabbed my bag and waved good-bye at my friends, phone in hand. They all watched and nodded.

But other than noting that, I didn't look back. Just grabbed my bag and hotfooted it out of the hall to the quieter outside.

I hit speed dial and Bea answered before the phone rang more than once, but stammered so bad I couldn't understand her at first.

"Hey, Bea, it's going to be all right. Whatever it is, it's going to be all right." Her sobs broke my heart. "Just breathe, okay? Slow and steady."

"He's g-g-gone. D-d-dad. All his special things."

Behind her voice came distant bangs of metal against metal. Worse, they accompanied the unmistakable sound of Mom singing.

Bea switched to video call format. Just about everything

Emilio had listed about me applied to her. Her usual ruddy gold coloration had gone pinky-gold, not a good look. Dark lines marred the skin beneath her gray eyes. White teeth bit into her lower lip, which also looked a paler pink than usual. The dimples that often danced in her cheeks had vanished.

"All g-g-gone."

Her hand shook as she held up the phone, reversing the camera to show the living room. Most of it looked the same as usual. Two big, over-stuffed chairs in dark green and a matching sofa with a gray cat curled up atop a light green blanket. A walnut what-not that held trinkets, including school craft projects alongside Mom's beloved collection of glass cats and the antique ice cream dishes Dad had inherited from Gramma. A big television dominating one wall with small framed photos covering another.

"See, see, see." Bea pointed to blanks and empty spots. The dishes had gone, along with a third of the framed photos —the photos of Dad's family. Not everything, but stuff that meant a lot to him.

"What about his clothes and stuff?" I asked. "Where's he been sleeping?"

"Your room."

Not much of a surprise. He preferred my room when he moved out from the master bedroom, since it lay farther away. He moved back to the master at the start of last summer, but midway through he shifted to Rose's room, since she was staying with our maternal grandparents closer to Philly while working at a summer job.

Bea headed up the stairs, grabbing the cat on the way. Petting helped her calm down, for her breathing slowed and became less audible. In the process, she mashed the camera against the cat's fur so my phone showed a mat of black and gray hairs.

All the while, I headed across campus, trying not to trip

or bump into anyone. In short, being the cliché college student looking at nothing but the phone. People got out of my way at the last minute, or vice-versa. I ducked to the side a couple times to avoid collisions with other phone-fixated students.

And wished hard I had already reached my room so I wouldn't have to worry about bumping into someone, or accidentally share the conversation with anyone I wouldn't want to overhear.

The next moment, I stumbled and fell face-forward onto a soft surface.

My head whirled, every muscle ached, and nausea threatened. I nearly vomited—or suffocated, pressed against the bedspread. *My* bedspread, because when I managed to roll over and take in my surroundings it turned out I'd managed to bop into my dorm room.

I lay on my bed in my dorm room looking at a mini-version of my room at home, or rather, my once-and-future room. It didn't seem all that different from how I'd left it: bare bones and stripped down apart from a couple of travel posters still on the walls. Most of my clothes were with me at college.

The bed was covered with a dust sheet, tucked in at each corner with a perfect three-point fold that Dad tried to make me and my sisters use but Bea and I always failed. The closet held none of my clothes and some of Dad's, but at best half.

Bea kept pointing out things missing—she had a better eye than I, noting the bags with all Dad's extra phone and computer cords had gone, along with the annotated volumes of Shakespeare's plays that he kept at his bedside for light reading before going to sleep.

"Looks like he's moving on." With rotten timing. "What does Mom say?"

"She won't say anything, except she wasn't g-going t-to g-get in between him and us and so we'd have t-to g-get our answers from him." Bea heaved a big sigh, but at least she'd settled down some.

Dings announced Rose texting us on both ends.

Bea switched back to voice-only and conferenced Rose in.

I texted Mom and Dad to ask what was going on. Rose no doubt did the same, as an almost-perfect big sister. My vertigo didn't improve so I lay flat on my bed listening to my sisters chew it over.

And wondered what triggered the meltdown. All of us knew they'd split sooner or later, but thought they'd made it this far so they'd stick it out until after Bea went to college next fall. Did I want to know the why?

My head kept circling as though I floated atop virtual ocean waves. My stomach settled enough that I nabbed a protein bar from the stash under my bed.

Despite my distraction, I was the first to notice Dad's text sent to all three of us.

<<My heroes>>

He liked to call us that because he and Mom named us for leading characters in Shakespearean plays. My Dad in a nutshell: accountant by day, frustrated Shakespearean actor by night. Playing small roles in the local amateur Shakespeare theater troupe's twice-yearly productions ranked as one of his greatest accomplishments in life. So of course he insisted we all be named after Shakespearean characters. Mom wasn't quite so in love with Shakespeare, but said okay as long as she got to pick which ones. Thus they ended up with Rosalind Celia, Viola Olivia, and Beatrice Portia, the last because Mom considered Hero a stupid name and passive character.

Dad promised to pick up Bea for dinner on Friday and teleconference me and Rose in . . .

<<And then I'll share all.>>

A promise and a threat.

8

The next day started off worse. I slept badly, woke late, and skipped breakfast to run to Professor Noches's class. Then bungled my presentation. Major disgrace.

No one to blame but myself. I'd procrastinated, knowing I could finish it in an evening. My accidental teleportation spell left me wiped out. I might not've slept much, but neither did I manage anything else.

The professor didn't say much at the time. He pointed out, in a kind manner, all sorts of things I could have included, and then let me sit down while the next student presented.

Sweat trickled down my face and back, leaving me chilled and sick to my stomach and wishing I were anywhere else. Unable to meet even my friends' eyes, though Gloria sitting behind me gave me a comforting pat. No excuses. I screwed up.

In front of Alex's father, no less. Who'd never been anything but polite and encouraging to me and all of Alex's friends. Last year he often let us invade the house, raid the refrigerator, take over the living room for games. Sometimes he cooked and other times we did, though we always cleaned up at Alex's insistence.

Professor Noches asked me to stay after class a bit. Lips tight and hands braced on his hips, he looked me over—up and down. And resembled Alex to the point I almost imagined he, rather than his father, confessed his disappointment in me.

"You can do better, Viola."

"I know. I'm sorry."

"It causes me wonder if you want to be here."

"I do. Everybody who's taken it says—" My mouth snapped shut when he held up a hand.

"No course is for everyone. It is no shame to withdraw, if you decide it does not suit. The add-drop period does not end until tomorrow."

"Are you saying I should drop?" A heavy lump seemed to form in my stomach.

"No, not at all." He shook his head. "But if you stay, you must do better. Think bigger. More creative. Make more connections."

"I will. I promise, I just . . ." I bent my head and bit my lip, hard, rather than pour out excuses since I couldn't explain the key reason I'd not finished my presentation, i.e. magicking myself across campus by accident.

"Very well. You can do this, Viola, but you must want it." He nodded.

The day went downhill from there. I nearly fell asleep at work; skipped practicing my oboe in the afternoon to catch a nap before dinner and orchestra rehearsal; and worried all the time about what Dad meant by promising to tell all. He didn't answer my texts, Mom texted back she refused to get in the middle of anything and to let her be for a while. Bea and Rose started texting possibilities, but that petered out.

With my own secret hanging over me, I had a hard time participating.

Small surprise I wasn't my usual self at orchestra, but at least I managed not to hit too many sour notes.

This time, Evan stuck around afterward and walked me over to his mother's.

I didn't realize he meant to do that at first. Unlike last time, I took forever packing up my oboe. Grabbing the sweatshirt I'd slung over the back of my chair, I caught glimpses of him idling by the door with his arms crossed over his chest. He wore jeans and a white T-shirt with a message glorifying violins at the expense of all other instruments. His violin case sat between his sneakered feet.

He drew attention. Partly because most days he booked it out of the room as soon as we wrapped, but also due to his good looks. And that dang T-shirt, which it seemed like every violinist wore at least once and sometimes all at the same time by arrangement. Then again, I had a dozen or more pro-oboe T-shirts in my bureau.

"Got yourself a new admirer?" A clarinetist I hung out with sometimes jerked her head his way and gave me a wink. "Nice catch."

"It's not quite like that."

"From where I'm standing, it looks just like that." She shut her case with a snap and gave me a gentle nudge. "You go, girl."

Sure enough, when I passed through the door he fell into step alongside me.

"I'll walk with you to my mother's." He matched my stride, not making me stretch it although he had the longer legs.

"No running this time?" I stuck to the paved sidewalks rather than cutting across the grass as he had before.

"I'll get my exercise in other ways." He glanced up at the dark sky.

Cooler breezes blew this night, making me shiver as they carried the scents of autumn: crisp and earthy with hints of falling leaves and decaying apples as the campus had too many crabapple trees. I stopped and untied the sweatshirt from around my waist. Pulled it on over and reduced the number of goose bumps on my arms.

Evan shook his head and chuckled at the message on the sweatshirt—that no oboe player ever had too many oboes.

"I'll take care of that." He jerked his head at my oboe case. "Send it home for you, if you want. Since you don't know the way of it yet."

I agreed fast enough. He refused to work the spell until we reached a patch of shadows between lampposts. Then he did it twice, for his violin and then for my oboe. Try as I might, I missed the important bits of how he managed it. No bangs or claps of lightning, just a light slap of a hand against each case. Maybe a flash of some sort of energy that made the hairs stand up on my arms—or I imagined that.

Either way, I benefited by not carrying my oboe case all the way to Evan's home and back. The more so as most of my muscles were still sore from the run two nights ago and last night's spell.

Maybe that's what made me bold.

"Can I ask you something personal?" I asked if I could ask instead of just blurting out the question, because I'd found sometimes it was better to ease into things. In this case, it got me an answer of sorts. Albeit, not straight out.

"You can ask." He gave me a sideways glance. "I don't promise to answer."

"What's it like, being a swan . . . flying?" I held my breath and tried to keep from stepping on any sticks or dried leaves.

"That's a big question, and not something I can answer, either."

We walked in silence for a few more steps, then he stopped and whirled to face me. "I'll try, on one condition. Give me equal value in return."

"Fair enough." I faced him.

"You don't even know what I'm going to ask. Trusting aren't you?"

We'd gone about a quarter of the way around the lake. A thin layer of bushes and trees separated us from the rocky lakeshore. The path stretched off to either side, while behind us lay a chunk of forest—tangled trees and bushes left as nature preferred. A faint odor of decaying vegetation mixed with the musty smell of the lake. An owl hooted from a not-too distant tree. The college maintained this as a pocket wilderness, encircled on one side by the college and the subdivision on the other.

A lamppost glowed several feet away, close enough to make Evan's form and features visible but far enough to leave us in degrees of shadow.

"I guess I am, at least within reason." I trusted him enough to walk alone with him this far. Granted, I still had my phone in my pocket. "Besides, who says you know me well enough yet to ask anything super personal."

"You sure of that?"

"No." I took a deep breath, lungs protesting. "But go ahead. Ask."

"Why did you turn, even after I warned you?" He shook his head and kicked at a large piece of gravel.

"Warn? Or was it a dare?" Crossing my arms over my chest, I tucked my hands under to keep them warm. A defensive measure, of course, but one I made without conscious thought and refused to undo because otherwise he might not notice. Or I might be analyzing everything more than him.

"Maybe. Maybe not."

"So who goes first, with answers?"

"You, because you said yours would be less personal." He mirrored my stance, but laid his hands over his crossed arms rather than under.

"Okay. I turned . . ." I pulled my lip between my teeth, then let out a huffing sigh. "I'd had a shitty day, for one thing. My younger sister called from home reporting trouble between my parents. Again. And . . . you want personal? I saw some of my friends getting together without me. That hurt."

"Why didn't you say anything? Confront them?"

He might say that, since he'd assumed a posture of power while I'd taken one of protection.

"Because I'm not that brave."

He grunted.

"Maybe you're one of those people who're super confident, and it's just too foreign for you to get. Good for you, but I'm not that way. If you were shy or lacked confidence, you'd understand. At any rate, I didn't ask." I ducked my head. "I ran away."

"I get that. I do it, too." He cupped my cheek with a warm hand. Not exerting any pressure for me to turn my head and meet his gaze. Skin to skin. A caress and wordless affirmation of understanding.

Which emboldened me to let my arms hang by my side, lift my chin, and lay out the rest.

"Then I saw you. As the swan, I mean, and . . . it was just so beautiful and graceful. Swooping in to land. Plus you changing from swan to you, that was beautiful too. And, I guess, when push came to shove, I wasn't willing to give up that moment of beauty to forget sorcery."

"When I can't deal with things, I fly away." His hand dropped from my cheek to grab my fingers and squeeze. "I didn't use to spend so much time flying, letting the swan take over. Back in high school, I had more things to do. More distractions. But now . . . there's nothing like it. I've never done hang gliding, but maybe that would be close. It's just us and the wind as the earth falls away beneath me. It can be tough sometimes, gauging the wind. We've been blown off course and nearly hit trees, but it's worth it for that . . . utter tranquility. Beauty."

We stood staring at each other for several minutes. Wings flashed across his eyes for a moment, then they returned to being shades of green and yellow.

Then he shook his head and pulled back.

"It's stupid, really. The more we do it, the harder it is to return. Though I always do, so far."

He kicked at the path, then started off. After a few steps, realizing I hadn't moved, he glanced back at me.

"You staying here?"

"No." I joined him and we fell into a pretty good pace. Not too fast or slow. His legs were a bit longer, but he kept his stride matched to mine.

At first we walked in silence, but something in his words nagged at me. It didn't fit. Took me awhile, but I put two and two together without getting four.

"You said you changed because of the curse the other night, but you can change if you want to, too?"

"It varies. Most of the time I have to change form, whether or not I want to. Sometimes I can choose, and that's when the swan flies away. But we always come back."

"What's the curse if you can do it when you want to?"

"Nothing you have to worry about." A ghastly grin appeared on his face, turning it into something akin to a mask. "Ask me sometime when I'm more myself, and maybe I'll tell you."

"You're not yourself right now?"

"It's too good a night for flying." He grabbed my hand as

we walked, entwining our fingers. "But I promise I'll see you all the way to my home."

We reached his home a few yards further. The gate opened at our approach, without a hand touching it. The hinges didn't creak this time. His mother must've oiled them, or had someone do so. The gate opened smooth and easy, so light and well-balanced a baby could move it.

Despite my sweatshirt, the fingers of my free hand turned cold as icicles while my palm sweated. I tucked my hand in the front pocket of my sweatshirt.

"What's wrong?" Evan nudged me.

"Nothing."

"Tell me. Can't be worse than what we shared earlier." He'd turned antsy, too, fingers twitching against mine. He rapped his other hand against his thigh.

"Your house is big. At least twice as big as my home. And your mother's . . . intimidating."

"Yeah, she's my Mom but I know what you mean. She's the chief legal counsel for the Webmasters of Fate, which doesn't hurt, but she comes by it naturally anyway. My uncles, her younger brothers, say she's always been that way."

My game of choice might be frisbee, but Bea loved video games and in particular Webmasters of Fate's natural history series. She'd squeal if she knew I'd met someone who worked there.

The lawn seemed even longer than last time, with the house a beacon of light at the top of the incline. My calves ached, but at least my knees didn't knock.

Evan accompanied me all the way up to the kitchen door, same one I entered and exited through last time. He let go of my hand and yanked the door open, yelling for his mother. Made my ears ring. A faint pasta-and-tomatoes aroma flitted past me and then evaporated, leaving the kitchen smelling of citrus detergent.

Regina emerged from a room farther in with a pained look. At first glance, she presented a very different appearance from her son—tailored silk blouse of royal blue and navy trousers instead of T-shirt and jeans—but instead of shoes she wore tan slippers with violins on them. Her collar bore an enamel pin in the shape of a violin.

Different styles of clothing aside, they shared looks and passion for the string instrument.

"You couldn't have rung or texted?"

"Nope." He remained outside the house, standing on the step. One hand gripping the frame, he leaned back and stared up at the sky.

I stood on the ground behind and to the side. Although I glanced up, nothing caught my eye. The winds had picked up, sending clouds skittering across the sky; dark shadows against the deep blue. A typical almost-autumn night. On the other hand, it might be cool for flying.

"How long do you think you'll need tonight?" He rolled his neck and shoulders, flexing his arms, and returned his attention to his mother who now stood in the doorway.

"An hour should do. Just the basics to start, then time to ponder them. Why?" She shook her head, lips tight. "You're not going up now, are you?"

"If I go now, I might make it back in time to walk Viola to campus."

"You don't have—" I said, or rather started. I gave up pretty fast.

"That's an excuse—" Regina grabbed hold of his arm.

"The point is to make sure—" He shook his shoulder and arm but didn't loosen her hold.

"You have to fight—"

"Viola gets home safe."

"Don't give in to the—"

"If I'm not back, make sure—" This time he managed to get his arm free.

"It's you I'm worried—" She grabbed his other hand.

"Stop trying to distract me—"

"I'll drive her, if need be."

"The night sky's calling." A big shiver rippled through him, feet to head. First his legs bent and straightened, then his back arched and he threw his head back, dragging in deep breaths.

Regina fell back a step. Rallying, she wrapped him in a tight embrace. "You have to fight it. Don't give in. Don't ever give in all the way."

He ducked his head as he pulled away, again. For a second, an expression of relief settled on his face. The next moment, he winced and gritted his teeth. Turning around, he ran down the yard stripping off his clothes with every other step. First he yanked his shirt off and tossed it high—the light fabric floated for a moment and then vanished in midair. He kicked off one sandal then the other, each arcing high then disappearing. Last of all, requiring a hop or two, he pulled off his shorts and underwear and threw them off to vanish as well.

He didn't reach the fence. Instead, he built up enough speed that he leapt into the air and changed into a swan, pumping his wings to clear the gate and angle up into the sky.

White wings bright, then turned shadowed as he flew away. Regina and I watched until he disappeared from sight, at best a faint gleam of white that could be a star.

Gorgeous. I would've put up with all the lessons and strife and details, for the chance to gain wings and fly.

I turned away, but Regina still watched the sky. She clasped her hands, eyes glittering with tears.

"Be warned, my dear, sorcery has limits. All sorcerers have limits. I'm considered a skilled and powerful practitioner, yet even I couldn't protect him against this."

※   9   ※

My first sorcery lesson started about five or ten minutes later. Regina pulled herself together while starting tea again. I sat at the same table, in the same chair, though this time I didn't have my oboe to worry about. Watched her, again, setting the table with all the usual accoutrements of sugar bowl and creamer, cups and saucers.

She threw questions at me all the while, a skilled multi-tasker. Open ended queries extracting information about every incident in my life these past seventy-two hours, give or take, since I first saw the swan turn to Evan—ending with me confessing the accidental teleportation.

Her eyebrows rose high and she whisked over to sit opposite me. Had me hold my hands out flat, palms up. Hers she stretched out over mine, palms down. Millimeter by millimeter she lowered her hands towards mine. Holding in a steady position took a fair amount of effort, as my muscles started to want to move. It seemed a bit silly, as though we were recording a scene for a fantasy movie and the sorcery would be added in special effects weeks or months later.

A crackle broke the silence. Tension filled the air between our hands, which turned hot and heavy. Hairs stood upright at the nape of my neck and along my arms. Power arced between us—invisible, but there.

"That answers one question." Less than an inch separated us when she pulled back and ran a shaky hand over her head.

"Which is?" I rubbed my hands together, despite sparks of static electricity shooting along my arms.

"You don't have much in the way of power reserves at the moment. The teleportation spell cleared you out. Your body has regenerated some power since then, not much but nothing to worry about. The rate of regeneration tends to fluctuate over the first months and will level out later on, though it will vary over your life. Follows the same basic rules as physical energy—stay healthy, get sleep, eat nutritious foods, avoid stress." The kettle whistled and she whisked away from the table to return with mugs of darkening liquid. Chamomile, by the scent.

"Is the whole clearing out thing good or bad?"

"Neither, it just is. Though I suppose it's as well." She held her hands over the cup, fingers shaking, then lifted it and took a sip. "I'll show you a very simple spell, which you can practice over the next days until your levels increase."

"Okay." The cushion beneath me squeaked as I shifted in my seat.

"But first, the basics. There are five core components to any sorcerous spell: intent, belief, desire, power, and a symbol that links them all and makes sorcery manifest."

That seemed simple enough so I nodded, ready for complications.

"Now, most humans generate some degree of sorcerous power by breathing. People who don't believe in sorcery discharge this automatically, in a variety of ways including static electricity, sneezes, hiccups. We can discuss that another time, if you're interested."

With excellent timing, a jolt of static electricity or nerves made my whole upper body twitch. Regina watched me, eyes dark. The steaming cup of tea in her hands hid her mouth, so I couldn't say for sure if she'd sent the jolt or not.

"How much sorcery a person generates varies. Some sorcerers say it's genetic and runs in families. Others disagree, throwing up this or that example of weak members of strong lines or vice-versa. And then there's the school that argues we all start small and build our ability to generate magic over time. All of which constitutes a lot of hot air." Regina made a tsking sound.

I held out my hands parallel to each other and brought them together. My eyes saw nothing, but my arms shook. Closing my eyes, I almost caught the thousand mini bolts of lightning flashing between my palms. With another jerk, I dropped my now sweaty hands and wiped them on my pants.

"The thing to bear in mind," she continued, "is that how much power you have access to at any given moment limits what spells you can work. The more complicated a spell, the more power required. Though we're still figuring out what constitutes a complicated spell because some things that seem simple aren't, and some that aren't ... Don't worry too much about whether or not you have power. Indeed, it's best to keep your levels low when you're learning. Reduces the likelihood of accidents— such as teleporting—unless you want to try that again."

She leveled a hard look at me, one eyebrow raised in inquiry. The pain and exhaustion following my accidental teleportation flashed through my head, and an echo made my muscles ache for a moment.

"I'm good." I shook my head. "No need to try that again. So. Power. You need it to work magic."

"Yes. That is a constant." She nodded. "One must possess at least a spark of power, no matter how minute, although how much power is required for any spell varies depending on the other factors."

Quiet fell for a few minutes. A low ticking filled the air, from the grandmother clock standing in a far corner. Reading hands instead of a digital display took a few moments' thought. Not as much had passed as I would have guessed. A touch on the smart phone indicated the same time, and that I'd received several texts from friends and my sisters—without it making so much as a chirp.

"I've silenced that for now." Regina nodded at my phone. "Only urgent matters—by your lights, not mine—will make it ring or beep."

"Got it." I turned the phone face-down and took another sip of tea, hoping the steam would hide the flush in my cheeks.

"Excellent." She held up a hand and folded down one finger. "Power." Folded another. "Intent: you have to have some idea of what you want to happen, the more detailed the better. It's considered unwise to give the universe too much scope in deciding how to carry out your intent. Sometimes the universe—or God or the Spirit of Sorcery—has a nasty sense of humor."

"Is that how Evan wound up being a swan part of the time?" I'm still not sure how I had the courage to ask.

"In part." She winced, then sent me a dark look and folded a third finger down. "Belief is also an important component of any given sorcerous spell. You have to believe it will work. Doubt is fatal to ambition."

"But I already believe, isn't that why I'm here?"

"No, belief as an element of spells is separate from acceptance of sorcery."

"So you can do magic even if you don't believe in it?" My head started to hurt.

This sent us down a rabbit hole that ate up at least ten or twenty minutes. When we got back on track, she folded down a fourth finger.

"Then there's desire. The spellcaster has to want a spell to happen."

Made sense, so I nodded, happy to find at least one part of magic was simple.

"Last but not least, there's the symbol. This encapsulates the desired end result in some way—there's always a connection—and thus links the intent and belief to the power that makes a given spell work. The symbol can be anything that makes sense to the caster as representing the spell, although it's simplest to use existing symbols." Regina picked up the half-full creamer. Half-rising, she placed it at the far end of the table and sat back down, well out of arm's reach.

She glanced back and forth between the creamer and me, then frowned. Got up from the table and walked over to the mantel, where she selected a white swan feather from the array laid out. She set the feather next to the creamer before returning to her seat.

"Hold still."

The hard note in her voice had my spine straight and still in a moment. I hardly dared drag in anything more than shallow breaths.

"Would you agree that crooking a finger represents summoning someone—or some thing?"

"Yeah."

"Then watch." She turned sideways, she extended her hand. Her index finger and thumb were extended, but the other three fingers curved in toward her palm. With a flick, she crooked her index finger at the creamer.

Leaving the table with a rattle, it flew towards her. She caught it, settling it back on the table.

"Now, you try it with the feather. You must want to summon it, believe you can, visualize it coming to your command . . . then crook your finger and make it happen."

Five ingredients to make sorcery.

Power—a little crackled in my hand as I extended my arm. Enough? I had no clue.

Belief—she'd just proved it could be done, so surely I'd manage it.

Intent—I wanted the feather to come to my hand, but how? Zoom? Float? I opted for the latter, trying to visualize an air current bringing the feather to me.

Desire—check, bring on success.

Symbol, though. Much as I agreed crooking a finger meant summoning someone, it seemed sort of . . . wimpy for sorcery.

Especially when my first try failed.

And my second. Third. Fourth.

"You have to will it."

My teeth hurt as I pressed them together to keep from giving Regina a glare. Some teacher.

Beneath the table, my free hand clenched into a fist. I fixed my gaze on the lean fall of down at the far end of the table. From Evan, no doubt, whether or not it was the one I'd got after watching him turn the first time. That had belonged to me for a whole day and I wouldn't mind having it back. Or this one.

With a sharp gesture, knuckle cracking, I crooked my finger in summons.

The feather rose from the table and tumbled down-over-quill at me so fast I didn't react before it smacked me in the face. I counted myself luck the down hit me rather than the quill end.

"Yes." Regina nodded and clapped. "Get the action wrong, nothing happens. Get it right, and it's magic. Sometimes we even manage to get the symbolic action so calibrated that we can convince mundanes to work it. Then we call it science."

This time, she let me keep the feather.

❦ 10 ❧

Evan didn't show by the time the lesson ended.

Regina worried. She tried to pass it off with a flick of her hands. Nevertheless, her body vibrated when we left the house and walked down the path to the gate. Full dark and no moon meant I followed her outline and didn't see her expressions. Storm clouds covered the sky. A bitter breeze blew, carrying the taste of ozone.

My fingers chilled fast, until I tucked them in my sweat-shirt pockets. Soft down brushed my left hand, and I stroked the feather tucked away just in case Regina regretted letting me take it. A promise that somehow, someday I'd learn to fly, though I also promised myself I'd always come back.

I didn't want anyone in my family to have to worry over me.

We reached the fence with still no sign of Evan anywhere. Not even the slightest flicker of white plumage against the dark sky and waters. Regina stood there for a long moment, holding the gate. Then, instead of retracing our steps back up the path, she led me around the yard.

First we turned and paced over soft, sweet-scented wild

grasses all grown at least ankle high, marred by the occasional fallen leaf. No bushes or trees grew against the wrought-iron fence—the garden designer had left a clearance of at least six feet between the fence and any larger landscaping elements. Yet I couldn't match the scene with my vague memories of seeing the yard by twilight. All plants and grasses to me at the time—and now all shadows.

Once or twice security lights embedded in the ground flickered at our approach, but Regina waved a hand at them and they stayed dark.

We walked in darkness and silence.

Down to the corner and then up along the fence separating Regina's land from the next-door neighbor's property. Around the sides of house. Back down next to the fence separating her land from the pocket wilderness Arden liked to call a forest. Across to the gate. And around again.

We walked as close as we could to the fence or side of the house in a big circle. Or square. Or a weird combination of rectangles.

Three times.

"Is three some kind of charm, after all?"

"What do you think?" She asked in a voice steady, but thin.

The Socratic method of teaching was never my favorite. I always suspected teachers of having specific answers in mind even when they promised us they didn't. Easy enough to come up with an answer, though.

"Yes, because it can be a symbol."

"Numbers are symbols, letters are symbols, words are symbols, actions are symbols." Regina gave a sharp laugh.

"Is there anything that can't be a symbol?"

"Not really."

We'd reached the gate again by this point, ending the third round, and this time she headed up the path, shoulders slumped. She deviated at the last moment, following a side path I hadn't noticed to a different door and into the garage.

Before flicking on the light, she took one last look back for any sign of Evan or the swan.

Nothing.

She pressed a button glowing with faint red light, and the overhead light popped on. The garage door groaned and squeaked, chains rattling as it rose. The breeze blew away the faint hint of oil in the air.

The garage held two cars, neither of which I recognized. Cars had four wheels, four doors, and engines, and drove the same way. That's all I needed to know. I got in the passenger side of the lower-slung car, which might've been a hybrid or electric since the motor made almost no sound whatsoever.

"Which dorm are you in?" She didn't ask me until she'd already pulled out of the garage and begun winding back and forth out of the subdivision. Since we had to go wide around the Arden Forest Preserve separating the subdivision from the campus, we had time.

"Locust Hall."

"Hmm. I don't remember that one. You'll have to give me directions."

"It's at the corner of Campus Drive and Professor Street." I held tight to the belts strapping me into the seat as she took a corner faster than I'd expected. Then again, she must know this area like the back of her hand, drive it every day to get anywhere.

"It would be." She gave a harsh laugh. "Enemy territory."

"Excuse me?"

Shaking her head, she took another corner tight— coasting at the stop sign and not actually stopping.

"Practice the basic spells you learned today, as often as you can to keep your power levels low. As you become more accustomed to sorcery, then you may risk letting your levels get higher. Most sorcerers waste magic left and right unless they're saving up for a big spell. It's safer that way." She clicked her tongue. "Elsewise, a pinch of power's all that's needed if belief and desire, even momentary, are strong enough to compensate, and the next thing you know you've worked a spell you never truly intended."

"Got it."

I started to list the basic spells she'd shown me thus far—summoning, pushing away, simple things like that—except something about her words nagged at me. Working back through them, they reminded me of Evan's warning about curses.

"Is that what happened with Evan? A spell that worked out different than he meant?"

"If I were charitable, I would say yes." The car wheels squealed as she accelerated onto the main street leading back around to campus.

"Then . . . was it a curse?"

A bitter laugh. Her fingers clenched tight around the steering wheel, knuckles white under the streetlights.

"There are evil sorcerers in the world, and evil magic. Men who think nothing of robbing a woman of her child. My son, my Evan . . . it wasn't his fault at all. He was three years old! I tried to protect him, but I failed and he has to live with the results of my failure. A nightmare, for at best he spends a limited amount of time as himself. For the rest, he flies away . . . sometimes I don't see him for days.

Yanking on the wheel, she pulled over into the parking lane and stopped the car. She grabbed my left hand in both hers, holding tight. A faint peppermint scent clung to her warm skin.

"Help me. Be his friend. When he does manage to return and change back . . . Be an anchor, to keep him here as himself."

What could I say? It didn't sound too bad, at least not the part about being a friend. Having a friend.

"I'll try."

Regina stared at me for a long moment, then nodded. Let go of my hand a finger at a time—until her phone dinged and she lunged for it. Her lips curved into a smile, and she heaved a sigh of relief.

"Evan texted, he's home." She pulled back into the driving lane.

As we approached the campus her shoulders stiffened. She tapped her fingers against the steering wheel. Bit her lip.

"Come back next Tuesday, and I'll show you some more spells. We can do this for a few weeks, though I'm setting things in motion to find you a new teacher on campus."

"You're what?" I mirrored her straight, stiff posture. I hadn't realized she meant to find me a new teacher so soon.

"This is perfectly normal, passing students along. Doing sorcery is a personal activity—what spells you work reflect who you are, your beliefs—it also reflects your heritage, culture, imagination . . . I can only teach you spells and ways to construct spells that I know. Others can teach you ones I've never managed—or even dreamed of."

She pulled up to the curb in front of the dorm and put the car in park, then gave me a wry look.

"There's also the matter that I'm . . . not welcome on campus. Oh, I have friends and allies, but many other sorcerers do not like me. Hatred isn't too strong a word in some cases. They might even stoop to playing dirty tricks on you if they learned you were my pupil. I recommend you keep that a secret just in case."

Took me a while to parse through that. Not welcome on campus? Student affairs reminded us at orientation every year that parts of the town didn't like the college and vice-versa. Complaints about drunk students making messes or college officials buying up property on the one side and overly strict noise ordinances or zoning issues or something on the other. Or whatever.

"But you do come to the orchestra concerts, right?"

"Yes," she nodded. "Those visits are negotiated to the nth degree and I never overstay my welcome. So for your sake both in terms of learning more and not running unnecessary danger, I will arrange another teacher sooner rather than later. But stay my son's ally. Please?"

❧ II ❧

That Friday night became one of the worst, best, and stupidest of my life.

I managed to eat dinner, though I forgot what I ate right after except that the taste of barbeque sauce lingered on my lips for a while. Left most of my friends talking about which parties they might hit—those that wanted to party. Gloria asked if I planned to come along. I don't know what I said, but she promised to text updates about where they were in case I decided to join, and kept her word.

Other than that, nothing really registered. Not even whatever I did to pass time in my dorm room while waiting for Dad's call.

His big explanation.

At least he was willing to talk. Mom kept referring us to him and asking us to give her time to adjust. This didn't help ease the gut-hit of them separating but not announcing it in an open manner, but she didn't bad-mouth him or anything.

I wore the same thing I had all day, jeans and a T-shirt

bearing rather more wrinkles than before. Rammed fingers through my hair to make it look decent enough, based on the reflection on my phone. The storm had left a chill in the air, and some of the trees had begun to turn colors. Outside my dorm room window green leaves shaded into light orange.

The harbinger of change? Or merely a symbol?

After much fidgeting and fussing, I settled on the bed cross-legged. Leaned back against the wall and waited.

And waited.

And waited some more.

At last, the screen lit and the ring tone I'd set for Dad way back when pealed out. A flick of my finger, and Dad's face appeared in miniature.

"Hold a sec and let me get your sister back here."

Things went dark, then a moment later the screen divided into Rose on one side and Dad and Bea on the other. Dad must've had his arm around Bea's shoulders to get her close enough for them both to be in frame. His hand bobbled off and on, so I couldn't always see all of her face or his but he managed to keep some of each visible all the time.

His brown hair had thinned more and started grizzling around the ears. Still, he had a nice smile and sparkling teeth as he greeted us all together.

"My heroes."

"Hey Dad, Bea, Rose."

We did the whole rounds of greeting each other, with Dad beaming and nodding.

"So, what's up? What's the deal?" Rose cut to the chase.

He heaved a sigh and lifted the hand from behind Bea's back to rub his forehead.

"I'm sorry to say, your mother and I have reached a cross-road. Her life is going one way, mine another."

Bea and I let Rose take the lead. Sometimes we'd fight her

for it, but not now. Easier to let the wanna-be future lawyer do the heavy questioning.

"Yeah, we figured that much. But why now? Why not over the summer, or wait until the end of the year?"

"We tried, and talked about that, but it didn't work out that way. Because of good news. The best. Something I never anticipated happening again."

"Oh God." Other than that single exclamation, Rose remained speechless for a moment or two, her face showing dawning shock, horror, and resignation. Same on Bea's, inasmuch as I could see any of her.

"You're leaving Mom for another woman." A lump formed in my throat.

"Your mother and I left each other, in all but sharing the house, last year."

Rose grimaced. Bea flinched. I rubbed my stomach, which had started to hurt.

He sighed and rubbed his forehead again.

"Yes, there's another woman in my life. Grace Medina. She's part of the theater troupe. You saw her last year as Paulina in *A Winter's Tale*. We started talking after rehearsals. Having coffee. Enjoying each other's company. Long story short, I've moved in with her."

More than enough to deal with.

Except it wasn't all.

"Grace is pregnant."

Classic tale, though one I'd hoped not to see in my family. No wonder Mom didn't want to talk about it. Nothing about Grace Medina's name rang a bell. I did a web search soon as I could and her image popped up on the troupe's website—still didn't strike any memories. Younger than Dad, though I couldn't tell how much. At least she looked to be way older than me or Rose, but . . .

How did I miss it? I lived at home until all of a couple

weeks ago. Granted, I'd worked a couple of part-time jobs. But he had to have been seeing her then for the math to work out regarding pregnancy. Yet somehow I noticed nothing except him being irritated at having to move from my room to Rose's.

My breath caught in my lungs and shivers racked me. The walls seemed to close in around me. I had to get away.

Go for a run, or go partying?

On a Friday night there were parties everywhere and always in certain buildings near campus. Students had to live on campus their first two years. Most stayed on for all four, but every spring the most party-hearty rising seniors managed to find each other and stake out claims on off-campus apartments and houses.

Several lay within easy walking distance of my dorm. So close that the steady beat of the bass reached as far as my dorm room—which faced campus, not the street.

A quick glance at my phone indicated parties two, three, and five blocks away. All three with great music and atmosphere, according to the latest tweets from Gloria. She and Ruth were dancing their way through them. Ruth sent a text also, a quick photo of Alex standing in the background of a party, looking bored.

<<Poor guy needs a buddy. He's missing you!!!>>

I didn't change my clothes or take anything more than my phone and ID with me as I headed for the closest.

Stepping out of the dorm, I followed the sound of drums and guitars blasting through the night, although the song was forgettable. Music ranked nowhere on my list of reasons to party.

The sun had set some time ago and little pink remained in the sky. A light chill hung in the air, along with the tempting smell of someone baking apple pie. If I'd known where, I'd have detoured.

Streetlamps provided ample illumination, as did houses where the inhabitants hadn't yet pulled their curtains, such as Professor Noches. He had a two-story cape on the corner across from my dorm. Evergreen bushes lined the sidewalk leading up to the porch. Weathered gray siding blended into the night, but the wide front windows gleamed with light. He sat in an easy chair in the living room, reading something. Although I couldn't tell from the distance, his mouth probably pulled tight in a frown as he waited out the clock. A noise ordinance prohibited loud music or other nuisances after ten, and everyone knew he'd call the police if students holding parties or anyone making noise didn't turn everything down before 10:05.

Acquaintances galore filled the house at the far end of the block. Much less well-kept than the Noches's. Might've been nice once, but Alex said students had rented it every year since the college first started letting juniors and seniors move off campus, and it looked it. The bare yard mixed bald patches with grass of uneven height. Scuff marks on the porch columns and exterior walls.

The front door hung wide open, showing plain white walls hung with posters of sports teams and actresses in provocative poses. All the furniture—navy blue couches and beat-up tables and chairs—pushed back against the walls. Three white couples danced, or groped, in the middle of the living room. Two guys with red cups sat on the couch watching, both in short-sleeve shirts and jeans, one with his boots propped up on the edge of a recycling bin and the other barefoot with lots of black hairs springing up from his pasty toes.

The wood floor proved tacky in places with some notable splotch marks, only one of which seemed fresh. A heavy tang of sweat hung in the air, along with something cloyingly sweet . . . and beer. Lots of beer. The recycling bin held a pile of empty beer cans and bottles in a heap, plus more lying around. People must be trying to hit baskets, and not picking up when they missed.

A big punch bowl sat in splendor on the coffee table along the far wall: red plastic with a yellow dipper and a pile of red plastic cups.

"Have a drink," one of the guys on the couch called out to me. He hiccuped as he raised his plastic cup high and drained it.

"Thanks, I will."

I didn't drink the punch partly because I didn't want anything sweet. The guys who rented the house didn't have a reputation for hard drugs, just alcohol and marijuana, but for safety's sake I refused to drink anything from an open bowl unless I saw hosts drinking from it. And even then, conditional on having a designated driver or someone I trust to see me home safe.

Instead of punch, I headed further into the house.

Laughter followed a splash, plus calls of "drink it, one go!" in the dining room. Five or six people clustered around a table covered with red cups playing beer pong. As I circled around them to reach the kitchen, I got a good view of a second beer pong game going strong on the patio in the back-yard, plus more people dancing and drinking in the yard below. Cheap Christmas lights hung this way and that from the wooden fence enclosing the space. Rather pretty, if one kept one's eyes on the lights.

I grabbed an unopened bottle of beer from the bottom shelf of the fridge. Wrapped my hand around the cool glass. Found a cheap can opener in the shape of an orange slice and popped the top. Gulped it down too fast to do more than gasp at the cold, malty goodness.

Then snatched a second one.

Regina's warning not to drink alcohol or do drugs had flown in one ear and out the other. Parents and college officials and community members constantly advised students—especially women—not to drink or at least not to excess and yada yada yada. It got old fast, and Regina's warning seemed just another in that bunch.

The first edge of hallucination hit a few moments after I'd chugged the first beer and grabbed the second. As I straightened up, my head bobbed on my neck. Nothing big, just a sign I loosened up. Unfortunately, the world didn't stop moving around me. The bobble rippled through my body and all of a sudden I had a queasy feeling—which at least meant I didn't take the cap off the second beer and drink it down too.

Worse, my eyes couldn't quite focus. Everything seemed to be moving up and down, but not all together. Rather in waves, as though my glasses turned into transparent televisions superimposing wavelike motions on everything else.

I set the beer down on the counter and pulled off my glasses. Wiped them off on a clean patch of my shirt, then put them back on. That did the trick, wave illusion gone.

"Hey, toss me a beer, will you?" The guy who'd propped his boots on the recycling bin stood in the kitchen doorway, arms braced on either side of the frame. Maybe he thought it made him look sexy. Handsome he might be, with broad shoulders and a lean waist, but the blank look on his face did not appeal to me.

Plus, the posture pulled up his shirt to show a snakeskin belt threaded through the loops on his jeans—but he'd forgotten to fasten it. The buckle was shaped like a snake head and draped limp along his thigh.

Yet when I handed him the bottle I'd put aside, the buckle began to move on its own. Bit by bit, it pulled itself up so the head faced me. The forked prong extended and rippled as the snake hissed.

The instant the guy grabbed the bottle, I leapt back. Gripped the cabinet edge tight as the cobra belt watched me.

"What's your problem?" He stomped to the door leading out to the back yard, then turned around and pointed a finger at me. "Don't break any of my beer."

He kicked a foot my way, giving me a good look at the hard sole of his leather boot, then slammed the door behind him.

I stayed in place for a few breaths, trying to breathe deep. All seemed well with him gone. So, still being stupid, I turned back to the fridge for another bottle. Curved my hand around the cool glass and went for the can opener.

That's when I spotted the strange creature standing in the outside door. Not in the doorway, but half-in and half-out of the actual door. As though the door didn't exist. Maybe, for the creature, it didn't, since my vision seemed to waver. Everything else stayed solid as it varied back-and-forth from almost-not-existing to almost-solid.

The monster was a miniature bull about five feet tall, two very long horns extended from either side of his head—and each mottled like snake skin. The horns began to writhe and the ends turned towards me, revealing snake heads with diamond-bright eyes and forked tongues. They hissed in unison.

The bottle fell from my hand and rolled off somewhere.

I bolted out the door. People yelled and pushed back as I stumbled through the dining room and living room, but no one followed me. Escaping the house, I swayed. My stomach clenched and my head throbbed with pain. Sliding sideways, I took a few shaky steps and clutched at the porch railing. Hazy images of snake heads seemed to circle around me, until I closed my eyes. Shivers racked my body, every hair standing on end and goose bumps lining my arms and legs.

Another loud, dual hiss filled my ears and I dropped to floor of the porch, cowering against the solidity of the wood railing. Just a hallucination. That's all. A figment of my imagination.

"There are no snakes here. No snake-headed cows here." I repeated the words, hoping the denial would banish them away.

"Viola? Are you okay?"

I jerked as a warm hand touched my shoulder. An instant later, I recognized Alex's voice. Didn't dare open my eyes, but let go of the railing and grabbed hold of him instead.

"It's okay. Deep breaths, now." He sat down next to me and pulled me into an embrace. Wrapped his arms around me. Stroked his hands over my back. Cradled me on his lap. Let me hide my face against his shirt, soft and worn with a slight rip over the center of his chest. Just enough to let his scent—sweat, grass, a tang of marshy musk, and a hint of vinegar—seep out. "Everything's okay. I've got you."

The shivers reduced in number and vigor, dissolving under the warmth emanating from his body. From his caring. No more snake hisses.

"Get a room!" Someone jumped on the porch, making the floor-boards screech.

"Fuck off." One of Alex's hands left my back long enough to make a rude gesture or two, but the other drew comforting circles across my shoulders.

I dragged in a deep, shuddering breath and let it out. Then dared crack one eye open. I hedged my bets, though, using the eye on the side of my face pressed against his chest. I got a flash of a light blue polo shirt stretched over smooth muscles. So I tried opening my other eye.

Something hissed and I snapped both eyes shut, trying to burrow further into him and away from anything that might be a snake, real or hallucinated.

"What's the matter? Can't you tell me?" Alex stroked my hair. "Whatever it is, I'll help or find help."

Part of my brain screamed not to tell him, that he'd laugh. Mock me. Tell our other friends and make me an outcast. All the while another part cautioned that I might be breaking some sorcerer-rule.

But alcohol loosened my tongue.

"Hallucinations. Snakes and cows with snake horns."

"Sounds awful." He pulled back a little. Readjusted his seat, giving a few grunts as I slipped off his lap and he flexed his leg muscles. He settled me to his side, both of us leaning against the railing and his arm curving around to hold me against his side. His fingers drew small, calming circles on my shoulder. "A bad trip? What did you take? I've never seen you on drugs before, but—"

"Not drugs, beer. That's all. One beer, no more. Never ever been this bad before." I didn't drink often because alcohol relaxed me from head to toe—tongue most definitely included. Rose joked a couple of beers turned me into a babbling fool.

"You hallucinated on a beer?" He shook his head, some of his hair brushing across my face. "Some new craft blend?"

"Nope, just your basic cheapo brand." I shivered, the taste lingering in my mouth. "I didn't even get to drink more than one. Some guy came in wearing a stupid snakeskin belt and fancy cowboy boots and belt started to move and the boots grew into this hazy image of a cow . . ."

"You saw all that on one beer?" His fingers stilled on my shoulder.

"Yeah."

He didn't respond. Just sat next to me, not moving other than the rise and fall of his chest. One minute, two . . . I wasn't sure how long, but he kept not doing or saying anything or reacting in any way.

"Alex?"

"I'm here." A hug, then he pulled away and laid his hands on my shoulders.

I kept my eyes shut.

"I'm going to try something, okay? See if I can figure out what's going on. Either you're drunk or on drugs . . . or you're not." He squeezed my shoulders. "So trade eyes with me, will you? I want to see the world as you do."

"Whatever."

By this time, I'd mostly got over the hallucination. Not all the way, but enough I could face opening my eyes.

Heat had already started to make my cheeks flush—not from too much drink, but incipient embarrassment.

"I need you to say if you're okay with me trying this, all right?"

"Will it help?" I asked.

He drew in a deep breath.

"It'll eliminate at least one possibility."

Not the most encouraging words by far, but he hadn't gone anywhere. Or laughed or mocked. Instead, he'd been sweet and comforting, and . . . I refused to remain the quivering mass I'd turned into. I had a spine and could use it.

"Okay."

"Keep your hands here." Alex grabbed my wrists and

lifted them so my hands rested on his face covering his eyes. My fingers settled on his brow, thumbs aslant his nose.

Then he did the same with his fingers on my face. Only his fingertips touched me, hands cupped so as to not press against my glasses.

"Blink."

I did.

"Now open your eyes." His hands slipped away. He pulled mine as well, clasping them within his.

Drawing a deep breath, I opened my eyes . . .

A familiar face appeared before me. Head tilted to the angle I'd had mine and glasses askew. A moment or two later, realization dawned that I looked at myself only without the reverse effect of mirrors.

Alex meant seeing through my eyes very literally.

He was a sorcerer.

And now he knew I was one as well, or he wouldn't have been able to cast the spell.

If I saw through his eyes and he through mine, then at least he didn't see the not-so-lovely view of my face stretching wide in astonishment, mouth hanging open.

"You're a sorcerer!" The basic fact blew everything else out of my mind—blasted out thoughts of snakes and bulls and dads starting second families.

Alex. My friend Alex. My first college friend. The man I'd played hundreds of frisbee games and cards and studied with. The guy whose house I'd been in countless times. Whose father I'd met. Whom I'd spent an evening or two once upon a time kissing. Who . . . .

No. Couldn't be.

Yet I couldn't deny the evidence in front of me. I looked out of his eyes at myself.

I blinked and held my eyes closed hard. For a moment I watched my own eyes snap shut and the skin around crinkle.

An instant later my vision cut out. My body jerked. I snapped my hands up over my own eyes—not Alex's—and held them there.

"It's safe to look." Alex touched my shoulder, then drew back. "You have your sight back."

"That's not funny."

"No, and yet it's glorious."

I cracked my lids at that, glaring at him.

"This is so tremendous." He beamed back at me. White teeth flashed as his mouth opened in a wide grin. "How long since you turned? Can't be much, or I'd have seen you on the list—"

A wild shriek rang out from inside the house, followed by gales of laughter.

Alex glanced to either side and frowned. Shaking his head, he grabbed my hand.

"We can't talk about this here. Come with me."

I let him guide me along the sidewalk to his house. Easier to follow along than resist. We retraced the steps I'd walked earlier, this time with Alex muttering under his breath all the while.

"When did it happen? Did whoever turned you at least get you a teacher? What kind of sorcerer lets a newbie go loose without warning them not to drink or take drugs or—"

"She did warn me," I said. Soft, because his words had triggered memory of the caution—I started to realize the depth of my own stupidity and that she'd meant me to follow her advice and avoid even beer.

All the same, Alex paused long enough to glare at me. "And you didn't listen?"

"I forgot. It's been a hard night."

He studied my face, and didn't push. Just ran his hand through his hair, shook his head, and went back to leading me up and into his home.

As soon as he opened the door, the pungent vinegary smell of adobo made me start. My mouth watered a little, and my stomach rumbled.

The living room looked as tidy as on all my previous visits. Bookcases filled with books lining one wall. Framed photos of family members hung on the opposite wall and lined up along the top of the wood mantelpiece. A couch and two matching comfy chairs, upholstered in a nubbly gray fabric.

Everything in its place and a place for everything. My gaze went right to the one thing out-of-place: an almost empty plate on the side table next to Professor Noches. It held stray grains of rice and chicken bones, the source of the wonderful smell.

The professor looked up as Alex shut the door behind us with a click. His eyebrows rose, and he set aside his book as he stood up and pulled his white polo shirt down before it could ride up.

"Emergency assistance required." Alex waved a hand at his father.

He shot Alex a puzzled look, then gave me a warm smile, with a touch of concern. "Are you all right, Viola? Here, have a seat."

I must've looked pretty dazed, for the professor took my elbow and guided me to sit on the couch. The over-stuffed cushions creaked as I settled down.

"Carrot or tomato?" Alex asked.

"Huh?"

"Carrot, then." Alex stretched out a hand toward the kitchen. A moment later a bottle of carrot juice flew through the door into his hand with a smack. He pulled off the top and handed it to me. "Drink it up, every last drop. It'll help ground you."

I'd heard a lot of things about carrot juice, but not "grounding" as a benefit. Nevertheless, I tilted the bottle back and let the sweet liquid trickle down my throat. Warmth spread through me, accompanied by a fuzzy sensation as though I'd donned a pair of ultra comfy pajamas..

When I finished it, Alex handed me another and I drank that, too.

"Thanks." More warmth let my muscles ease. My stomach rumbled, couldn't help it with the professor's leftovers so nearby.

"Doing better?" Alex gave me a visual once-over, then nodded. "How about some dinner? I'll fix you a plate." He took the empty bottles and his father's plate with him as he left.

"Is this a recent development?" Professor Noches settled back into his chair, hands steepled as he studied me. "It's wonderful news, of course."

"Yeah, new. I guess. If you mean since I turned. A couple days." The actual number escaped me at the moment. "Less than a week."

"Ah, then that may explain your, er, distraction yesterday?" He nodded, lips curving in a broad smile. "Welcome to the world of sorcerers."

"Thanks. I take it you're a sorcerer, too?" The number I knew had just doubled, but it didn't sink in, not really. Too many shocks. By this point, I'd gone numb, nodding and accepting everything. Processing and analysis could wait until tomorrow—or whenever I had the strength to deal with it all.

"Runs in the family." He waved at the images covering the wall. Popping up out of his chair, he whisked over to the mantel and selected the center photo. He settled next to me on the couch, and the cushions creaked again. "Last summer!"

I took the photo from him, the wood frame still warm where he'd held it. Easily twenty inches long, it weighed more than I expected. I let it slip enough to brace the bottom against my thighs.

At least forty people ranged across the panorama. The women all wore beautiful formal gowns and the men had embroidered shirts worn untucked over trousers. Some sat or knelt on the ground, others sat in chairs, and a third row stood behind with a night-time cityscape in the background. Perhaps Manila. The professor had told the class the first day he was a naturalized citizen and loved both his countries. An older man and woman sat the center. White-haired and beaming, each had a yellow boutonniere pinned on, and they held hands. Good will and energy radiated out from one and all.

Not a magical photo as such. No one moved.

I searched the faces two times over before I located Alex, behind and to the right of the older woman. He had a broad smile, and his cream-colored shirt with a band collar and subtle gold embroidery set off his face and shoulders. The professor stood next to him, smile almost as wide, and on the other side . . .

"He's a sorcerer, too?" I pointed to Emilio. Perhaps I should have guessed, for the professor said sorcery ran in the family and Alex and Emilio were cousins. One more sorcerer that I hadn't known I knew.

"Yes, everyone there."

"Wow. That's a lot of sorcerers."

"It is all well and good to have friends who are not sorcerers. Most of Alex's friends in high school were mundane. But there is so much about sorcery that mundanes never understand that it doesn't do to marry someone who isn't a sorcerer." The professor shook his head and clicked his tongue. "If they never turn, you end up keeping some of yourself from them as though you are living two separate lives. Or worse, if they do turn they are angry at you for not having told them before."

He took the photo back, running a finger over the central

couple and then himself and Alex. Turning his head, he gave me a smile but it had a bitter edge not present in the image.

"Now you have turned there is much to learn, but Alex will help."

"Of course I'll help, but what are you showing her?" Alex swept around in front of us, able to sneak up because the thick rug muffled his footsteps. "Ah, Lalo and Lala's fiftieth wedding anniversary. That was a great trip. Making the arrangements was a beast, but worth it."

He lifted the frame from his father's lap and returned it to the mantel.

"Now, come and have something to eat, it'll help." He turned his gaze from me to his father. "Will you join us? I spooned up some maja blanca for dessert."

Alex had laid out three settings at the dining table, a small plate of chicken adobo for me and bowls of coconut pudding for him and his father with a third set aside. The chicken smelt so good, and nearly melted in my mouth. I managed a few bites of the pudding, after. They talked with me at the table, but I didn't contribute much.

After we were done eating, the professor raised no objections when Alex took me up to his room to talk. He did give Alex a speaking look and reminder to "mind himself," but returned to the living room and settled back into his chair with his book.

I'd visited the house before and knew the way to Alex's room—up the stairs and to the right, across from the bathroom. Alex lived at home, of course, to save money since it would be silly to live in the dorms in the same town. Especially as most of his family believed in adult children living with relatives until they struck out on their own. Emilio also stayed there, in the spare room, although he was still out partying somewhere.

Alex's room hadn't changed since my last visit. Still neat

and tidy, if not to the same degree as the living areas down-stairs. The bookshelf boasted rows of books and video game consoles. The desk held his laptop and a textbook. A comb and framed photo of a young Alex with his father sat atop the walnut bureau but nothing else. A blue T-shirt hung over the back of his slat-back wooden desk chair and he hadn't tucked the blue and white striped bedsheets under his twin bed, just pulled them up over his pillow. Posters covered his walls, all of beautiful landscapes from around the world.

He gestured for me to sit on the bed, and swung the chair around to sit backward with his forearms and head resting on the top slat.

"Why didn't you tell me you turned?"

"I didn't know I could. How should I know you'd be a sorcerer too?"

"You'd have had about a one-in-three chance of being right." His foot tapped against the floor, setting up a low racket.

"And I'd know that how? It's been less than a week! What I don't know about sorcery is . . ." My body sank further into the mattress. "Everything."

"Okay." He ran a hand through his hair, leaving the strands in disarray. "I get that. I just wish—" He shook his head and looked away.

"I'm sorry." Repeating the apology doesn't seem to make any difference. "I didn't know I could tell you. For all I knew, I'd already met the only sorcerers around."

"That might be true about anywhere but here." He stared at some speck on the wall or something. "Arden's one of the top colleges for sorcerers in the nation. Nationally, there aren't many sorcerers. Two percent of the population or less. But here . . . almost a quarter of every new class are sorcerers, and by the time a class graduates the number rises to at least a third. Plus half the faculty and staff are sorcerers."

"That's . . ." It was all too much to take, on top of everything else. The numbers went in one ear and out the other. I managed to grasp that a lot of people around here were sorcerers and I'd hurt Alex by not realizing I could tell him.

"Did you know the registrar's a sorcerer, too?" He still wouldn't look at me. "She runs a magical report that compiles a list of all students who are sorcerers, so the faculty can identify new-turned and make sure they have access to the additional classes and tutorials offered for sorcerers. I check the list as soon as it comes out, every Monday, and your name has never been there."

"I told you, it was just this week." Then his words, or some of them, registered. "You've been looking for me on the list?"

"Of course." Alex's neck bones gave a snap, he swiveled around to look at me again so fast—eyes wide and startled. He planted his feet firm on the floor with a solid stamp.

"Why wouldn't you just talk to me? Tell me about sorcery?" My turn to be upset. I threw up my hands in disbelief. "We've known each other for over a year and you haven't said anything, and now you're yelling at me for not telling you. Well excuse me, but go yell at yourself in the mirror!"

"I couldn't tell you." Of course now that I'd got angry, his voice became the epitome of calm.

"Why not, some kind of law?"

"It never works out. Do you think it hasn't been tried? That I haven't tried in the past?" He grimaced and recommenced tapping a foot against the rug. "No, telling people who aren't sorcerers about magic just doesn't work. At least not around here."

We both stewed for a few moments or minutes. An unpleasant variation of our old waiting game, seeing who'd break first.

But I couldn't stay angry for long. Hated having friends or family—anyone I cared about—angry at me for long.

"I'll forgive you for not telling me if you do the same."

"Deal." He got off the chair, making the chair legs rock against the floor. A few steps brought him to the bed and he sat next to me. The mattress dipped enough to send our hips sliding into each other. He took my hand and held it between both of his. My fingers weren't cold, but I warmed at the touch. "I just . . . I've been wishing you'd turn since last spring when you came so close."

"What about last spring?" I kept my voice even, although he'd started stroking my fingers. The scrape of his callused fingertip sent shivers down my spine.

"Right before finals, you saw . . . something sorcerous." He glanced away then turned a wry smile my way. "You asked me if I'd seen it too, which I had. For almost a day you kept turning it over, whether or not you'd seen it or hallucinated. Then I had to listen to you talk yourself out of believing."

A series of trembles rippled through my body. I shook my head, not denying him but trying to process that I'd come close to believing in sorcery before. Searched my memory for a few minutes but found faint scraps of memories at best. Nothing real, nothing I could hold onto.

"It's okay if you don't remember. Don't force it." He cupped my cheek with one hand, eyes gazing right into mine. "The important thing is, you've turned now."

"All it took was—"

He clapped a hand over my mouth before I could say anymore.

"Don't tell me. Not now. Not unless you want to." He lifted his hand a moment later.

"Why not?"

"Because it's special. It says something about you and what you can believe in. The general advice is for turned sorcerers never to share the details of why they turn except with people they truly trust."

"That's . . . I guess it makes sense." So I didn't tell him.

He moved on to another topic immediately. "You didn't know how many sorcerers there are around here, but you do have a teacher, right?"

"Yeah. Regina Roth."

He froze. His whole body went still, including his lungs. After a moment, he let out a long, slow breath with a faint whistle. Drew in a deep breath, and then repeated the name, syllable by syllable, as a question.

"You know her?" Not only had I forgotten Regina's warning not to drink alcohol, but her comment that many people at the college didn't like her.

"I've never met her, not really, though I've seen her around." He stared off into the distance, then flashed me warning glance. "My father hates her. Don't ever let him know she's your teacher unless you want to see him blow up."

"She said she'd turn me over to someone on campus once I know the basics, anyway."

"Good."

I could almost see wheels turning in his head, wanting to know the details of my turn, but that soon passed. Instead, he beamed at me with such gladness and hope I couldn't help but smile right back.

"You're a sorcerer. Finally. We're not supposed to hope anyone turns, but of everyone, you're the one I most wanted to turn."

He leaned in, moving slow enough that I had ample time to pull back. If anything, I bent forward and met him in the middle.

Of all that happened that night, kissing him made the most sense. Brought continuity from my life before—before the swan, sorcery, my father's news, and everything else.

We'd fooled around the spring before, but he'd stopped.

Not this time. His lips were warm and soft against mine, tasting of coconut pudding. Figuring out how to angle our faces without my glasses poking him took a moment, but after that . . . it was just him and me, with the rest of the world falling away.

Our arms slid around each other's backs, pulling closer.

"*Alejandro!*" A stern woman's voice blazed in both our ears.

We bolted a foot apart and pressed our hands over our ears until the reverberations died down.

"Tiya Amelia must've put that spell on when she and Tiyo Roberto brought Emilio here last fall." Alex laughed. He slipped back along the sheets to sit next to me, but didn't do anything more than nudge me with his shoulder. "She's all for equality between sexes and genders, but wants everyone to abide by strict moral precepts and chastity until marriage."

"If that's the kind of warning a kiss gets, I'm not sure I want to know what anything more gets." Much as I wanted to kiss him again, not if it meant risking my ears.

He brushed a finger across my mouth.

"Later."

❧ 13 ❧

I woke in my own bed the next morning alone and exhausted. No energy and no will to rise and face the day. I'd left the window ajar, enough that when raindrops hit the glass they slid down and dropped onto the sill. Watching the raindrops fall was about as much as I felt up to doing.

A rainy Saturday morning. Cool, with a breeze that snuck through the gap and the plinking raindrops to make the room chilly and damp. The top sheet and the sunburst quilt my grandmother gave me for my fifteenth birthday had slipped down to my waist in the night, and left my shoulders and arms to shiver because my oversize T-shirt didn't offer much warmth. I yanked the covers back up, determined to stay in bed as long as I could.

That left me nothing to do but turn over all the events of yesterday. Too much, too fast. I still couldn't handle it all.

So when my phone rang, I leapt out of bed and snatched it from my desk. Whirled on one foot and dove back under the warm covers.

Even though I recognized the ring tone, and this wouldn't be an escape from yesterday.

"Hi, Mom."

We went through usual spiel of questions. Were my classes going well, did I enjoy them. How about my work-study job. Better yet, what had I gotten up to with my friends. Practiced music.

I tended to tell little white lies. Mom didn't need to hear about ups and downs with grades as long as they were up enough. Or how boring I found half my work at the college archives, although the rest I enjoyed. Or my tendency to practice the oboe five days a week instead of seven.

This time, I left out so much more. Swans. Magic. Friends who turned out to be sorcerers.

All of which made talking with her that morning harder than usual, until we got to the point of why she'd called, or at least the main point: the obvious ulterior motive of checking on me post Dad confession.

"Your father told you."

"How'd you figure that out?" I asked.

"How do you think? I am still living in the same house as Bea."

"Is she okay?" I switched my display to check for texts, but nothing new from Bea and just a general "how're you doing?" from Rose. A quick message from Dad—that could wait. One from Alex saying he'd be busy today but looked forward to seeing me at dinner and study group on Sunday. A couple from fellow musicians, including, hmm, one from Evan that I also saved for later because I didn't want to think about sorcery while talking to my mother.

Who, of course, hadn't paused for me check texts but kept on talking. I might've missed a line or two, but it didn't feel like it when I tuned back in.

"Your sisters are both more adaptable than you tend to give them credit. Bea will be fine." Mom gave extra emphasis to the last word, as if saying it that way made it so. "If anything, she seems relieved that matters are in the open at last and we can move forward. You're the one I'm more concerned about."

"Me?" I sat bolt upright, so fast my spine crackled.

"You had a harder time in high school. Home was your refuge when everything else went sour. I want you to know it still is. I'm still here in the house, and I don't plan to do anything drastic fast."

Oh God. I hadn't even thought about the ramifications of them actually separating and getting divorced. Of either not wanting the house we'd lived in my whole life. Of not having it as a place to go to escape from school, when that turned bad, or to return to from college.

But she'd said she planned to remain.

"No selling the house."

"Not in the short run. At least not as long as Bea's still in high school. After that, we'll see. But I'll always have room for you."

My head started to swim and I lay back down. Everything changed so fast.

Not just for me, though. Mom didn't know about my other changes—and this one had to be hitting her harder than me, although . . . "You're calmer than I'd have thought."

"I've had more time to work this through." She paused, then gave a long sigh. "Your father and I had some good years, then bad, and now we're moving in different directions."

"You don't mind . . . about the baby?"

"Does it sting a bit that he found someone else so fast? Maybe, but we've been on the offs for a while." She gave a low chuckle. "As for him starting a second family—and think of it that way, please, a second family not a new one because he and I are divorcing each other, not you and your sisters—he can have it. Dearly as I love you, I have no desire whatsoever to face another round of endless diapers and sleepless nights. In fact, if he ever irritates me again, I will take great delight in imagining him up to his knees in infant diarrhea."

"Eugh." I spent some time babysitting while in high school, and that brought back very visceral memories.

"Too much information?" She laughed. "I'm sorry. Though please keep that image in mind if you're ever tempted to skimp on birth control before you're ready."

Also not something I wanted to talk to her about, especially given the night before with Alex and his promise of "later."

I felt better about Bea and Rose by the time Mom and I ended the call, though not so much I didn't text them both to see how they were doing. Then waited around while snug under the covers because neither of them texted back any too fast.

I used the waiting time to practice the summoning spell Regina had showed me, and that Alex had done so well the night before.

My first attempt went awry, but nothing happened beyond a fizzling sensation in my fingertips rather akin to pins-and-needles. The second try worked out a lot better—except, I made the mistake of getting my three-quarters full glass water bottle from where it sat on my desk.

The heavy glass hit my hand with a loud smack. It hurt so much I couldn't breathe for a moment. I dropped the bottle onto the bed as a red welt formed on my palm. Alex had handled summoning bottles of carrot juice fine the night before, but those were plastic bottles not glass. I made a mental note made not to try summoning anything heavy.

For my next practice, I aimed for the protein bar left out on the desk.

Unfortunately, my timing was off. I let myself get distracted by a knock on the door and called out "yeah?" at the same moment as I started the spell.

Gloria took my word as permission to enter, just as the protein bar in its blue-and-white wrapper glory whipped across the room and smacked into my other hand. With less force and impact than the water bottle, but it still smarted. I decided to use less power next time—something I preferred to consider versus facing the consequences of Gloria's entrance.

She stood full clothed in a pale-yellow wrap-around top and jeans, hair pulled back in a pony tail and monarch butterfly earrings chiming at her ears. Quite the contrast to me, semi-prone and still in my nightshirt.

After glancing at the desk, then at the bar lying in my hand, she grimaced.

I braced myself for having managed to turn someone else when I still didn't know what I was doing.

"Crap, you turned?"

Her words registered a moment later, and my jaw dropped with a click.

"Wait a minute, you're a sorcerer too?" Alex's words last night about how many attended Arden came back to me with a kick. One out of four or one out of three . . . overall or of everyone I knew? If sorcerers tended to hang out together, then knowing one might mean knowing lots. "Who else?"

"Oh God, you not only turned, you're so new you're green." Gloria pulled my chair out, wood legs scraping against the tiled floor, and dropped down in a frustrated heap. "I don't have time for this."

"I haven't asked you for anything." I slid around the bed until I sat with my back pressed against the headrest.

"You're new. Everyone's supposed to help you, cut you some slack until you settle in." She shook her head and rolled her eyes. "I knew I should've gone to a more mundane college."

"Well, excuse me for turning and ruining your life." I crossed my arms over my chest, tucking my hands under. My palms still smarted from summoning the bottle and bar, which lay atop the covers by my side, but my fingers had gone cold.

"It's not your fault." Not much of an apology for so much resistance to my turning. "It's just . . . I liked having mundane roommates. Not having to constantly check my room for stupid practical sorcery jokes that my cousins send my way. Being able to open packages from home without having things explode in my face."

"None of your packages ever exploded."

"That's because you were around. Or Terri, before she got so scared she ran out of here as though her hair had caught fire." Another eye roll.

Oh God, how many of my friends had been keeping this secret all the time?

"Was Terri a sorcerer, too?"

"No, that's the whole point." Gloria waved a hand at me. "She saw something somewhere, though, and talked herself out of believing in it, but transferred just to get away. But you," she pointed an accusing finger my way, "you had to turn. Don't tell me what did it, I don't want to know, just tell me you haven't gone all the way yet and can go back."

"Too late."

"Crap and double crap."

"What's so bad about me turning?" Although still tucked under my arms, my hands had balled into fists.

"Not bad. Don't mind me, I just . . . don't like change." She took a deep breath. Standing up, she pulled on the hem of her shirt and rubbed at an invisible wrinkle or two, then gave me a twisted smile. "Congrats. Welcome to the insanity of sorcery. You've got a teacher?"

"Yeah."

"Good. Well, live and learn." Her face brightened a little, and she snapped her fingers. "And hey, now you can join our sorcery study group. This semester, we're meeting every other Monday evening in the library. The tower room."

"*Sorcery* study group?" Memories flashed before my eyes— Gloria entering the library with Ruth and Emilio and others, then leaving with Alex in tow. A sinking sensation formed in my belly. "Did you meet last Monday?"

"How'd you guess?"

Irony in action: half the reason I ran around the lake, and discovered magic, was to get away from seeing my friends meeting without me—to study sorcery!

❧ 14 ❧

The discovery still stung the next day, when I headed into the library myself to study with my friends. Not for the sorcery group, but the regular Sunday evening meet-up.

Saturday's drizzle had morphed into a solid sheeting rain mixed with unpredictable wind gusts. Everything got wet. My sneakers squelched and oozed as I stomped along the paths. My leggings likewise sopped up rain. My light blue polo shirt was drier, but that wasn't saying much. The wind gusts kept sending rain sideways and even up under my umbrella. At least I'd splurged on a good backpack to keep my laptop safe.

A layer of moisture coated my skin, damped my hair, and trickled down my spine. Worst of all, drops splattered my glasses so I viewed the world through a hazy blur that ranked little better than going without.

A last burst of wind blew me into the library. I folded my umbrella and resisted the urge to shake myself like a dog coming in from the rain. Stepping to the side, so others could enter or leave, I sought the driest part of my shirt—which proved to be my collar—and dried my glasses. Mostly.

Library staff had laid out rubber mats to reduce the amount of water on the slick floors—plus "leave one / take one" umbrella bins on either side of the entryway. Umbrellas of all sizes and colors stuck out of the bins, but I hesitated and weighed mine in my hand. Hardly special and not worth much, but better than having no umbrella.

"Go ahead and stick it in a bin." One of the staff called from the desk nearby. "I promise there will be enough for you to take one when you leave."

The signs posted next to the bins encouraged people to leave wet umbrellas there, and pledged anyone wanting an umbrella would find one to take. Fair words, but how could they make them true?

I froze for a second, then slipped my umbrella into the nearest bin. A faint fizzle of some kind of power sent a burst of static electricity up my arms. Air fluttered around me, as though an air handler nearby had kicked on. My shoes still squelched as I crossed the floor, and my clothes and hair clung to my skin. All the same, I'd moved at least one or two steps closer to damp from sopping.

Maybe the library had a sorcerer on staff.

On that thought, I swung by the desk—though I didn't dare ask about anything other than whether the tower room was reserved—and then headed up the far stairs. I took the first set of steps at my usual pace. Perhaps a little slower, given my shoes hadn't completely dried.

Or for other reasons. The tension making the muscles in my legs twitch, and swirling as a heavy weight in my belly. I shouldn't be scared or uncertain. I'd made this climb so many times before.

All of that was before . . .

Before the swan, magic, and Evan.

Before I learned my friends kept secrets from me.

I changed, not the rest of the world. Everything else remained as before. Everyone else . . .

Such a stark lie I couldn't even make myself believe it for a moment.

Everything had changed. Gloria wasn't happy about my turning, though she'd tried to put a nice face on things, and she hadn't spent much time in our suite since. Avoiding me? Or just spending the weekend hanging with Ruth? Maybe the latter, but I suspected partly the former.

Alex had been much more welcoming and I'd gotten a couple of texts from him, but hadn't seen him, or Emilio or Ruth or Gordon.

Not unprecedented. We all did have our own separate interests. Several weekends last year everyone went off doing their own thing. Though: that happened all of three times, and I could name the days if I wanted to, that's how close a watch I'd kept.

So as I climbed, part of me wondered if anyone would be there. Well, someone would be there, because the room was already reserved, but maybe not by my friends. It might be we'd start splintering off in different directions. By the time I reached the last landing before the final approach to the tower, I'd slowed nearly to a stop.

"Hey, Viola!"

I jerked and my foot slipped. My hand on the railing, fingers gripping tight, saved me from a fall. Glancing up, my eyes met Alex peering over the railing down at me.

"Don't startle me like that!"

"Sorry."

He ran down the stairs, steps light and shoes dry, likewise his jeans and black T-shirt. He all but smacked into me, as though he'd meant to grab me in a hug, but stopped at the last moment. A hand's breadth of air separated us. Warmth emanated from him, not only due to his wide smile.

"Hey, you're still soaked." His brown eyes gave me the once-over.

"Well, we all can't dance between raindrops." I patted the hem of my shirt and end of my ponytail, which, while wet, weren't anywhere near as bad as before. The shirt did cling extra close to my chest and waist, though, and Alex's gaze lingered there for a few moments.

"Let me take care of that, until you learn to do it yourself. Okay?"

"If you mean help out with the damp, then sure."

He snapped both his fingers.

Another ripple of energy surged through me and every hair on my head seemed to crackle. Shoes, leggings, shirt, hair, everything lost dampness in a moment. He might've dried me up a bit too much, but I'd take it without complaining. Rather, "I've got to learn that one."

"I'll show you, if your teacher doesn't." Alex glanced back up at the top of the stairs, voice dropping. "Before anything else, I wanted . . . there's that quiz radio show recording at the Big Hall Wednesday evening. Do you want to go?"

"I thought it was sold out." An extra warmth spread through me, separate from the sudden, sorcerous dryness.

"I've got tickets." He waved a hand and they appeared in his fingers long enough for him to flash them at me. Twisting his arm back and forth, the muscles rippling beneath his skin because he had a short-sleeve shirt on, showed he had nowhere to hide the tickets. Waving his hand a second time, they vanished.

"Is that real magic or stage?"

"Real, but I can do some tricks, too. Doesn't hurt." He made the tickets appear and disappear again. "So, yes or no?"

He'd picked something he knew we'd both enjoy, and got the tickets somehow. How could I refuse?

Though I couldn't resist teasing him, just a little.

Pretended to pause and think it over—my cheeks turned hot and I must've blushed red because he smiled and didn't look at all surprised when I agreed. "It's a date."

"Good." He leaned in closer, as though about to kiss me, but at the last minute shifted to the side and whispered in my ear. "No anti-fooling around spells here."

"Alex!" Emilio appeared at the top of the stairs. Threw his hands out to either side—waving at me and giving his cousin the finger—then gave a big huff that made his chest rise high and fall. "What are you waiting for? We're all here."

"He's as bad as his mother." Alex shook his head, then turned around and waved back with the same finger. Emilio stuck out his tongue in response, but grinned back. "We'll be right there." Alex grabbed my hand and pulled me up the last set of steps.

The wide doorway at the other end of the narrow landing held two doors. Both had a trio of arched windowpanes set into them so that anyone passing by—mostly library staff when they made their rounds counting heads—could see what we did and that we weren't up to no good. The doors lay opened as wide as possible.

Thus I had an excellent view of Gloria, Ruth, and Emilio. He'd booked it over to the table, sitting opposite the women. All of them had laptops laid out on tables and textbooks open. Chemical formulae covered the whiteboard mounted on the far wall, an oddity since only Emilio was studying chemistry this semester.

The windows to either side of the whiteboard offered dramatic views of the campus, lake, and forest—in good weather. Little flickers of light shone between gusts of rain and wind this night. No sign at all of white swan wings, although to be fair it was lousy weather for flying.

Alex pulled the doors closed behind us.

"Surprise!"

The instant the latches clicked, the room changed. Balloons in all colors of the rainbow appeared out of nowhere. Something exploded, tossing green and white ribbons and confetti into the air. Horns rang out a triple blast, followed by three chimes of an alto bell. The sweet smell of fresh baked apples and cinnamon filled the room—because the laptops and textbooks disappeared from the table, replaced by a pie and carton of ice cream—and the number of people doubled.

Last but not least, the chemical formulae on the whiteboard changed to read "Welcome to Sorcery, Viola!"

"What . . ."

Ruth burst into an off-key rendition of the words to the tune of happy birthday, and by the second line everyone else had joined in. Most, alas, with no better pitch than her.

I wavered a little, adjusting to all the changes . . . and all the people I could now add to my mental list of fellow sorcerers. This kept growing, and doubling, and much as I appreciated knowing I wasn't alone, I wouldn't mind if my world didn't keep turning over and changing so fast.

Emilio, of course, I knew to be a sorcerer; Professor Noches had told me as much. But Ruth I hadn't guessed at. Or Lina and Marta, two fellow sophomores who I'd played frisbee and hung out with many times last year—the same two students I'd seen Alex, Gloria, Emilio, and Ruth with last Monday—at their sorcerous study group.

Alex whisked my bag away from me to set in a corner with other backpacks as Gloria and Ruth led me to the study table. A fresh apple pie plus vanilla ice cream and bowls and spoons lay there. Gloria dished up a big piece of pie into a bowl and topped it with a massive heap of ice cream, then handed it to me.

"Welcome to sorcery."

"I thought you were mad I'd turned."

"Well I am, but I'm also happy for you." She served herself and Ruth, then moved away from the table so others could help themselves. "I thought it would never happen, after all the times you ignored sorcery last year!"

"Way to welcome her." Ruth gave her a gentle nudge with her elbow. "Pay no attention to Gloria. You know she just doesn't like change. I'm happy for you."

Ruth gave me a warm hug, albeit an awkward one because we both had bowls of pie and ice cream at risk of getting poured down each other's back.

"Thanks."

"New sorcerers almost always wreak wonderful havoc. We're going to have so much fun! Right, Gloria, Alex?"

"Yeah, fun." Gloria rolled her eyes, but her lips curved in a rueful smile.

Most people had pie by then, but no one had taken a bite, so I dug in and moaned from the exquisite melding of hot apples with cinnamon, flaky pastry, and cool, smooth ice cream.

Emilio waited until I'd finished eating before he gave me a hug, with a wink and a quirk of his eyes toward Alex.

The other students contented themselves, and me, with shaking hands and pats on the back.

I missed one face as they passed me around for congratulations. Gordon usually met up with the rest of us here every Sunday night.

"Where's Gordon?"

"He texted me earlier—went on a weekend trip to NYC and got stuck in traffic on the way back." Alex shook his head. "We wouldn't be having this welcome for you if he were here, as he hasn't turned."

"Probably won't." Gloria sounded relieved.

"You never know. He might turn in his eighties. Stranger things have happened."

This left a slight mournful edge to the evening, because Gordon had been one of us since day one. Yet although I sort of wished he were a sorcerer too, that couldn't taint the warmth and welcome of the evening. One of the best sensations in the world: being welcomed by my friends into the fellowship of sorcerers.

❧ 15 ❧

Soon as I busted out of my sociology class the next morning, I had my phone in my hand. The hard plastic case warmed in my hand as I entered my pass- word and checked my texts.

This made me one of many phone zombies wandering the halls. At least I recognized the dangers, and pulled off to the side. Leaning back against the dingy, whitewashed plaster, I ignored as best I could all the other students and occasional professor or staff member pounding the halls. I do mean pounding. Collectively, they made the floor shake and created enough vibration to make my teeth ache. Half of them jabbered on their phones, or to friends, and the other half texted away, and avoiding collisions at the last minute. Sighs. Groans. Moans.

Sometimes, the corridor offered the best kind of people watching in the world. Not this time.

I scrolled up and down, and would've gone sideways if I could've. Ever since Friday, I'd been trying to catch Bea for a proper back-and-forth conversation—calling or texting, didn't matter, as long as it was one.

Bea's lunch hour should be prime time for contact.

We'd texted asynchronously since Friday. Me checking in to see how she was doing, and her blowing me off.

Rose too, but not quite so bad. We caught up a little Sunday afternoon—texting each other in real time—enough for me to know she stayed pissed at Dad for his timing, while relieved to have everything out in the open. She also alerted me that Dad said he planned to head her way this week to take her to dinner and "explain things more," and I could expect the same.

But Bea kept texting back she was fine and nothing more, no detail.

Just "believe me!"

And I did, but . . . I also wanted to hear and be sure, because this kind of news would've thrown me for a loop if Dad had broken the news at the start of my senior year.

"Ahem."

I jerked and my elbows pressed tight against either side of my chest. The hard wall behind me kept me standing, but gave me nowhere to retreat.

Unfortunate, for the woman before me inspired the urge to shrink away. Not, mind, due to any unkindness on her part. A gentle smile curved thin, pink lips and amusement lurked in warm green-brown eyes.

Of middling height and roses-under-beige complexion, Professor Helen Maia carried more weight than the Surgeon General would approve, though she wore it well under a long, flowing tunic of forest green that stopped above her knees, and black trousers below. She'd shod her feet in classic style black Crocs. Her short, dark brown hair showed mismatched earrings: a brass star dangled from the right and a white-and-brown feather with black marks, no longer than three inches, from her left.

Not the kind of description that, in the mainstream U.S., equated to power and command—yet these exuded from her every pore. The very air crackled around her.

It didn't hurt that I recognized her on sight as a major bigwig in the psychology department. The kind of name passed among majors as a someone to be sure and take at least one course from, which I hadn't had a chance as yet.

But she gave one of the lectures all freshmen were required to attend last year. One of the more interesting ones, too, because she focused on how much psychologists and researchers didn't know about people, and various ways the research we read might be or was flawed or biased, and the importance of more people exploring more questions in more ways with more other people.

"You're Viola, are you not?" She held out her hand. "Would you mind stepping into my office to talk? This won't take long."

I froze for a moment at the sound of my name in her calm, alto voice. Her hand stayed extended, unmoving. Fumbling, I transferred my phone to my left and placed my right in hers—then jerked again as an electric shock ran through me.

"Of course."

We shook hands. I rubbed mine afterward, as it felt a bit numb. Although lacking any clue as to what she wanted with me, I followed along anyway as she led me past the cluster of students waiting outside her door.

"Go ahead and sign up. Office hours start at two and there are plenty of spots left." She smiled at the other students, and pointed at the notice beneath her nameplate. A clipboard hung from a hook below, bearing a half-filled sign-up sheet. A pen dangling from twine tied to the metal clip.

The next moment, she swept me into her office and my

ears popped. All sounds from the corridor melted away. My shoes squeaked on the industrial tile floor, the same pale yellow as the hallway.

The latch clicked as the door shut behind us. Turning my head, I caught two or three students peering through the long glass window inset in the door. They shaded their eyes with their hands, as though straining to see in, and then moved away.

The office itself was long and thin, with windows at one end. She'd positioned the big L-shaped walnut desk bearing a large monitor and several neat piles of paper so that when she sat at her computer she faced the view over the main academic quad, with the forest in the distance. Nice and light, even at midday with the sun overhead rather than streaming in.

The side walls each bore one large piece of art. To the left, a large oil painting of a forest, although on closer examination all the trees turned out to have human forms. Opposite hung an immense photograph of endless sand dunes flowing into one another under a blazingly blue sky.

The walls at either end, in stark contrast, held at least two dozen pieces of children's artwork, from a rainbow colored hand-print to a family of stick-figures with a mother, father, child, and dog. Or cat or some other four-legged beast, as all I saw of the pet was legs, ears, and tail.

At her gesture, I sat down in a plain, low-backed, short-legged metal armchair upholstered in maple-colored cloth, and let my backpack sink into a heap between my feet. The chair cushion gave a duck-like squeak as I dropped onto it. A moment later, a faint odor of mint filled the air and the chair shifted around me. The seat rose just enough that my feet rested square on the floor. The arm rests likewise shifted to the perfect height for me, and stretched thinner so they supported my arms from elbows to fingertips. The back didn't move.

"What is this?" I almost jumped out of my seat, resisting because I caught the calculating look on her face as she watched the chair adapt to my body.

"A prototype I'm testing for a friend who doesn't like chairs made to fit so-called average body types. She prefers furniture that adjusts to the dimensions and preferences of whomever sits on it." Professor Maia walked a half-circle around me and the chair. "I don't think she's quite there yet, but this is close."

"Not there yet?"

"No."

I twisted around to watch the professor as she stood behind me and laid a hand on the back of the chair. It creaked and jerked, then moved in an inch or to and adjusted to provide support for my lower back.

"It's like sorcery."

"That's because it is." She raised an eyebrow at me, a small smile on her face as she rounded the desk to take her own seat on the other side. "Although mundane students tend to assume there's technology at work. Much though there is to dislike about technology, or at least the way too many people use and abuse it, it does give a great deal of cover to those of us who practice magic."

"You're a sorcerer, too." Not a question, not at this point. "Is there anyone who isn't?"

"Oh yes, the vast majority of this country's population are mundane." She gave a rueful sigh and shake of her head. "But you are far from the first to turn to sorcery and find many sorcerers among those you know. You may well feel as though you are constantly discovering them among your acquaintances, friends, and family for some time—in places and people you never dreamed might have a magical other life."

"Is that a . . . a warning?"

"Does it need to be?"

"I dunno. You're the expert."

"Expert in what sense, though?" She raised an eyebrow. "There is the old joke about the shoemaker's children going barefoot. I sometimes see a resemblance to myself."

I had no idea how to react to that, so I kept my mouth shut.

"Well, that's tangent I hadn't planned to take quite that way." Another rueful sigh, followed by a warm smile. "My first purpose in bringing you here was to welcome you. Which I do."

"Thanks." Dozens of questions blew through my head, of which three lingered longest. How had she learned I turned? Why did she care? What did she want with me?

"I also want to ensure you become aware of the resources the college offers that are now open to you." She rapped neatly trimmed, pale-pink fingernails against the surface of the desk. "For instance, any class you take from a sorcerer instructor may have an optional sorcerous component. There are sorcerous support groups, including one intended for students who turn into sorcerers while here at Arden. I'll send you information on that, though it should also be included in the packet you'll receive from the registrar's office in a day or two, since your name showed up on the list as newly turned. And I recommend checking out the sorcerous version of Arden College's website, which lists a lot of resources to help you adjust."

"Should I be writing any of this down?" I twisted my backpack straps between my fingers, the coarse cloth rough against my skin.

"We're used to finding newly turned sorcerers among the students. There's a whole machinery that springs into action.

You'll get a lot of emails." She leveled a stern glance at me. "Be sure to read them."

"Okay." My glasses had gotten a bit steamy for some reason. I took them off and cleaned the lenses with the hem of my shirt. The world turned to a blur of colors until I put them back on, and the professor's face resolved into a wry grin.

"Are you wondering why, in that case, I'm involved?"

"Maybe."

"Regina asked me to find someone suitable to be your next teacher, once she's shown you the basics. She mentioned you know her son Evan and he turned you."

"Yeah." I startled as her words registered. "Regina asked you?"

"I am, alas, the person who turned her many years ago." She grimaced, mouth wrinkling as though she'd tasted something sour.

"So she's a turned sorcerer, too?"

"Indeed. You can talk to her about the stresses and strains of having your world flip upside down in a moment. I, fortunately or unfortunately, am a born sorcerer. Raised in a sorcerous family, and Regina tells me, often, that no matter how much I sympathize I do not and cannot understand what turned sorcerers face." She must have read puzzlement in my face. "Regina is my second cousin. Just far enough removed that none of her parents, grandparents, or siblings worked sorcery, unlike mine."

"How does that work?" Evan had mentioned it being difficult to stop doing magic, being magic.

"It varies. Most born never lose sorcery. You have to want to very much, so far as I know. Although there are some cultures and practices that include banishment from sorcery, or curses. Then there are many groups within the U.S. whose concepts of magic do not emphasize either-or, either you do sorcery or disbelieve. Very confusing, I know." Professor Maia shook her head, a quick, violent motion. "But that's a tangent for another day. The point now is that Regina asked for your next teacher to be turned as well, which narrows the field quite a bit. I can think of one or two who might be suitable. I presume you would also prefer a turned?"

I agreed, for lack of any real idea what the difference might be. My head whirled as I started to appreciate how little I knew.

"Very well." Professor Maia gave a sharp nod. "I'll see who has the time to take on a new advisee. It may take a week or two to settle on one, but Regina is willing to keep teaching you until then."

"Sounds good to me."

"Excellent. I'll be in touch as things work out."

I started to rise, but the chair grabbed me—pinching my waist until I plopped back down.

"Before you go, a few pieces of advice, if I may." The professor didn't acknowledge my movement, apart from a glint in her eyes. Instead, she wove her fingers together and leaned her head upon her intertwined hands. "I realize that unasked-for advice is often ignored, and you are at liberty to forget what I have said the minute you leave this room—but I hope you will remember."

"Okay?"

"First, take things easy. You do not need to learn all you can at once. Indeed, as a new sorcerer you are powerful for the simple reason that you don't know yet what others have written off as impossible or too complicated to pursue—or inadvisable for personal, societal, or cultural reasons. Go at whatever speed feels most comfortable, but I recommend dipping your toes rather than jumping in with both feet. It's the best way to avoid accidental unpleasantness."

"Take it easy. Got that." No problem, but I frowned at the

last part of the warning. "Accidents like . . . turning men into pigs?"

"Ah, someone's introduced you to the Greek classics?"

"Evan mentioned Circe and accidental sorcery."

"He would." She chuckled, then shook her head and her voice lowered. "Accidental sorcery is, indeed, a risk but there's a very simple way to avoid it."

The professor folded her hands and waited. I broke first. "And that is?"

"Don't want anything too much. Especially not the impossible." She tilted her head to one side, lips curving likewise. "At least, not yet."

"I don't get . . . what does wanting have to do with it?"

"It's one of the elements of sorcery."

"Oh, right. Desire."

"That's one way of putting it," she said. "You have to desire, want, focus, *will* something to happen for sorcery to take place. So for these first months, take life as easy as you can. You have time."

"All right." Simple enough advice, though a lot easier for her to say than me to follow.

"Also, remember that turning into a sorcerer doesn't make you a different person unless you want that to happen. You're still you, just with newfound power."

That also made sense, so I nodded—and waited. The room grew so silent the loudest sound became the scrape of air passing through our mouths. Her gaze turned inward, a tortured expression twisting her face for a moment.

"Likewise, the people you knew before whom you now discover are sorcerers are the same people they always were. Please, do not hold it against them that they did not tell you about sorcery."

Faces flashed before my eyes: Evan, Alex, Professor Noches, Gloria, Ruth, Emilio . . . the others at the party last night . . . Professor Maia. All these people I'd met in some capacity before, without knowing they practiced sorcery.

So many. But I could deal with that. They'd all been welcoming enough, with the partial exception of Gloria.

So, no problem taking this other advice as well.

Until the next day.

❧ 16 ❧

Professor Maia's advice was the last thing on my mind the next morning when I slipped into a chair in Professor Noches' classroom and waited for him to arrive.

Things sounded the same as always, most of the students tapping away with fingers on phones or laptops, or feet against the floor. A little chitchat here and there, nothing worth listening in on. Someone had left a dry-erase marker uncapped on the ledge beneath the whiteboard at the far end, so the room stank a bit. Wooden chairs, all scuffed and pulled up around a big, old table. The top didn't have too many scars, but underneath (not that I looked, but the table legs alone told the story) were carved dozens of not hundreds of initials and graffiti.

Most of us in the class were there, only one missing. We left the chair at the head of the table for the professor because he always picked that seat. Gloria sat opposite me, head bent over her phone. She'd turned the streak in her hair pink, and paired it with deep-purple earrings, a matching wrap-around shirt, and black leggings.

Much more striking than my plain green Arden T-shirt, with loose threads in the tag that made the back of my neck itch. My jeans offered little cushioning against the hard wood seat—this chair, unlike Professor Maia's, didn't adjust and as a result my heels dangled while my toes brushed the floor.

A series of quick steps down the hall preceded the door flinging open and crashing shut behind Professor Noches. He wore a light blue, button-down shirt, navy trousers, and brown shoes. He'd run his hands through his hair a few times, leaving it rather disheveled. He dropped his laptop onto the table from no more than an inch in height, but it landed with a thud suitable to an elephant stomp.

Every spine stiffened and every head turned his way. He stretched out his hands to either side and smiled at us.

"I bring you good news." He turned his head around the table, counting us off and saying our names—all the way from Gloria to me. With a graceful move, he dropped into his chair and pulled up to the table. "Fifteen students. Fifteen sorcerers, plus me. Viola has turned."

All eyes fixed on me, except Gloria and the professor. My nerves jangled as they worked through the meaning of his words and then burst out into a ragged but wholehearted cheer.

Meanwhile, I finally remembered—and put together—something the professor had said the other night when he learned I had turned.

Every single person in Professor Noche's symbology course was a sorcerer. From the first day of class to the Tuesday after I accepted sorcery, I'd been the sole person in the room with no clue. The professor taught them sorcery around me. Over my head. Through me, without my realizing.

So the other students weren't cheering me turning so

much as that the course would now openly be about sorcery. Most of them didn't know me other than as a fellow student in this one course. I'd taken classes with no more than one of them before. They didn't care about me turning—only that I was no longer an obstacle to getting direct sorcerous instruction from the professor along with the regular course content.

In turn, he rejoiced because he no longer had to tread a fine line in teaching them sorcery without making me aware that there were layers I missed. The college wouldn't allow professors to limit classes to sorcerer students. Instructors could design courses for sorcerers, and market them to students who were sorcerers, but if any mundane registered they had to get sufficient value.

Realization didn't dawn on me in a moment, but over the course of the ninety-minute class. A time during which it became very clear very fast that I was in over my head. Most of what they said might as well be in a foreign language. They described spells to do this, that, and the other—and the different types of symbols used to make them manifest. Nesting spells within spells. Setting contingencies so spells triggered under specific conditions.

Me? All I knew was how to summon things from across a room, and I couldn't even manage that without hitting myself in the head or chest half the time instead of having the item land in my hand.

Every student in the room made me feel small whether or not they intended to. In no small part because the sorcerous community had as many biases as any other.

To give Professor Noches credit, he tried to include me. Made sure that others explained what they meant when they referenced this spell or that, this famed sorcerer or another. Gloria helped as well, texting me links to sorcerous websites with simple, illustrated how-tos.

Both of them in the process further pushing my ignorance into my face no matter how well-intended.

And reminded me that Helen Maia had made a big deal about people being the same whether or not I knew they did sorcery. She meant well. Perhaps she hoped to ward off what started in that class. A falling of scales from my eyes letting me realize the extent to which people I trusted kept secrets from me.

It wasn't personal.

Disbelieving in sorcery freed a person from being subject to it. Way back when, a bunch of influential former-sorcerers renounced sorcery so thoroughly that they shifted mainstream Western culture away from magic—and in the process reified and strengthened the idea that disbelief had power.

Thus Western cultures, such as the mainstream U.S., tended to divide everyone into one of two categories—sorcerers who accepted magic, believed in it, and could work it on the one hand and non-believers who existed in total denial of the sorcerous world on the other.

Under that stark division, my friends had no choice but keep silent.

But understanding didn't mean acceptance.

Every other word in class drilled into my head how much I didn't know—and how much my friends had kept from me.

I didn't go to lunch afterward. Skipped meeting up with any of my friends. Instead, I went to work and stewed.

All the secrets. The unwitting betrayals.

I counted the hours until I could meet with someone who'd understand: Regina.

17

When I returned for a second lesson, Regina allowed me past the kitchen. A mixed blessing, for I missed the familiar table—though she still provided ample tea, this time oolong. Merely seeing the dining room and living room confirmed that Regina had a lot more wealth than anyone I knew. More even than some of my classmates from back in middle school when I still got invited to birthday parties by people I considered friends.

First thing on stepping through the doorway into the dining room, I wiped my hands on my jeans. My fingers weren't sticky or dirty or anything, but just in case. The thin green sweater I'd pulled on over an Arden T-shirt earlier started to stick to me as a layer of perspiration covered my head and shoulders. I removed the sweater, laid it over one arm, and turned up my sneakers to check the soles as discreetly as possible to make sure I didn't track any dirt or leaves in.

Gold-striped wallpaper covered the dining room walls, complementing the gleaming cherry dining table and chairs, and the maple floor below. A hint of lemon-scented polish hung in the air.

In contrast, the hallway smelled of rose and lavender, thanks to a perforated china bowl on a side table holding potpourri. The wide front door had an arched window inset, frosted in intricate patterns. Opposite, stairs led up to the second story.

Evan had vanished earlier, after walking me over from orchestra and making me promise to let him walk me home. He muttered about having a paper to write, and the distant sounds of music filtered down from the upper floor. Not classical, but a hip-hop song fading into the heavy beat of rock.

When I walked into the living room, every step on the gorgeous red and blue rug and thick padding below felt as though I danced on a cloud. Heavy gold frames surrounded paintings hung from the ceiling. Large oil paintings of a couple drew my eye, both dressed in the fashions of the late nineteenth century. An immense seascape rested above a carved marble mantlepiece. An open door to the far side of the fireplace showed a book room beyond. A mirror mounted on one wall reflected the contents: a gleaming mahogany desk with two laptops against ample built-in shelves holding all manner of books from gilded leather bindings to modern paperbacks.

A plush sofa upholstered in deep blue sat on one side, with two matching armchairs on the other. Regina placed the tea tray on the table between the chairs. At her encouragement, I tried to perch on the edge of one of the chairs, but sank in and slid back. Definitely a mama-bear seat—too soft and cushy.

"Helen said she talked to you about finding another teacher." Regina added cream and a few flecks of sugar, then handed me a cup.

"She did, yeah." I took a sip, but found the liquid too hot

and set it aside to cool. It had a citrusy aftertaste that lingered on my lips. "She said you asked her to find someone who turned, not someone who was born a sorcerer."

"I think it's important. Do you agree?"

My neckbones crackled as I nodded.

"I've heard of sorcerers who turned and had no trouble adjusting." Regina's gaze turned inward, and her smile slipped from her lips leaving her face tired and flat. "They're the exceptions. The rest of us, we have trouble."

"It's not like getting plunged into another world where everything's strange but that's expected. Everything looks the same, and then all of a sudden my friends start talking about sorcery and they have this whole other language. They keep mentioning things I don't know and events I've never heard of. It's sort of as though I should celebrate and jump right into learning spells without . . . " I sank deeper into the chair, trying and failing to put my frustrations into words.

"The first days, months, years, can be very frustrating." She nodded. "Most born have no comprehension of how much change turned sorcerers face, and the adjustments required. Oh, they pay lip service, even speak a good line but, when it comes down to working with the turned, too often the born exhibit frustration rather than patience."

Neither of us spoke for a while, just drank tea. The warmth seeped through my body, loosening some of the tension.

"I'm sorry you ran into this so fast, that I didn't say anything to warn you," Regina said. "Maybe that was the wrong thing to do, but I hoped things had improved since when I turned. That you'd find a warmer welcome."

"Oh, they're happy enough. My friends that is, and the professor, and everybody. But . . . how do you deal with all the secrets?" I ran my fingers through my hair, yanking a hank out of frustration, and then forced my hands to return to my lap.

"People I thought I knew, friends . . . Professor Maia said to remember I'm still me, and they're still them—the people I thought they were—but it's hard knowing they had so much going on that they never shared with me. Never even considered."

"Helen speaks from her own experience. She turned me, which I'm sure she still half-regrets." A half-laugh escaped her. "You'll have to find your own way to move past the secrets, whether through forgiveness or acceptance or . . . It may help to remember that your friends likely didn't tell you about sorcery out of fear. That if they told, and you didn't believe, you'd laugh. Make a joke. Make fun of them. Turn them into the butt of jokes."

"I wouldn't!"

She said nothing, just sipped her tea and watched me with dark, tired eyes.

"I wouldn't have made fun of them." My gaze fell first. "But maybe I'd have laughed. Thought they were joking or playing a trick on me."

"From what I've seen, turning is easiest when the only sorcerers one knows are strangers or casual acquaintances. When there's no long, established relationship, no real intimacy to be ripped and remade. When you don't find sorcerers among your nearest and dearest, and realize they've been hiding half their life from you." She shuddered and gave a low snarl, lips pulling back from her teeth.

I stiffened, watching her out of the corner of my eyes as I sipped my cooling tea.

Another shudder rippled through her, then she gave a deep sigh and flashed a bitter smile my way. Took a swallow of tea, cup rattling against the saucer as she returned them to the tray.

I opened my mouth, about to ask a question, then snapped it shut because it was too personal.

"Go ahead. Ask whatever you wish." Regina folded her hands in her lap and watched me. "I'll hold nothing against you for asking, though I don't promise to answer. I'll at least tell you when I'm not going to share something with you."

"How old were you when you turned?" Not the question I'd almost asked, i.e. what had happened when she turned.

"Twenty-eight. Two years married. Three months pregnant. The electricity went out one night, and Helen used a spell to make her hand give off light—the same spell I mean to show you as your second lesson, for it's a good step from fetching things."

Regina made a fist and then opened her hand for an instant. Rays of bright white-gold light flashed. I closed my eyes and covered my face with my arm. After a couple of breaths, I lowered it and opened my eyes a crack. A faint after-effect made everything a bit faded, but she'd closed her hand and dispelled or otherwise put out the light.

"Helen tried to pass it off as having a mini-flashlight—we didn't have smartphones with flashlight apps in those days— but I'd seen her before the lights went out and she didn't have anything in her hand or anything near her that could be a source of light." Regina shook her head. "So stupid of me, to turn into a sorcerer over such a small thing. At least you turned from something unusual."

"Was it hard? Finding out she was a sorcerer all along, and she'd never told you?"

"Yes. Her, most of her side of the family, plus my husband and his. So many all around me. All those dinners and conversations that I realized I'd missed half of as the only one not in the know." She tilted her head, giving me a long look. "Does that sound familiar?"

"Most of my friends, at least people I thought were friends, are sorcerers." I nodded.

"They are your friends, still." Regina shook her head.

"Don't let my bitterness poison you. Forgive them, if you can, or withhold judgment until someone else you know turns."

"One's my roommate, who's pissed that I'm a sorcerer because now I'm not offering protection for her from her relatives playing practical jokes. No, that's not fair to her." I twiddled with my fingers. "She's at least being honest that it's a mixed blessing for her. One of my professors and everyone in his class is just happy now that they can be open about sorcery. And then there's Alex, who's delighted I turned—and upset because I almost did last spring and then went back at the last minute."

At least none of them had turned me—or had they? Alex had mentioned my witnessing sorcery last spring. Or worse, what if I'd turned because I caught Rose or Bea doing magic? Which hadn't happened, but how could I ever tell them I'd started to practice sorcery, in case they ever turned. No bright ideas sprang to mind, but I'd have to come up with something.

"I wish I hadn't turned." Regina said.

The problem of facing my sisters consumed me enough that I nearly missed Regina's low-voiced reply. Swiveling around to face her, she didn't meet my gaze.

"Do you? Really?"

"If I hadn't turned to magic, my son would not be cursed. I might not still be married to my now ex-husband. We argued a lot even before. But at least he couldn't have taken it out on Evan. My disbelief would have protected him." Her head bowed low, shoulders slumped, hands tucked into her lap.

"Would Evan have been born a sorcerer, then?"

"No, not so far as I've seen." She shook her head. "Babies, infants, toddlers, rarely manage to combine all elements to work sorcery anyway, albeit with exceptions. Children born with one parent who's a sorcerer and one who isn't usually don't become sorcerers until their teens, at the earliest."

"Evan once said he wished he hadn't been born a sorcerer." The moment the words escaped me, I wanted to call them back. He hadn't asked me to keep this as a secret, but I didn't ask either.

"So he says."

"You don't agree?"

"He loves to fly. Though he didn't grow wings until after the curse, I wonder if he would not have caught his father working magic some time, or Helen, and still wound up changing to a bird." A snort escaped her and she gave a huffy laugh. "Helen certainly does so often enough, and she has no curse to blame."

"There's more than one way to fly?" I straightened, shifting forward in the chair so my feet sat flat on the floor. Just once to grow wings and rise above the earth without an airplane around me . . .

"There's more than one way to do just about anything." Regina gave me a sideways glance.

Hot blood rushed to my cheeks, and I looked away.

"Helen's way of shape-changing is much harder and more demanding. I recommend at least two years of mastering sorcery before you consider attempting it. But you are here for a lesson, and it's time you learned another spell or two." Regina clapped her hands. All the lights in the room went out. A little illumination from across the front hall, where the stair light remained lit, let us see our way around. "Let's start with the light spell that turned me. You'll find it handy in many ways."

For this, we moved to the sofa. The firm cushion squeaked once when we sat down, and otherwise remained silent. Regina angled so her arm aligned with mine. Arms, not bodies. She left space between us. All the same, every time she exhaled, the air blew across my bangs.

"A very simple spell, all told, and easy to learn. Take an open hand. Make a fist. Imagine holding a miniature sun or moon within it—a flashlight—something small and safe, warm but not hot, capable of shedding light but not blinding. Then open your fingers."

A little more complicated in actual practice.

First try led to failure.

Second try I came so close. My brain ached as I strained but things didn't connect.

Third time proved the charm. Everything clicked—power, intent, and all the other elements.

I unfolded my fingers and a soft white-gold light filled the air. Everything sprung into sharper relief. Shadows shifted into lighter degrees of gray. Regina's face became a mask of planes and angles, until she smiled.

Presto! Let there be light.

18

I triggered the light spell several times on the walk home.

Thin, wispy clouds formed irregular lines across the sky, so thin they did little to conceal the waxing crescent glimmering overhead. A light breeze twisted through trees and bushes, making branches rustle and leaves fall. The pine trees exuded their perfume, albeit with a tang of decaying leaves, but the air held enough warmth that I tied my sweater around my waist and went bare-armed.

And bare-handed.

Such a perfect night to summon a little starlight to one's hand—much better than using a flashlight or flashlight app. A softer light, which illuminated and cast gentle, even weak, shadows. Didn't heat my skin at all, and maintaining it required little energy from me. I felt no more tired than usual after a long day. On the other hand, the spell required constant attention. Not concentration, but even a momentary lapse of awareness caused the light to flicker and fade.

Evan accompanied me. A silent presence for the first third of the walk. We passed through the yard down to the lake and headed toward campus. The light spell deepened the shadows under his eyes, giving his face a skeletal appearance. He wore a dark gray shirt and black jeans tonight, all of which had me fancying a ghoul marched along beside me.

Though he glanced often at the water. Muscles stiffened, upper arms tight against his side and jaw fixed. His fingers twitched. He walked on the right, closer to the lake. The rippling waters glittered, reflecting moon and starlight between the movements of clouds overhead.

As the path neared a rocky promontory, with little in the way of bushes or brush between us and the short, Evan lagged back and let me pass. A moment later, he caught up—on my left side. He gave a soft sigh, some of the tension draining from him. He rolled his head on his neck, spine cracking.

My attention slipped, and the light spell faded. All the same, I could see his face well enough.

"Are you all right?"

"Fine."

"Really?" I slowed and turned my head, pointing to the left where he didn't walk anymore and the right where he'd moved. "Then why swap sides?"

"The moon's pull is strong, that's all."

Rather than returning to my normal pace, I let my steps remain slow. Glanced at the reflected light dancing over the water, and imagined some of the brightness turning into the reflection of white wings overhead.

"Do you need to fly?"

"I always need to fly these days."

"Why these days?"

"Because I'm stuck here, at Arden." He made a disgusted noise.

My head snapped back as I stopped in my tracks, then turned to give him a close look over. Most Arden students flourished here. Not all, true, a couple transfers trickled away every year—my former roommate Terri among them—but I'd spent most of my first year among people so enthusiastic about all that Arden offered that it rubbed off on me.

"Didn't you want to go here?"

Given the wealth visible in his home, Regina had to have enough money to send him wherever and not worry about costs. I hadn't questioned his living at home before because, well, every local student I knew lived at home to save money. Even Emilio, who wasn't local, and most definitely loved Arden, lived with Alex and Professor Noches so his parents didn't have to pay for a dorm room.

"I grew up here." Evan shook his head. "The only town kids who go to Arden are the children of professors and staff who can't afford to send them anywhere else. The rest of us want like hell to get out of here and go someplace new. Almost all my high school friends escaped. One didn't, but I don't see much of him anymore."

We hadn't moved far from the lake. The forest rose up behind us, but otherwise the air remained clear. The angle of the path to near and far shore left the lights of several academic buildings visible in the distance, but they cast dim reflections in the water.

"It's so stupid, you know? Things weren't so bad when I was still in high school. Two, three times a week I'd go out playing soccer with my friends or hang around in my house or theirs chilling and shooting the breeze." Evan bent and picked up something from the ground, a fallen stick. Long and thin with a couple of twigs still attached. He stripped the twigs off with quick twists, casting them away into the underbrush. "But they're gone, and Mom won't let me live in a dorm, so two or more times a day I walk by the lake and the swan alter starts agitating to fly more."

Pulling his arm back, he threw the stick. It whistled through the air. The dark blur arced, then fell into the water with a soft plop.

Turning away, Evan gave a wry smile.

"Sorry for whining all over you. I blame the moon."

"Are you sure you don't turn into a wolf instead of a swan?" A stupid attempt at a joke, although I didn't know why.

"If I turned into a wolf, someone would've shot me and put me out of my misery by now."

Nothing came to mind as a suitable response. He didn't speak, just gestured for me to start walking again. When I did, he fell into step alongside me—again on the forest side farther from the lake. The path moved away from the shore, and overgrown bushes filled the space between us and the water.

I'd let the light spell lapse and not re-cast it. The lamp-posts gave plenty of light, but left pools of darkness. I tripped over something, a root or crack in the path, and started to fall. Evan caught my shoulders and braced me. His warm hands slipped down my arms, steadying me, until I pulled away, ready to move on.

"You okay?"

"Yeah."

He kept hold of me, his right hand tangling with my left, as we started back on our way.

"Is there anything I can do to help? About the curse, I mean. Having to turn into a swan, not wanting to." My words tripped over my tongue, coming out more garbled than I wanted. My cheeks heated, though at least he couldn't see.

"I get it." He shook his head. "You don't have to do much. Be a friend. Let me rant, blow off steam. And . . . don't let go, not until we're on campus, okay?"

His hand tightened on mine.

"Will you be okay, going back home?"

"I'll call Mom to pick me up. As long as I'm on campus, or with her, I'm safe enough." He gave me a fake grin, white teeth flashing in the lamplight far too broad. "Why did you end up at Arden?"

Patent attempt to change subject, but I allowed it.

"Accident of fate." I said.

"Sounds like there's a story there."

"Not much of a one."

"Come on, I shared with you. You owe me."

My cheeks heated again. Thank fortune he couldn't see —much.

"So my Dad's a Shakespeare nut. Mom's better, but also a fan. I mean, they named me Viola Olivia, okay?"

"You won the Shakespeare fellowship." His grin turned real, as he guessed the punchline.

"I entered the contest sort of as a joke. Write a ten-page essay about what Shakespeare means to me? It was half bull-shit . . ."

But I'd practically sweated blood over it. I hadn't heard of Arden before the day Dad came home from rehearsal with a flyer advertising the contest, because Arden sent copies to every Shakespearean theater company in the Northeast, no matter how amateur. Dad took my jokey first draft seriously, reading it and offering a ton of feedback. After that, I revised and polished, and he critiqued, until I grew sick of it and sent the application on its merry way.

Then I won. Four years full tuition plus a stipend that covered part of my room and board. It wound up being cheaper than just about any other way to get a bachelor's degree. No way could I turn that down.

"Hey, if you won that you didn't write crap. You did good. Congrats."

"Thanks." A warm sensation flooded through me.

His hand tightened, as we drew close to campus and the path neared the water again.

"So how do you like sorcery now?" A false lightness to his voice suggested he wanted distraction.

"Magic's fine. It's everything else that's . . . changed."

"Like what?" he asked.

"Oh, just . . . finding out how many of my friends are sorcerers. Some happy I turned, some not. My roommate asked me if it was too late for me to not turn."

"Smart woman. I told you not to believe sorcery. I'd give it up if I could. To not be cursed."

"Would you?" My turn to stop in my tracks. "I've seen you run off to turn into a swan. You leapt into that, as though it was all you ever wanted. You looked happy. If that's a curse—"

"It is."

"How?"

He rubbed his forehead with his free hand, not letting go of me.

"When I was very young, three or four years old, my father disowned me. To get back at Mom. It wasn't me he was angry with but her. All the same . . . even before then, he never called me by my name, because my mother chose it. He didn't want me."

"God, that's . . ." I squeezed his hand tight. "I'm sorry."

"His loss." Evan's jaw tightened and his fingers shook against mine. "Unfortunately, he made sure I couldn't stay near Mom, even when I was little. There's no pleading with him for mercy. Mom's tried to free me. She does her best to keep me safe as much as she can. She begged him to help me."

Evan shivered. A chill ran through me, and I echoed the movement. Had trouble imagining Regina kneeling to anyone. Or begging. She seemed so strong and sure, yet her love for Evan shone as clear as the sun. He mattered enough to her.

"He refused. Doesn't see or hear me. Pretends I don't

exist." Evan grunted. "Now every time they see each other they get in the most raging fights."

And I thought my family mixed up. My parents' break-up seemed simple in comparison. Both my father and mother tried to belittle the other or argue in front of me and my sisters. Guilty relief flashed through me. I glanced away. Shivered as the night started to cool—and Evan shared the dark side of sorcery.

"Isn't there anything anyone can do to break the curse?"

"Every sorcerer in the family tried, including Aunt Helen who's better than all the rest combined." He gazed upward, shook his head. "If she can't do it, who else could? It's thanks to her that I go to college at all. She makes sure I get to be me the same hours the same days each week so I can take classes and play in the orchestra. But even she can't break the curse. Says it's grown beyond her."

Took me a moment or two to work through that, and connect Aunt Helen with Professor Maia.

"The worst thing is," he leaned his chin on the top of my head, words muffled, "the swan is sometimes the best part of my life. It's where I feel . . . whole . . . when we're flying away from everything else. Sometimes I wonder what would happen if we just kept going."

19

Evan's words haunted my sleep and inspired my dreams. My arms stretched out to either side, pumping hard. Skeins of muscles covered with skin and feathers raised me high in the sky. A wind blew up, buoying me ever higher with strong gusts carrying a tinge of smoke. Other birds rose to either side, squawking and honking as we straggled into an uneven V. I flew second on the left, following the leader. The world dropped away below, becoming little more than a blur of blue and green.

Sunlight warmed my wings. Winds caressed my feathers with every beat. At first I flew with others during full daylight.

Then the sun went down. A gorgeous sunset, filling the wide-open expanse with streaks of a dozen different shades of red. Red sky at night sailor's delight, right? Not that I was a sailor or over the sea.

I soared on alone.

A rippling surface manifested below me as I coasted on the wind. Floated. Began to sink lower.

Not toward the lake. Rather, a forest filled with tall trees and branches reaching my way filled my vision. My aim was off.

I flapped my wings, trying to change course as I realized I'd overshoot the water and crash into the woods.

Then sat bolt upright in bed, covered in sweat under my nightshirt, cell phone alarm blaring.

My torso swayed as my hand reached over and slapped the off button, for a very different image filled my mind: me and Evan standing hand in hand at the border between campus and forest—and a figure out on the terrace in front the library, staring at us. For a moment the outline against the light reminded me of Alex, but the truth soon hit.

Alex's cousin Emilio saw me with Evan.

It wasn't a question of if he'd call me on it, but when.

He ran into me, accidentally on purpose, on the way to lunch. Ironic that he chose the very same terrace where he'd stood the night before.

I had my head down as I left the library after work, phone in hand and scanning for new texts from my sisters. Paid my surroundings little mind. An average fall day, with just enough of a nip in the air to warrant wearing a thigh-length, green cable-knit sweater over my white shirt and black leggings. Comfy black flats with good soles on my feet. Backpack slung over one shoulder, not holding much this time other than the book I hadn't finished reading for my afternoon class.

Cloudy sky overhead, a far cry from the sun in my dream. Other students walking to and fro, most of us carrying cell phones and managing not to bump into each other. Strong smell of coffee from a damp stain where someone had spilt and left a half-crushed paper cup behind.

A grunt startled me. My hand clenched around my phone and I raised my head to see Emilio sweep across my path.

Emilio bent over and nabbed the cup with two fingers.

Straightening back up, he tossed it. The white and brown mass arced high and landed square in a nearby trash bin.

"Nice toss."

"I can make it almost as well without sorcery as with." He brushed his hands together, minute flecks of dust glittering in a rare, full beam of sunlight as they fell to the ground. His hard-soled boots thudded against the pavement as he strode over to my side.

First and foremost, height differentiated Emilio and Alex. Emilio had enough additional inches to look down on his cousin—and me. This close, I had to crane my head back to see his face.

Even at a distance, I wouldn't mistake them for long. Alex favored T-shirts and jeans, where Emilio went for polos that he always left unbuttoned at the neck. He had a looser way of moving, too, not as efficient as Alex. More swing in his shoulders and hips, and he took up more space when he stood thanks to setting his feet farther apart.

Plus, Emilio used a citrus-based cologne whereas Alex tended to smell of musk and mint, so I registered who fell into step with me as I headed off towards the dining hall. He cut to the chase quick enough.

"You were over by the forest last night."

"Yeah." I glanced around to make sure we walked far enough from anyone else not to be heard. "I was coming back from a sorcery lesson."

"Your teacher couldn't give you a lesson on campus?"

"No, she—"

He snorted. "I wouldn't have thought the person you were with last night would use female pronouns."

"How would you know from a distance?" I rolled my eyes. "Anyway, that's not my teacher, that's her son. He walked me back to campus. Evan's a student here, and a violinist in the orchestra."

Emilio didn't say anything for a while. The thud of his boots almost drowned out the softer slap of my shoes against the sidewalk. Then he stopped and turned toward me.

I stopped too, but not by choice. An invisible wall manifested around surround us. Hard as glass to the touch, and imposing a heavy silence. All the distant clamor of campus life that I took for granted—people walking and chatting, lawnmowers in the distance—vanished. Pressure built in my ears, as though I was cruising in an airplane at thirty-thousand feet.

"What's this?"

"A cone of silence." He waved a hand, lips tightening. "Not for beginners. You'll learn it sometime."

"Why do we need it?" I run a finger along the invisible surface, which did indeed angle down as though forming an immense cone with a point high above us. My breath shallowed, filling the tops of my lungs. "Will we be able to breathe?"

"Of course, it's air-permeable. And I won't keep you long. It's . . ." He ran a hand through his hair, leaving the strands in disarray. "Look, I'm not asking what you're doing with your teacher's son. Don't mess up Alex, that's all."

"Mess him up how?" I turn around to face him, shoulders pressing against the cone's angled surface. "I'm going out with him. Seeing what happens."

"He likes you, a lot. That's not a secret, you know it." He flipped a hand at me. "Last spring, when you backtracked on sorcery, he took it hard."

"All we did was fool around some." Not that I recalled exactly how much, or even many other details. I remembered were kisses, caresses, and a sense of loss when he pulled back.

"That's not necessarily all you did."

"What don't I remember?"

"I don't know." He shook his head. "I wasn't there for it all. But for those two days, Alex could've walked on water."

I closed my eyes and rubbed my temples. The same memories returned to mind, still vague. Emilio's words sparked a flash of Alex smiling bright at me. His arms wrapping around, in a close but not too tight embrace. His head resting on my shoulder as his whole body vibrated with excitement and possibility.

Not so mine. Both in memory and in the present, my arms dropped to my sides and pressed tight against my chest. My shoulders stiffened and my chest seemed to shrink around my lungs. Even the warmth of Alex's body against me couldn't loosen the discomfort welling in me.

And I didn't even have the reality of him near me now.

A bitter tang flooded my mouth, as ripples of fear and betrayal ran through me. Much the same as I'd felt the other day, in Professor Noches's class—but worse because they centered around Alex keeping secrets from me.

I shook my head and torso, shattering the reverie and tension although the bitter taste remained.

"What turned me?" A lump in my throat made me sound hoarse. I swallowed, and fumbled with my bag to retrieve my water bottle and take a long swig.

"I don't know." Emilio shook his head again. "But a better question is why you got scared and walked everything back then, but not now. What turned you this time that you could accept?"

Before I could open my mouth and spill anything out, he waved a hand in the air.

"Forget I asked, but don't forget why." He blew air out in a huff. "Something scared you last time. Don't let it scare you again."

"It's too late anyway. I've already accepted sorcery."

"Fair enough, but have you accepted Alex?" Grabbing my

hand, he squeezed my fingers close. "He deserves someone willing to care about all of him. It's not just my cousin we're talking about, but my friend. You're a friend too, but Alex comes first. If you're going to walk away from him for any reason—because of magic or because you like someone else better—do it now, or don't do it at all. No dangling him on a string."

Dropping my hand, he strode forward. The cone of silence shattered into a million flecks of ice that glittered in the sun as they fell to earth and vanished.

He didn't leave, though, but walked with me over to the dining hall and stayed for lunch. Gloria and Gordon showed up as well, although Alex skipped as usual for Wednesdays.

Emilio's warning didn't scare me. If anything, it gave me the warm fuzzies to see how much he cared for Alex to warn me off. Though it also left me worried.

Not about Emilio's concern that I might dangle Alex and Evan on strings until I decided which I preferred.

I already knew. Alex, hands down.

I liked Evan, but as a friend. He might resemble book boyfriends from fantasy novels, but I'd never wanted to date any character from a book. Evan was handsome and attractive, but also moody as hell. The kind of brooding that made me hope he was in counseling with a good therapist who understood sorcery, because the things he'd shared last night raised fears he might someday fly away never to return.

What nagged at me wasn't Emilio's comments about Evan, but those two days last spring I'd almost turned. I had to strain my brain to even recall the kisses.

The lack of knowledge weighed on me through the afternoon, dinner, and even the date.

I fooled myself into believing I hid it well, laughing at all the funny lines—or at least those that tickled my funny bone —but afterward Alex walked me home only to stop halfway.

Of all places, he chose the point where the sidewalk passed through an arched bridge connecting the two main academic buildings. Pools of light filled the wide passage, from lanterns set at either side of either end. All the same, the space had a shadowy feel given the carved stone walls and large wooden double doors on each side. A few curled, dead leaves and twigs had blown into the archway and wound up wedged where the path met the walls, giving the air a tinge of dust and decay.

Alex wore a gray shirt and pants, very sober and eye-catching. I'd changed into a blue knee-length tunic over tights.

"What's wrong?" He held my hand, his fingers warm and smooth.

"Nothing much, really." I opened and shut my mouth a couple times, searching for words. Didn't want to lie. "It's been a great night—"

He laid a finger across my lips, a light pressure, until I stopped. Shaking his head, he let his hand drop to the side, but kept hold of me with the other.

"Tell me."

Not a command or a plea, and I don't think he worked any kind of spell. All the same, I looked down and away. Avoided his gaze and took a deep breath before speaking.

"I keep thinking about last spring. About almost turning, and then not."

"Okay." As before, he didn't push or plead. Just waited, patient and silent.

"What did I see that made me believe? And . . ." I lifted my head and met his shadowed gaze. "Why wasn't it enough?"

"I can't tell you the last part." He slid both hands up to cup my face. "If wishes were dishes, you'd have turned and never looked back."

"But you know what I saw." I laid my hands over his, fingers chilling in the night breeze.

"Oh yes."

My turn to wait in silence.

"You sure want to know?"

"Is it wrong?"

"No. I don't know." He ran a hand through his hair, same as Emilio had although Alex's shorter hair was fine enough to fall back into place. "I've never been much around people who recently turned before. Most sorcerers I know were born that way. Or turned long ago. This isn't . . . nobody talks about it much."

"Why not? You'd think it'd be a big topic of conversation. If nothing else, figuring out what kind of spells to avoid doing in any kind of public in case you turn someone."

"I didn't do a spell." Alex moved backwards, leaning his head against the stone wall.

"What happened?"

His turn not to meet my eyes. Mine, again, to wait. And wait. Until he sighed, swallowed, and broke.

"You saw someone walk right through me. As though I wasn't there."

"Walk through you." I whispered. Vague memories started to coalesce and pass before me. Not, at first, of the event itself but the preceding circumstances.

"It was just after lunch, a day or so before finals started. We were walking . . ." I turned around in a circle, shoes shuffling against the flagstones. "There."

I pointed toward the middle of the academic quad. The main path across campus, wide enough for four people to walk next to each other.

Back then, we didn't walk side-by-side, as we had tonight. Instead, we took up more than our share of the path. I lagged behind for some reason that escaped me, while Alex blazed on ahead.

"I said something to you."

"'Wait up.'" Alex nodded, arms crossed over his chest and he leaned against the wall.

"You stopped."

"Always."

Our eyes met at that. I nearly broke off, but I'd triggered the memory strong enough that it played on in my mind's eye.

Back then, Alex turned. At first he smiled at me, then his face went blank. Jaw tightened. Hands fisted.

Hurried footsteps sounded behind me, coming closer. Before I could turn and glance around, a woman passed me in a huff. Tall and straight-backed in a navy pantsuit, she strode down the center of the path and left no more than a hands' breadth. Didn't say anything to me, even so little as "excuse me" or "on your left."

Kept on her merry way to where Alex had stopped in the middle of the path.

And walked through him. For a moment, the two of them occupied the same space—then she went on.

Leaving him hunched over behind, shoulders heaving and arms clenched against his belly. He arched his neck and lifted his head, showing eyes squeezed shut and teeth locked in a grimace.

"It wasn't just anyone, was it? You recognized her."

"That's almost what you said back then." Alex in the now tucked his hands in his pockets, shoulders tight. "After babbling about her walking through me first while you helped me over to the nearest bench."

"Your skin was cold as ice." Even the memory made me shiver. I hustled over to his side and wrapped my arms around him. This time he blazed with warmth, enough to dispel the chill although the muscles of his arms and back were tight and ropy under my fingers. He leaned into me, arms looping around my waist. "So who was it?"

"My mother."

"Your . . ." I blinked and drew back far enough to study his face. If anything, he looked tired. "I thought she was dead or something. I've never heard you or your father mention her. Not so much as her name."

"Oh, she lives." Another huff. "But she hates my father. No, hates isn't a strong enough word. Detests. Abhors. And because I look like him, she pretends I don't exist. Since she's a sorcerer, the wish becomes the reality. For her, I don't."

❦ 20 ❧

One minute before Professor Noches's class started, a surge of dread rushed through me.

Until then, everything seemed fine. Ordinary, even. Me in my typical student attire of T-shirt and jeans, sitting in my preferred seat. My phone in my hand with the message app open texting Bea and Rose, also as usual. All the other students present and accounted for. Gloria across the way. Still throwing the occasional glare my way when I practiced summoning or light spells—I'd got quite good at fetching things to me.

Outside, the grounds people mowed the lawns. The low hum of the motors reverberated in the room and, when they swept near enough, rattled the glass windowpanes. The noise was an irritant, but not the smell of fresh-mown grass they left in their wake. Though one of the students, I don't remember who, decided this made an opportune moment to lecture us on how the smell was blades of grass yelling for help because they'd been hurt.

Out of the blue, a wave of energy pulsed through the

building. Inaudible, invisible, intangible, but most definitely *THERE*. A sudden lurching of the stomach. Dizziness, with everyone who wasn't seated before dropping into the nearest available chair. Added electricity in the air, similar to the pressure change right before a storm hit.

I grabbed hold of the table edge. My fingernails dug into the ridges of the wood. Blood pounded in my veins. A small surge of bile filled my mouth. I swallowed and it went back down, but left a sour taste behind.

Then a second wave.

A third, steady and pounding . . .

In exact time with the clop of hard-soled shoes against the hall flooring.

Then the waves of energy or whatever stopped.

Professor Noches appeared in the doorway. He paused there, head high and jaw tight. He'd dressed for the day, as usual in a gold-toned polo shirt and brown slacks, with his hair parted on the right. Beads of perspiration dotted his brow. His gaze fixed on the far left of the room. Bit by bit, person by person, he scanned from left to right, pausing for a long moment to stare at me.

No more dizziness or surges of bile, though the protein bar I'd had for breakfast sat heavy in my stomach.

The whole room crackled with static electricity. Amazing that none of our hair stood straight out from our heads, it was that strong.

The professor closed the door behind him. The hinges squeaked, a familiar sound that took on an ominous note, and then the latch clicked.

Walking to the front of the classroom, he took his usual seat at the head of the seminar table.

"Let us begin."

He didn't call on me at first, and just as well since I was

still raw and new, but neither did he look at me after that one long glance.

I'd never seen him fidget before, but two students presented about symbols with sorcerous overtones and all the while the professor's fingers twitched. At first he rapped his nails against the table, but realized this was distracting and moved his hands to his lap.

He wasn't the only one affected by energy lingering in the air. Everyone seemed to develop some kind of twitch. Fingers quivering, tics in cheeks, feet tapping away at the floor.

At length, the discussion following the presentations turned to different approaches to sorcerous symbols. A lot of terms were tossed around—simplissimus, evidentialist, fantastical fundamentalist, cerebro-psychiatric—but I had no idea what any meant. Nor did I have any openings to inquire unless I wanted to wave my ignorance in front of everyone.

Some of my frustration might've reached the professor, for he wrenched the discussion in a different direction.

"Let's go back to the core. Many schools of thought consider the first symbols you imbibe to be fundamental. Since we have a new turned sorcerer amongst us, think about the first spells you learned—not through doing by accident but instruction and practice under the care of your first teacher. What was your first spell, and why did your teacher pick that?"

After glancing between me and Gloria, seated on opposite sides of him, he started with her.

"Oh God, that was forever ago." She dug in her backpack and pulled out a glass water bottle. It sloshed about, half full, as she set it on the table where everyone could see. "I learned how to refill a glass or mug or anything that had held liquid."

She waved her hand, and the level of liquid rose.

"An interesting choice, but why that?"

"I was always running around and getting thirsty, but

short as I was I couldn't reach the faucets to get water to drink." Gloria twisted off the top, she took a swig. "My Tia Isabella got tired of me always asking for more to drink, so she showed me."

Gloria proved unusual. No one else shared her first spell, but others had things in common. Two learned to make light first. Three to summon lightweight objects across short distances.

Before long the question came to me.

"I've learned two spells so far."

"We all must start somewhere." Professor Noches gave me a kind smile, although his gaze narrowed. "What was your first spell?"

Energy still filled the air. The hairs on the nape of my neck stood up and my leg muscles quivered. I bit my lip, trying not to let my teeth chatter, but managed to squeeze out an answer. "Summoning, same as half the class."

"A classic choice." The professor nodded at the other students, without moving his gaze. "What was your teacher's rationale?"

"I don't know that she had one." I frowned. "She'd just told me about the basics of sorcery. About desire and will, power and intent, and all, and this was a way to have me work through them. She showed me, and then had me practice fetching a feather."

"A swan feather, perhaps?"

"Yes." I still had it, tucked in the top drawer of my bureau.

"Something that wouldn't injure you or disintegrate if you summoned it with excessive power. Fair enough."

I jerked as his gaze left me. The sense of static electricity in the air faded for the most part. The air closest to the professor still sparked, although only when I looked at him from the corner of my eye and not head-on.

He went on to hand out the next week's assignment. We were to research different cultures' approaches to symbolism and magic and situate or classify our own training in relation to these. My ears heard and my hand took notes, but I didn't listen.

With every moment that passed, the sense of a storm building increased.

The professor asked me to stay after class for a moment. He smiled and watched the other students leave, then his smile faded as he focused on me.

"How long have you known Alex?"

"Since orientation last year."

"He brought you home, into my house, that same weekend. You've been his friend for some time, for which I thank you. I know he is very pleased you've turned." His hands swept the reaction papers we'd turned in earlier into a neat pile before placing them in his briefcase. "You are so new, you may not yet recognize the dangers sorcery can pose. I worry for you, if your teacher does not do well by you."

He patted the bag, then shifted to face me head-on.

"Who is your teacher?"

Everything remained calm for a moment. His gaze grabbed me, and I froze. Felt a sudden sympathy for prey animals when they're caught and know they can't escape.

"Who is your teacher?"

Alex's warning rang afresh in my head, but I couldn't not answer such a straight question. Nothing came to mind other than the truth.

"Regina Roth."

"Ah." Professor Noches slammed a fist into his other hand. "Emilio mentioned your teacher was off-campus, and I wondered. How often have you seen the swan?" He waved a hand in the direction of the lake.

I blinked, the answer slipping out of me without thought. "Three or four times."

"Over how long?"

"A week and a half?"

"She encourages this insanity. Puts everything at risk." He slammed a fist against the table. The air crackled and sparked around him. He pointed a finger straight at me. "Find another teacher."

"But she's been—"

"She will understand one way or another. I'll tell her myself that she shall no longer teach you or anyone who comes near my son."

Without another word, he stormed out of the room. A trail of orange and white sparkles glittered in his wake, until they fell to the ground and dissipated.

I stared after him, mouth agape, for several minutes at least—until all the sparks died out. My hands fumbled as I pulled my phone from my pocket and speed dialed Alex.

"Hey, I'm just out of class." His cheery voice sent a warm ripple through me. "What's up?"

I drew in a deep breath, lungs aching, and sighed it out.

"Viola?"

"Your father knows who my teacher is."

"Where is he?" A harsh grunt escaped him. "Is he headed over to . . . her house?"

Slams, footsteps, and voices echoed down the hall as folks streamed into other classrooms. Several students passed by the seminar door and glanced in, but no one entered. Feet scuffing against the tiled floor, I slipped over to the window and peered out.

A straight figure marched across campus, the form and way of walking marking him as the professor.

"Maybe. He's headed for the lake."

"Damn. If they fight, last time they nearly set the woods

on fire." Something slammed on his end. "I'll text Tiya Helen. Maybe she can stop them."

"Why does he hate Regina so much?"

"The greatest loves turn to the greatest hates. They were lovers once upon a time. Husband and wife even." His voice dropped in volume. "She pretends I don't exist, but she was my mother."

21

I ran along the lake path. The humid air wrung rivulets of sweat from me, slicking my nose and face to the point I stopped every couple of minutes to wipe off my glasses frames so they didn't slide off. More perspiration coated my torso and legs. My shirt stuck to my back and breasts. Sometimes, while I cleaned my glasses, I tried one or another number on my phone. Calling or texting, didn't matter which. Alex didn't answer. Evan the same. Helen Maia, Regina . . . no one answered.

Stupid of me to head off after Professor Noches. What could I do? I knew two spells and no more. Yet off I ran anyway. He headed to Regina's to fight because of me. Not over me—I recognized the difference. I'd slipped into an ongoing dispute, the latest reason for confrontation. All the same, if it weren't for me Professor Noches wouldn't have headed off to confront Regina.

Regina was Alex's mother, which made Evan Alex's brother. Or half-brother? No, twin, since they were the same age. At least, like me they were both in their second year at

Arden so they had to be twins unless one or both was adopted.

Being twins meant the professor was the father who denied Evan and cursed him to be a swan part of the time.

Which just about blew my mind. No way I could wrap my mind around it all. The professor always struck me as a nice guy, albeit a hard grader, and above all a loving father. If I saw him and Alex together once this last year I saw them a dozen times, and love shone between them. Frustration sometimes, too, yeah, but nothing to suggest the professor had a cruel streak or a penchant for vengeance and a willingness to slam an innocent child with a curse.

Then again, neither did the time I'd spent with Regina agree with the image the professor and Alex had painted of her, as a mother denying her son. She loved Evan as well as the professor Alex. Sure, Evan flew away from her now and then, and wanted to be free of this place, but he returned her affection.

If learning sorcery existed turned my world upside down, the news about Alex, Evan, and their parents made the world make no sense.

Either Professor Noches took a different route, or he got to Regina's way before me as I never caught sight of him on the way. Maybe I'd mistaken his reaction to learning she taught me. Or let Alex's worry infect me.

The gate lay shut. The wrought-iron fence rose high above me, embedded with who knew what protective spells Regina had cast above and beyond any mundane security measures. Bird calls and the plop of frogs leaping into the lake (or something like that) reached me—but no cries or shouts, and still no sign of the professor.

Wrapping my hand around the cool metal latch, I gave a good yank. Nothing moved. My hand ached a little from pulling, so I let go.

Then, with a creak even though the hinges had been silent the other night, the gate opened on its own. No word, nothing.

Drawing in a deep breath, I slipped through the opening. After my fifth step up towards the house, the gate closed. The latch clicked as it settled in place.

Everything appeared normal and fine in the yard—yet all remained far too quiet. The birds no longer called from the trees—or if they did, the calls didn't reach this far. I stuck my fingers in my ears then pulled them back out. Still quiet, with a faint pressure, reminiscent of the cone of silence Emilio cast the day before.

A flash of ruddy light flared up above the roof.

Dashing around flower beds and bushes, I rounded the side of the house, only to stop in my tracks, body swaying and head bobbing.

Regina's car sat in front of the closed garage, the driver's side door open. A red light flickered on the dashboard, but made no sound. A briefcase lay flat on the ground a few inches from the open door.

Several feet further, Regina and Noches faced each other. The front yard, with its decorative flower beds and bushes, hid most of the street from view and vice-versa—and just as well. The air around them held a whitish cast, as though a small, personal fog hung around them. Vaguely triangular, or curved? Was it fog or smoke, given the occasional flicker of orange-red sparks?

All visible signs—mouth movements, facial grimaces— indicated they yelled at each other at the same time and neither listened to the other. Nevertheless, not even a sliver of sound escaped.

"Regina! Professor!" My mouth opened and a scream emerged given the burn on my throat, but I couldn't hear myself any more than them, and they paid no attention whatsoever to me. One or both had thrown up a cone of silence. Or maybe two, one nearby and the other over the house and land?

Knees knocking, I inched closer. The air between them sparkled with flickering bits of light—or flame—as though they were dry logs on a fire about to burst into flame. A bunch of sparks combined into a flare that spiraled high and escaped the top of the cone. Puffs of smoke followed, leaving the air in the cone clearer, even as ever more embers emanated from them.

At least five feet separated them, but Noches's head snapped sideways as though he were slapped. Bloody scratch marks appeared on his cheek.

Regina's head and torso rocked back and forth as though hands grabbed her shoulders and shook her.

The sparks multiplied, darkened, and combined into flames. Sweat dotted their foreheads, glistening in the weird, orange light. My sweat from running dried, but new drops oozed out and a wave of warmth swept over me.

Then vanished.

A quick burst of ozone stung my nostrils. A narrow, targeted downpour of water doused flames and combatants.

The next moment, a large owl swooped down and looped around the cone of silence. Heavy wings of gray and brown beat at the air. The wings spread over a couple of feet at least, until the bird landed near me and snapped them into its body. Its head swiveled around, tufted ears twitching as large yellow eyes bored into me. Swiveling its head back, it stretched out its wings.

Instead of taking off, some kind of sonic boom went off. My teeth vibrated for an instant, a residual ache remaining after.

The owl vanished and Professor Maia appeared. Unlike Evan, she wore clothes. Black Crocs on her feet, black pants, a silver and blue tunic, and mismatched earrings again, this time a silver crescent moon paired with a small, white and brown feather. Her mouth pulled into a tight line.

With a flick of her fingers, a second downpour fell on Professor Noches and Regina. The foggy air dissipated, leaving two drenched people turning as one to frown at the new arrival. Both opened their mouths and started speaking.

"Enough!" Professor Maia threw up her hands.

Three mouths snapped shut—mine along with Regina's and Noches's although I hadn't said anything. My teeth met and refused to part, though they didn't grind against each other. I scraped one side of my mouth given a sudden soreness and the tang of blood in my saliva, but didn't bite my tongue.

"Regina, as host you will wait your turn. As will you, Sebastian, as an uninvited guest." The new arrival turned to me, one eyebrow lifting as she looked me over from head to toe. "Alex told me only that his parents were fighting, again. Given your presence here, I take it you can provide some further explanation?"

At a gesture from her, my jaw loosened. I drew in a deep breath and let it out on a huff, happy to be able to move my mouth again.

"Um, it's my fault."

"Don't take all responsibility on yourself." She shook her head. "They have a million old quarrels they cannot let go. You may have provided a reason for this latest confrontation, but that does not make it your fault."

"I told Professor Noches that R—um . . . " It didn't seem right to call him professor and her by her first name. "Ms. Roth was teaching me sorcery."

"Why would he be interested?" Professor Maia's eyes narrowed and she stroked her chin with a finger.

"I'm in his symbolism class."

"And you just turned. Sometimes the world works in mysterious ways." She chuckled, though she also shook her head and gave me a narrow look. "But that alone would not send Sebastian out here at a moment's notice. Nor explain why Alex called to report it."

To the side, Professor Noches—Sebastian—and Regina struggled against the spell. Neither moved any closer, to each other or Professor Maia or me, but a few specks of bright orange flecked into life between them.

Professor Maia gave a small sigh and waved her hand. A narrow burst of water drenched the sparks, and a gust of wind pushed the combatants a good ten feet further apart.

She did all this without ever taking her gaze from me.

"How well do you know Alex?"

"We've been friends for a year, or more." Heat rose in my cheeks, no doubt turning them bright red.

"Just friends?"

"Maybe more." I didn't meet her eyes.

"Yet you know Evan as well."

"We both play in the orchestra."

Professor Maia bowed her head and steepled her fingers. Silence reigned for a few moments, broken by a truck of some kind driving along the road.

"If you have to take sides, to choose between them . . ." She moved closer to me. To the side, Regina and Sebastian both stiffened. Neither moved, maybe they couldn't, but they leaned in. "Who would you choose? Alex or Evan?"

"What . . . is this some kind of joke?" I stumbled back a step as all three of them watched me with serious expressions. "They can't even have a friend in common?"

"No joke." Professor Maia shook her head. "I suppose they can have a friend in common, although I am not aware that they ever have. Let's try this another way. You cannot study with Regina and take a class with Sebastian. Who will it be?"

She wanted me to choose between them? Not fair or nice, especially with both of them able to hear my answer.

Sebastian folded his arms over his chest and turned his head away. Didn't cover his ears, though.

Regina gave me a small smile and pointed at her cousin, then grimaced.

"I can't d-drop the symbolism course." I stumbled over the words, then took a deep breath and slowed down. "We're past the add/drop date. It'd still be on my transcript."

Another car or truck rumbled past on the nearby road. I shivered as a sudden breeze swept through. A glance to the side showed Sebastian and Regina had traded postures; he nodded while she'd crossed her arms over her chest.

"Very well." Professor Maia clapped her hands together. "Regina already asked me to find you another teacher. I'll look for someone who's turned, but until then you will study under me, if you agree."

"Will it make things easier?"

"Oh yes." She hissed the last word, then uttered a deep sigh. Turned to face the other two. "Sebastian, your complaint is now moot. Regina is no longer Viola's teacher."

A wave of her hand set his mouth free.

"It's not merely the matter of teaching Viola. That Woman encourages the bird to steal my son from me." Sebastian snapped both his fingers. A breeze whirled around him, whisking away moisture. His clothes and hair dried, but remained mussed.

"We've been through this before." Professor Maia fluttered her fingers in the direction of the road. "Neither you nor Regina control the swan. And you're trespassing. Leave now, and Regina will waive claim to time on campus to balance your trespass. Won't you, Regina?"

"You're the one who lured the swans to the lake in the first place." Regina bared gritted teeth. She'd also managed to dry her clothes, and stroked fingers over them removing wrinkles. Seemingly unconcerned, but her hands vibrated. Indeed, her whole body emanated waves of fury.

Professor Maia gave her a hard look.

"All right. If he goes now, I won't claim additional time in recompense."

Sebastian gave her a stiff nod, then directed a kindlier look my way.

Before he could speak, Professor Maia laid a hand on my shoulder.

"Viola will be coming with me." Her fingers rested light, but her hold encouraged me to remain in place. "Go back to campus, and tell Alex all is as well as it can be."

He nodded again, not happy, and hiked down the driveway to meet a rideshare car that conveniently showed up to pick him up. Even from this distance, the driver seemed a bit bemused and goggled at us through the windshield before driving off.

The silence lessened as the soft hum of the motor faded into the distance. Birds called in the trees and a leaf blower kicked into action further up the street.

"This won't affect Evan, will it?" Regina started out strong, but her voice quavered at the end.

"No." Professor Maia removed her hand and made inscrutable gestures towards the road.

Regina sighed and gave a whole-body shudder. Turned toward me, she gave a rueful smile.

"I'm sorry I can't teach you more, but I leave you in good hands." Offered her hand to shake.

I took it, and she pressed mine between both of hers, hands warm.

"You will stay Evan's friend, I hope."

Professor Maia watched, a grim expression on her face, but didn't say anything. Her question about choosing between Alex and Evan echoed in my brain, but surely there was nothing wrong in staying friends?

❧ 22 ❧

"The least I can do is offer you lunch."

Other than that, Professor Maia said one other thing to me as we took a rideshare to her house—to call her Helen.

The drive proved a great disappointment. I'd hoped she'd show me how to fly, but instead she led me out to the road and summoned up a car and driver out of the blue instead. A confused driver, whose expression bore a distinct resemblance to Sebastian's driver's, turned a corner and came to a halt beside us.

The compact car smelt of sauteed onions and stale bread, no wonder Helen mentioned lunch. My stomach rumbled, though I was more thirsty than hungry. Above all, I wanted answers.

She'd pulled out her phone and was texting away, so I did the same. First and foremost, I alerted my boss that I wasn't doing well and wouldn't be in today. A half-lie, because no way could I handle work with so many unanswered questions dancing in my head.

Had a variety of texts. Bea asking me where I'd left a shirt she thought I'd borrowed and of which I had no recollection, then texted a second time telling me to ignore the first text which was meant for someone else. Then a long series of texts between Gloria, Ruth, and Emilio about lunch plans—and puzzlement as to why I wasn't answering whether or not I'd join them. Easy enough to send back that I'd been busy and would see them at dinner. They sent smiley faces in reply.

Another thread from Alex asking me where I was, what I was doing, over and over. I texted back that everything was fine now, and when could we catch up this afternoon—but he didn't respond.

Then a message from Rose alerting me that Dad would be headed my way soon and I should keep my ears and mind open when I met with him. This puzzled me for all of a few seconds, until I found the next text thread where Dad said he was heading up my way for a weekend conference, and could he take me to dinner tomorrow night?

Might as well get it over with.

By which time we arrived at a red brick ranch about halfway between Regina's suburb and the campus. Whatever I was expecting it wasn't this. So much smaller and simpler than Regina's house, or even Sebastian's. The front lawn had a lot of weeds and hadn't been mown for a week or three. A big, gnarled maple tree stood on one side, its leaves still green with a bare hint of red here and there.

The sidewalk leading up to the house had deep cracks. Several gray feathers dropped to decorate the bland concrete, and a moment later an ungainly pigeon landed atop them.

Helen took a look at the pigeon and muttered a curse. After tipping the driver, she rushed ahead of me and scooped up the bird. It fluttered its wings, but didn't resist her hold.

I followed her into the house. The door closed behind me with a snick, and a surge of warmth ran through me. The living room was a mess. A large box painted bright blue sat in one corner with stuffed animals and books spilling out of it. Toy railroad tracks covered the pale blue carpet. They made an elaborate loop around the sofa and matching chairs, complete with bridges, crossings, and two trains sitting stalled face-to-face. The end tables boasted table lamps and piles of books, both children's and meant for adults. Every single piece of art on the walls—all pastoral scenes, painted or photographs—hung askew. The disarray extended to the dining area, an extension of the living room, beyond which lay sliding glass doors leading to the back yard.

A glorious smell of freshly cooked onions and beans and garlic filled the house. Could be hunger, for it smelled better than anything I'd had in the dining hall in a long time.

"Julius!"

"Bonjou." A tall black man dressed in jeans and a tie-dyed shirt, barefoot and wearing thick glasses, walked in from the hall. He held a tablet in his hands, which he laid atop a pile of books. It teetered, but didn't fall.

"Hi, sweetheart. Did you know about this?" Helen held the pigeon out at arm's length.

"No." He adjusted the wire-framed glasses to study the pigeon, then extended his hands to either side. "I would never have consented, you know that." He had a strong Louisianan accent.

"Then we'll have to come up with better consequences." Helen placed the pigeon on the carpet. She braced her hands on her hips and glared at it. "Change. Now."

The pigeon fluffed its feathers and stretched out small wings. A small boom sent a ripple of vibrations through me.

A young girl, around six or seven, appeared in place of the bird. A miniature version of Helen and her husband, she wore jeans and a tie-dyed T-shirt mirroring her father but bright pink Crocs in echo of her mother. A wealth of crochet braids fell from a loose topknot, and small bell-shaped stud earrings glittered at her ears. She clutched her hands to her chest, chin pointed down.

"Feather please, Leonie." Julius walked around the girl to stand next to Helen. He held out a hand.

After a moment, the girl opened hers and dropped a single pigeon feather into his grasp.

"You know you're not allowed to change shape. What is your excuse this time?" Helen asked.

"I forgot my lunch."

Julius gave a curse. Sliding sideways through an archway into the kitchen, he returned with a lunch box. "I'll drive her to school. With any fortune, they'll take her back."

"Works for me." Helen shook her head, hands on her hips as she watched the girl. "We'll talk about this tonight. You have until then to decide what punishment to suggest."

Leonie wiggled and frowned, then glanced my way. Lifting her chin, she studied me. "Who're you?"

"This is Viola, a friend of your cousins'. Viola, my daughter Leonie, proof positive that wishing someone to have children like themselves is a very powerful curse." Helen bent down and stared into her daughter's eyes. "No more changing without permission, got that?"

"Yeah." The girl scuffed a croc against the carpet. Taking her lunch box from her father's hand, she clasped it as tight against her chest as she had the feather.

Julius gave Helen a quick kiss before slipping on sandals. He wrapped an arm around his daughter's shoulders and escorted her out to the garage. The door shut, and a car motor started—but the moment lingered in my mind's eye.

Reminded me of how long since I'd seen my parents do the same, if I ever had. Maybe when I was Leonie's age? I couldn't imagine Regina and Sebastian ever doing so.

The house became much quieter with only Helen and me left.

Helen served up lunch at the kitchen table in short order. The dishes were an eclectic mishmash of colors and styles, the utensils stainless steel, and the woven place mats made of thick strips of cotton ragging in primary colors.

The food tasted good no matter how served. I'd smelt the veggie gumbo cooking earlier, and it lived up to expectations. She added carrot and celery sticks to my plate that I could've lived without, though I ate some. The fruit cup appealed to me far more, with pineapple, bananas, papaya, mangoes, and guava. So good I finished every bite.

While we ate, Helen kept the discussion mundane, mentioning preparations for Homecoming next week. All very well and good, and I was looking forward to the costume ball that took over campus, but not what I wanted to talk about.

"Evan said turning into a swan was a curse, but you were an owl and your daughter a pigeon."

Helen paused, spoon halfway to her mouth. She gave me a considering glance. Took her time finishing the bite, then laid the utensil down on the table with a soft chime.

"Let me guess, you want to fly?"

My head jerked in a quick nod. Turning my gaze down and away, I scraped the last bits of fruit from my bowl.

"Very well. May as well begin there." Helen cleared the table, declining my offer to help. She piled the dishes in the sink and gave them a quick rinse before returning to her seat. The wooden chair creaked as she leaned back and crossed her arms to lay her hands on her shoulders. "There are three ways to change shape. One is to be cursed, which generally involves turning into a hybrid of more than one type of animal or bird, and almost always requires external assistance to dispel. I don't recommend it."

Lowering her hands, she used her finger to paint smoky lines of blue in the air. A roughly sketched gryphon appeared, with eagle head and wings and the body of a lion. Then, next to it, a winged serpent. Last, a being with a lion's head, goat body, and scorpion tail.

The images hovered for a few moments before dissipating, long enough to bring back memories of the steer with snake-head horns.

"Got it." I shivered. "Avoid curses."

"Then there's the kind of shape changing Julius and I do and which, God help us, Leonie figured out at far too young an age." She rubbed her temples, shaking her head. "It requires a very strict lifestyle to maintain—vegan diet for the most part, to ensure you don't curse yourself and change into a hybrid. Practitioners of this type of change also never wear anything containing animal products, not just avoiding fur and bone but also wool, unless we want to strip before changing. You can only have genetic material of one type of animal or bird on you—whatever it is you want to change into—at a time. Anything else risks a curse."

She gestured at herself, walking me through the substances she was—and wasn't—wearing. Linen tunic. Cotton leggings, undergarments, and socks. And whatever Crocs were made of.

My clothes almost passed muster. T-shirt, fine. Jeans, too. Sneakers, unclear.

"Give yourself time to settle into sorcery and then, if you want, I'll supervise a trial run."

This hinged on my willingness to commit to a vegan lifestyle for the duration, but I'd have promised anything. I didn't even care what kind of bird I changed into. Being able to fly would suffice. I bounced on my chair. The wood squeaked in protest, to the point I almost missed Helen's next words.

"And then there's the last way to change shape. This takes the form of a sorcerous dissociative psychiatric disorder wherein an individual develops a separate non-human personality or alter with sufficient strength and validity that when that alter is dominant, they shift into animal or bird form." Her gaze fixed on me until I stopped wiggling and held still. "This type of shifting is always done in the nude."

A long pause, while she kept staring at me.

Why? Obviously, I wouldn't be trying this kind of change.

Though, she'd said what kind of shape changers she and her husband, and daughter, were—but hadn't mentioned Evan. Deliberate? She had to know he changed into a swan on a regular basis, being his aunt and all.

A swan, not a hybrid of more than one type of animal, so his curse didn't fit how she'd defined it. Especially since he went back and forth between forms without any problem.

"Evan said he's cursed, but his curse isn't the shape changing kind."

"Not in the traditional sense, no."

"In the untraditional?"

Her lips twisted to one side, but she didn't answer.

I had no clue what he ate or didn't eat, but he favored the same kinds of clothes as me, cotton and other natural fibers. Or had he worn a leather belt with his jeans once? Leather shoes?

He always stripped before changing.

Oh.

"He's got that dissociative disorder?"

"Yes." She nodded, lines of weariness and sorrow clear on her face. "I blame Regina and Sebastian, not individually but together."

"What did they do?"

Her chair legs scraped against the linoleum as she pushed back from the table. A few steps here, then there, the rush of water pouring out of the faucet, and she returned. Shifting around the placemats, she moved one in stripes of blue and red to the center of the table and placed a large, water-filled shallow dish atop it. A scrolling design of Celtic blue dragons decorated the outside of the bowl, but the inside had an opalescent tinge.

"I introduced them, years ago. My cousin and my colleague. They struck sparks off each other from the moment they met."

"Yeah, I saw that much." The memory of flames spitting out of the cone of silence sent a shiver through me.

"But back then, the flame was sexual attraction."

She waved a hand over the bowl. Two figures appeared in the water, rippling as the liquid responded to the shifting air currents above. When the fluid settled, the faces made me shiver again.

Alex resembled his father. Once last year, while I and other friends were over at the Noches house, Sebastian pulled out photo albums and showed us Alex's earlier years.

But this version of Alex, this younger Sebastian, had a goofy, adoring expression as he gazed at a younger, stunning, Regina. Bits of light flickered around them, as though someone had hung a half-dozen strings of white lights and swathed them in layers of gauze.

Lovely and romantic, with a distinct sexual undercurrent to the extent my face grew hot as I leaned over, gazing into the bowl. I pulled back, and the effect diminished.

"For whatever reason, the fire didn't burn out fast. It lasted years before things soured. Long enough that they married and settled into life here before it all went wrong." Helen braced her hands to either side of the bowl.

The faces in the water shifted as she spoke. Lust and love turned to distrust.

"And all this while, Regina never knew Sebastian was a sorcerer. Or that I and part of our shared family also practiced sorcery." Helen rubbed her hands together, shoulders hunching. "Then I visited them on New Year's Day, when Regina was about three months pregnant. A horrid day, odd gray skies. I should've stayed home—but they'd both mentioned intentions to set past grudges aside and start anew, with the New Year, and I wanted to cheer them on. Instead I made things worse."

Her face appeared alongside the others, in a room that resembled Regina's living room. The fireplace struck a chord, but some of the framed photos lined on the mantelpiece I'd seen in Sebastian and Alex's home: an old photo of Alex's grandparents on their wedding day, and a family photo when Sebastian was a teenager.

"A storm blew up. Thunder and lightning. Heavy snow. Wind gusts that knocked down power lines."

Thick darkness layered over the images in the bowl.

"Regina found flashlights, but the batteries had all died. She blamed Sebastian for not checking them. He located candles, but no matches, and blamed Regina because she'd smoked before learning she was pregnant, and he suspected she'd used the matchbooks or at least moved them outside since she didn't smoke in the house."

Faint sparks flared amidst the darkness, sullen and orange-red.

"Those damn sparks started flying around them, for the first time manifesting as visible flames capable of setting things on fire no matter how small." Helen's voice grew tight. "I was worried, or not thinking, or . . . all manner of accusations have been thrown at me over the years. Suffice to say, I worked a spell for light."

The image brightened, showing Helen's worried face. Light shone from her upraised hand. Sebastian appeared relieved and irritated, Regina at first relieved, then awestruck until the awe turned to horror. She grabbed Helen's hand and ran her fingers over the smooth palm emitting light. Then the faces in the bowl dissolved into clear water.

Helen's tale matched the version Regina had shared with me close enough.

"You turned her."

Shoulders slumping, Helen nodded. "And she realized her husband and her cousin, plus untold family members and friends, kept secrets from her for years. She held that against him more than me. Refused to even try to understand why he didn't tell her. He insisted he mentioned it several times when they were first in love but she laughed at him, so he stopped sharing. Around that time, someone filed a complaint against him, putting his naturalization at risk. He blamed her. She denied it, and sometimes I believe her. Sometimes I don't."

"That's horrid." And made my parents seem much more sane and compassionate in comparison. "But . . . it doesn't explain how Evan wound up turning into a swan."

"Skip ahead about four years." Again, she passed a hand over the dish.

A new image formed, this time a swooping view, as though from a bird flying around. Over water, then along a shoreline until Regina's house appeared. Not the same as it had earlier. No tall wrought-iron fence rose between the yard and the lake, but instead a white picket fence lined with flowers. The path around the lake wasn't paved, nothing more than a depression in the grass.

In the waters, a pair of swans floated by, followed by a trail of six gray cygnets.

"Sebastian and Regina argued over everything, even though they no longer lived together. Everything. And on at least one occasion, both focused so hard on making their points and yelling over each other that neither noticed when their son left the yard."

A little boy played in a sandpit near the kitchen door.

He'd got dust all over him, covering his once-white shirt, blue shorts, dark brown curls, bright eyes, and sun-touched skin. No resemblance to anyone, just himself.

Sparks flew overhead. The boy hunched his shoulders and left the sandpit. Walking on bare, muddy feet he stumbled away from the house. Trampled around flowers. Marched alongside the fence . . . and discovered where something gnawed on the fence and left a hole.

Bending down, dusty bottom raised high, he peered through the hole at the swans and cygnets on the other side.

The image flashed in the water, shattering into a thousand pieces and reforming into a different vista. A pair of shorts and a shirt lay abandoned on the grassy path, as the swans swam by.

I blinked, for the new image looked close to the previous and yet something had changed. Then it dawned.

The adult swans led a trail of seven cygnets, not six.

"Regina and Sebastian called me when they couldn't find him. We searched for hours before we realized the swans had one too many cygnets."

Helen sighed, and the water in the bowl returned to normal.

"It took a week to convince him to turn back into a human. Probably the last time Sebastian and Regina ever cooperated on anything, but it worked. He returned."

"Oh God, poor Evan." I clapped my hand over my face, muffling my voice, and shaking at the idea of him as a child being so frightened of his parents' anger that he sought refuge with the swan family. And poor Alex, losing his brother for days. . . "Where was Alex?"

Pity shone in Helen's eyes.

"Sebastian and Regina agree on almost nothing, including his name, but both admit she gave birth to only one child."

One child.

A rill of light, airy notes floated from the soloist's violin, underscored by the occasional ripple of harp. My foot tapped the air to keep the tempo. Professor Rodriguez's hands danced above me, from high on his elevated block. My fingers curved around my instrument, the wood and metal smooth to the touch. A low ache spread through my shoulders and upper back. Tightening and releasing my shoulders offered some relief, but not enough. I wore the same clothes as earlier in the day, sat in the same place in the orchestra as every Tuesday and Thursday, and held my familiar oboe.

Yet for the second time in as many weeks my world turned upside down.

One child.

Worse, we rehearsed the second movement of Rimsky-Korskakov's *Scheherazade*, and as second oboe I had almost nothing to do. The first oboist played a solo, but I counted over sixty bars before playing any note and then the same one several times in succession. Afterward, more waiting before the rest of the movement required concentration to ensure the sounds I produced mingled with the rest of the orchestra. I'd have traded for just about any other piece or movement for the fall concert, because the long rests left me too much time to think.

One son.

Helen's words haunted me. At any moment, particularly when my attention strayed, they rang in my ears again.

Alex and Evan as two sides of a coin.

The first oboist's solo wound toward the end. I straightened in my seat and inserted my reed in my mouth, ready to start an animated tempo—and the conductor stopped. Gave quick comments to the soloists, and started the piece at the beginning.

More time to sit and glance over at Evan among the violins. Without, of course, letting him catch me watching him. Which required discreet angling of my head, part of the reason my shoulders ached.

His head bobbed in time, lips curved in a small smile. One hand wrapped around the neck of his violin. The base rested on his knee, brown polished wood bright against his dull blue jeans. He wore another violin-themed T-shirt, although the instrument obscured the images at the moment. His fashion sense resembled Alex, both preferring casual T-shirts and shorts or jeans, but otherwise they were so different.

He caught my gaze for a moment and winked.

I startled and instantly refocused on the conductor. None too soon, for this time we plowed on—then I had more beats to rest. Eighteen here, eleven there, nineteen elsewhere. Too much time to think, and not enough at the same time. Nearby, the first oboist soared through several solos. Usually, I enjoyed playing second but this once I wished for the solos, for something to concentrate on.

We took a break after the first full run-through. Others

got up and walked around, or ran for the bathrooms. I stayed in place. Stood and stretched a bit, careful to keep my back to the string section, but otherwise remained hunched at my stand with my instrument across my lap.

And my brain still stuck on the revelations of the day.

Putting Evan and Alex together as two sides of a coin—Regina's son and Sebastian's son—made no sense to me. Helen's scrying bowl had shown me the little boy being lured back into human form from swan. For a moment, he'd resembled the boy from before. Then he took a stumbling step and moved closer to Regina. In that instant, his appearance shifted. Not much, just enough for his resemblance to his mother to double or triple. His next lurching step brought him nearer to Sebastian. Again, his face and body, hair and skin, changed subtly to increase his likeness to his father.

Back and forth and back and forth. With every flip or flop, the differences grew until anyone with eyes to see might perceive the one being his father's son and the other his mother's.

But seeing wasn't believing. As the break ended and everyone returned to their place, I risked glancing Evan's way and found no resemblance, other than clothes, to Alex.

Then again, I never had seen them in the same place.

This semester alone, I could plot every time I'd seen Alex on a weekly chart. All the dots would fall into a pattern. Monday, Wednesday, and Friday afternoons and nights. Tuesday and Thursday mornings. Sunday nights.

Plus, thanks to Alex I now remembered watching Regina walk right through him because she disbelieved in him to the point he didn't exist for her.

Helen had assured me it was the same for Evan and Sebastian.

"Neither has budged for years." She'd shaken her head, mouth tight. "At first, they pulled their child back and forth as though a rope and they playing a game of tug-of-war. Whoever was stronger, more focused, and closer—that's who had a son they could see and interact with. From their perspectives, the other kept stealing their son from them. Other than when the swans did, instead."

White and gray wings filled the scrying bowl for a moment, as the number of cygnets following their parents changed from six to seven and back and forth. The shifts had a hypnotic effect on me as Helen's voice provided background narration.

"Alex or Evan, both kept running back to them and changing into a cygnet again. Regina and Sebastian blamed the swans on each other, and seemed to ignore the danger that they posed. That their child might choose to fly away at the end of the summer and never return. No matter how often I warned them, they did nothing. Harming their son and themselves in the process. They cannot move on, locked together in endless striving to protect their son even as they rip him into pieces in the process."

The high, lilting strain of the first violin brought me back. My body jerked. The first oboist glanced my way, but immediately turned back to her music as she waited for her solo. The room grew warmer, and sweat started to bead on my forehead and the small of my back.

But again, I had time to think and remember. One small section of my brain kept time, or at least listened close for the phrases a few bars before my first notes.

The rest returned to that recent memory. To Helen confiding her sorcerous triumph and tragedy.

"I worked the greatest and most complicated spell of my life, which is saying something." She laid out a bright, color coded chart on the table. "Sebastian and his belief in his son anchor Alex, as Regina does Evan. I split the time between them. Alex and Evan each get the equivalent of three days, with the last day left to chance. At the start of each semester, I work out their schedule based on what classes they want to take. If Regina or Sebastian want additional time, say to go on a trip somewhere, I make sure it balances out."

In primary colors—reds and yellows—the schedule for the semester specified when Evan had to turn into Alex and vice-versa, and the small portion of the week left up to chance.

Tracing the dictated changes with shaky fingers, I'd blinked several times in hopes it would vanish. No such luck.

"Haven't they ever heard of Solomon's decision and the woman who put the welfare of her baby ahead of raising the baby herself?"

"They know, but they also don't." Helen grimaced. "Remember, as far as each is concerned, the other's son does not exist. If either let go of that belief for so much as one moment, they are sure their son might die."

"Could he? They?"

"I don't know. When I cast the spell, I wanted no one but Alex and Evan to be able to break it. They could decide to unite into one person, or split into two. I never thought it would last this long." Her whole body slumped. "I hoped they'd unite in one—such a sweet, trusting little boy they were before . . . but I expected they'd choose to become two separate individuals, so I tried to make it so breaking the spell would allow them to have two bodies."

She rubbed her temples and gave me a rueful look.

"Now, even I can't break it, only adjust it evermore."

Drawn back to the music, I raised my oboe and counted the few measures remaining until my first notes. Pushed all thoughts of Evan and Alex aside, and focused only on the joy of music and being part of an ensemble, something larger than myself.

Yet weariness filled me, body, mind, and soul. Too much happened in the last weeks, days, twenty-four hours.

After rehearsal, Evan waited for me at the door as before.

I couldn't face him. Not then. Needed more time to elapse, to adjust.

So I took the weasel way out—left through the emergency exit. Shivered a little, though the evening remained fairly warm, just not as much as the rehearsal room full of active musicians. Darker sky, as we edged closer towards full fall.

The exit put me on the wrong side of the music building from my dorm. I had to go the long way around, with my oboe case banging against my side again.

I almost made it past the building and off into the shadowy paths leading to the residential quad, but my luck ran out. Evan must've noticed I'd escaped the room for he burst out the front doors and barreled toward me.

A week or so ago, I chased him from orchestra to his mother's house.

This time he chased me.

Feet pounding against the pavement, and lungs huffing away, I ran from him.

Would've done the same if he'd been Alex.

Raced home to shut the door and keep the world out.

Evan did some kind of end run. When I reached my dorm, he'd already arrived. His lanky body leaned against the doorway, arms crossed.

"Wretch, you knew I wanted to talk to you." He managed an almost perfect imitation of my tone and words from a week or so ago.

"Can't this wait?" My lungs ached from the run, and my side ached where the oboe case banged it.

"Don't you have a lesson?" He frowned.

"Not anymore. Haven't you talked to your mother?"

"Texts only." Evan shook his head. "What happened?"

"You don't know?"

He snapped his fingers and pulled out his phone out of

nowhere. After scrolling through his messages, he passed it over to me.

A brief exchange glowed blue and gray against a white background.

Regina: <<Take care with Viola. She'll need your help.>>

Evan: <<What's up?>>

Regina: <<Ask her.>>

What the hell? Way for Regina to throw me under the bus. My fingers itched to scroll up and read more of their texts, but I handed the phone back instead. Our hands brushed as he took it. He flipped on silence mode and slipped it into his back pocket.

Muffled voices approached from the street side. Unfortunately, the dorm opened right onto the quad and there was no good place to talk privately anywhere nearby.

Except one.

Heaving a sigh, I opened the heavy door and jerked my chin at the foyer beyond.

"Follow me."

Evan left a foot or two between us as I led the way up the stairs, but somehow his breath fell hot on my neck anyway.

"Gloria?" I checked our shared living room, but there was no sight or sound of her.

As far as I knew, Gloria had never met Evan or had any clue about his connection to Alex. Even Emilio hadn't breathed so much as a hint. Then again, given how good sorcerers seemed to be at lies and keeping secrets, I couldn't be sure of anything.

If Gloria didn't know Alex wasn't around twenty-four hours/seven days a week, I didn't want to be the one to tell her. Not without Alex's permission. Bad enough that I'd learned his secret and hadn't had a chance to talk to him.

But ignoring Evan until after that wasn't happening either. Whether or not he was . . . what, Alex's other half?

How was I supposed to even think about them? They weren't two sides of a coin, but two separate people who shared a body . . . maybe with a bonus swan added for good measure.

Evan waited, leaning against the hallway wall with a smirk on his face.

I wished he'd go away so I could deal with him after Alex. Tried to cast such a spell, to snap my fingers and have this all rearrange. Reaching inside to the well of power growing in me.

Snapped.

Small surprise, it failed.

He rolled his eyes. "I take it your suite mate may return at any moment?"

"She's a sorcerer." I grimaced. "And a friend of Alex Noches."

The smirk dropped from his face. He snapped straight, arms tight at his side. His mouth shaped the name, but he didn't say it.

"Come on in." I opened the door to my bedroom and pulled out the desk chair for him to sit on. No way was I sharing the bed. I wanted to have a clear view of his face at all times, so I turned on the overhead and aimed my reading lamp his way.

Striding into the room, he closed the door behind and stood in the center. Made a slow circle around, head nodding as he stared at the walls, desk, bed. Grinned at the travel posters on the walls. Then stopped in his tracks and picked up the feather from my desk. Examined it under the reading lamp, tracing every barb and sniffing the quill.

Returning it to its former place, he grabbed the slatted desk chair and turned it around. Sat down on it backwards, arms resting across the top of the back.

Neither of us spoke, waiting the other out. The silence

turned heavy, pressing on my lungs until I strained to draw anything more than a shallow breath.

"Do you know my father?" Evan broke first. Head tilted down, showing only the whorls of hair on his crown and white-knuckled fingers holding on to the chair.

"Yeah. I'm in his symbolism class this semester. And I've known him since last fall, after I met Alex."

His shoulders jerked at the name. Still didn't look up.

"What's he like?"

"Don't you know? You said . . . he was the one who cursed you."

"He did." He drew swirling lines on his pants. "That's what my mother's always said. But I've never been around him much. Seen him from a distance, mostly. When I was younger, I . . . he doesn't hear me. He walked right through me. Twice. After that, I stopped hanging around. It wasn't worth it."

"He's a decent teacher. I'd've said good before I accepted sorcery." I huffed. "But, well, I'm a bit down on him and my sorcerer friends right now for keeping secrets."

"It's not by choice." He glanced up, a rueful smile lightening his face.

"That doesn't make me feel any better." I slumped onto my bed and leaned back against the wall. "Anyway, I've been in class with him since the start of the semester, which is only a matter of weeks. I know him better as Alex's father."

Evan jerked again.

"He always welcomed me and Alex's other friends, when Alex had us over." I scratched my head, trying to guess what he might want to know. "Cooked for us—his chicken adobo is fabulous. Joined in games sometimes, but also let us hang out together without him hanging over us."

Evan didn't say anything. His head bobbed or nodded. I guessed the first, because he still faced downward.

"You told me about your curse." I inched down the bed, sitting close to the end so as to watch him more closely. "Why didn't you . . ."

I don't know what I wanted to know, but at least this time I managed to wait him out.

"Why didn't I what? Share that half of my life, my body goes off and does things and I have no memory? That at least once a week I find myself in parts of the campus without any clue why I'd be there? Because it wasn't me who was there." He reared up, his head high, eyes flashing, and mouth snarling. "I told you what was most important—that I spend at most half the time as myself, and sometimes I'd give anything to be able to fly away."

"Would it be you flying away?"

"Not just me. I don't . . . I'm subsumed, but I'm there and aware. The swan alter is in control."

White feathers reflected in his eyes for a moment.

Clatter from the hallway doused the light. We both froze as footsteps and loud voices speaking over each other penetrated into my room.

And then all was silent again, or mostly so.

The chair legs scraped across the floor as Evan moved it so he could see me on the bed, and the feather on the desk.

My pulse beat fast in my throat, and I dragged in a deep breath.

"Helen said you and Alex could split into separate people. She made the spell that shares your time that way. Why haven't you?"

He rolled his head back, staring at the ceiling. His arms remained braced along the top of the chair back, knuckles white as he held on.

At last he, too, drew in a deep breath and looked me in the eye. Again the brush of wings and feathers across the pupil and iris, then the brightness faded away leaving Evan's natural green and yellow rings around the dark pupil.

Kneeling on the chair, he stretched across the distance to pick up the swan feather and stroked it between his fingers.

"Aunt Helen's as deep in this as anyone, more than she acknowledges. We've tried every way we can think of to change her spell or break it, with no success yet. Every night the swan flies and returns is another attempt by some measures. Another failure." His hands curved inward mimicking talons and his lips drew back in a snarl. "She miscounted when she cast the spell. It presumes there are only two to unite or split."

❧ 24 ❧

Dinner with my father should have offered a distraction from my new, complicated daily life. I should've known better. The man who usually opted to eat off the beaten track, in local favorites and holes-in-the-wall with great food, for once made a totally mainstream choice of restaurant: the Arden Inn. It smelled good, at least, lots of butter and bread and sizzling oils.

A nice-enough place decorated with every style of Shakespearean-inspired art imaginable. I counted at least five busts or portraits in different sizes, along with scenes depicting iconic moments from various plays which my father spent much time admiring. At least the college didn't take the theme too far and make us sit on Elizabethan furniture. All the fittings were plush, forest green, and forgettable.

But soft. The pile on the thick carpet occasionally brushed my feet since I wore good walking sandals with trendy leather straps supposed to give them a classical Roman look. Plus, the chairs proved quite comfy, which I appreciated since I'd dressed for a warm day in short shorts that didn't mix well with wood chairs. I'd only changed shirts before Dad picked me up, from a worn Arden tee to a gauzy pink tunic suitable for partying later if I wanted.

My father wore one of his many gray suits, although he left the suit coat in the car and had removed his tie and rolled his sleeves halfway up. Gray flecked his dark brown hair, the same color as the silver frame on his glasses; I got my bad eye sight from him. He towered over me, well over six feet, when he pulled out the chair for me to take a seat at the green-cloth-covered table set with gleaming tableware and a small, lit candle in a crystal holder.

Unfortunately, one of the Inn restaurant's main attractions, other than the art and proximity to campus, lay in the view of the lake. The building sat on a small promontory and thus had a panorama overlook of the campus shoreline. If a brisk wind hadn't kicked up, we might have sat outside on the patio. Even from an inside table, right against the glass wall, I might point out any of the college buildings—or where the trail around the far side of the lake left campus.

An outcropping of rocks and trees partially obscured Regina's house, but I could still identify the general area I'd seen the swan turn to Evan and back again.

The view made me super aware of my phone in my pocket, certain unanswered texts, and the need to talk to Alex. We'd kept missing each other all day, partly because I didn't want to talk to him over texts but in person. Or at least voice to voice.

And based on the lack of response for most of the day, he wasn't himself Fridays until late afternoon.

Basically, this dinner came with the worst timing in the world. Much as I wanted to talk to my father about every-thing, at least everything family-wise not magic-wise, I *so* didn't want it to happen now. Later would be good. After I'd touched base with Alex. In person.

But fate conspired to keep us apart all afternoon, especially with Dad arriving early to take me to dinner. According to Rose, skipping this wasn't an option. Bea even texted earlier to ask when I was doing dinner with him. Both wanted reports afterward.

Small wonder my legs turned fidgety, toes tapping against the carpet. Muscles twitched. I kept my hands linked together in my lap most of the time to keep my fingers still.

The waiter laid a menu in front. I had to open the heavy green leather cover, embossed with the college's seal, and flip through the pages to settle on something to order other than water to drink—better not to risk sugar or caffeine given my antsiness.

The menu offered a brief distraction. Should I start moving toward a vegan lifestyle now to make things easy in a year or two when Helen made good on her promise to show me how to take bird shape and fly? Or indulge in all the meat and dairy before I had to forgo it.

Decisions, decisions, for which the trail of steak-scented smoke rising from a steaming platter carried to a nearby table did not help one bit.

I took the small steps route and went with the fish special. A moment later, the waiter whisked away the menu.

A flicker of white flashed in the corner of my eye. I whipped my head around to glance out at the view but couldn't find the cause. No swan anywhere to be seen. Good, though in my distraction my fingers started rapping against the soft linen tablecloth and cool glass of the water goblet.

Dad captured my hand and held it. His skin was warm against mine as he stroked and soothed away some of the shakes.

"I'm sorry."

"For what?"

"Disrupting your life? Letting you down?" His teeth

flashed as he smiled ruefully. "Being something of a cliché, the middle-aged man starting a second family?"

"We all knew you and Mom would separate sooner or later." I pulled away, tucking both hands in my lap. My fingers twisted the linen napkin until it wrapped around them and they finally stopped twitching.

"Indeed." Dad leaned back in his chair and stroked his chin. "How long have you thought this?"

"I don't know. Four years? Five? Seven? Ten?"

"I hope not ten." He shuddered. "Four is closer to the mark."

"Then why didn't you just do it then?" Under the table, I flipped the napkin over and started worrying at a stray thread.

"A variety of reasons. To be absolutely sure. To give us time to figure out what we wanted next. To ensure you and your sisters could stay in one place until you were ready to spread your wings and start flying away."

Accidental bad choice of words. I turned my head, staring out at the lake. A couple of ducks, or geese, floated on the waters close enough to be seen if not exactly identified. No white wings and arched neck, though.

"Then you break the last year before Bea's off." A huff escaped me, as I focused on the discussion at hand. "Good going."

"Your mother and I being together matters less to Bea. She values clarity over stability. She didn't like the uncertainty when we made the final move to split, but she's settling down now that things are clearer." Dad leaned forward, setting his elbows on the table. "She's not like you."

"What do you mean?" I turned away from the window. The napkin slipped from my hands and fluttered to the floor.

"Rose is the leader, Bea's the planner, and you're the peacemaker."

"How do you know?" Leaning over, I pinched the corner of my napkin and pulled it back into my lap, then tied it in a big knot around my fingers. "Pigeonholing us? I thought you didn't like doing that."

"Peacemaker doesn't describe all you are, but it's one of your core attributes."

"It's not like I go around spreading love and joy everywhere."

"That's not what I meant." The candle flame reflected in his glasses, almost exactly lined up with his eyes. I winced and retreated against the plush back of my chair. "Perhaps you don't do this with your friends, but I've seen it countless times in the family. Rose and Bea would get into an argument, and you'd convince them to make friends again. Didn't matter how many times you had to trundle between them, carrying messages, you kept going until they made up. Same thing with your cousins. Your friends, when you were younger. Even your mother and me. We'd argue about something, and you'd show up talking to each of us, putting the best interpretation possible on whatever we said, and trying to get us to see the good in each other."

With exquisite timing, the waiter brought over small salads. Lovely concoctions of greens with bright colored peppers, bits of cucumber, olives, and feta cheese. I wrapped my right hand around my fork to keep from shaking too much, and took a bite.

The crunch wasn't loud enough to drown out his voice.

"Being a peacemaker is one of the reasons you had such a hard time in high school. You kept making compromises, always the first to apologize even when you weren't in the wrong, hoping to smooth things over—only to get trod on again and again."

He dug into his salad, head tilting my way as he waited for my response. Well, he could wait all he wanted.

I fidgeted in my chair, head down and shoulders hunched. Trying not to think about all the times I'd gone along to keep people liking me, turned the other cheek to teasing and jibes until I finally walked away and stayed away.

"We failed you."

An ache started to develop at the top of my spine, between my shoulders. Gritting my teeth, I forced myself to straighten up. Still didn't say anything. Focused on transferring the salad from plate to mouth one bite at a time.

"I'm sorry for that, too. That I didn't pull you out. Homeschool you, or your mother and I could have separated then and one of us moved to a nearby town so you could start afresh at a new school." His voice had dwindled down to little more than a whisper, though I heard every word. "But we thought—I thought—you would take us breaking up worse, and miss your sisters."

Another bite, then my head shot up and I had to force the food past the sudden lump in my throat. My fork dropped and clattered as it hit the plate.

"So I'm the reason you didn't get divorced earlier?"

"No! Never that."He reached over and grabbed my hand again, squeezing tight. "I'm human. Humans make mistakes, that's what we do. Even with the best intentions. I . . . want to apologize for the ways I've let you down. And make sure you know that your mother and I are divorcing each other, but not you and your sisters. You will always be my heroes."

"I don't—" A glance around showed no one paying any attention to us. The other diners were busy in their own groups, and the servers fussing discreetly around. All the same I wished we were somewhere more homey, or back in my dorm room where I could break down and cry. "I thought you were supposed to be a hero too."

"Heroes make mistakes, too. And fall off marble pedestals." He picked up his fork and held it upright atop the back of his other hand. Then let it topple, though he caught it before it crashed down and clattered again.

My eyes stung from holding back tears, but I managed a small smile.

"Sometimes we try to be too many things to too many people. I'm guilty of that. Holding onto all of you, and sticking in the house with you girls and your mother, and keeping up appearances at work, until the theater group became the one place I could just be me. Then Grace and I started clicking, and . . . sometimes you have to let old things go to make room for the new. I didn't do that fast enough, or smooth enough. I hurt you and your sisters. And Grace, who's forgiven me but not forgotten."

That, at least, distracted him from analyzing me.

His face lightened as he talked about her with more energy and excitement than I remembered seeing or hearing in his voice in ages. He even pulled out his wallet, which held a photo of me and my sisters smiling at him, to show off an image of her and a sonogram of the baby. Grace had evidently agreed to keep with the family theme and give it a Shakespearean name as well. Another hero. Dad went off on that, suggesting some of the most godawful Shakespearean possibilities.

Fakery, of course, but he had fun and it rubbed off on me. A bit.

He was so cheery, I risked slipping my phone out of my pocket to check my texts.

Two from Rose asking how I'm doing. Others from Gloria and Ruth, out partying again. Emilio ditto.

And several from Alex.

<<Where are you?>>

<<Ten missed calls from you. No voicemail messages. No texts. What's going on?>>

<<Where are you?>>

lex waited in front of my dorm. Wearing jeans and a short-sleeved green polo shirt, sandals on his feet, he paced up and down. He held an orange frisbee disc, which he tossed from hand to hand.

When Dad pulled the car into the curved driveway leading to the dorm, Alex stopped and swirled around to stare at us. Dad put the car in neutral, reducing the throb of the motor to a low thrum. The vibrations rippled through me as I shifted in the passenger seat. Both windows were open halfway, letting the wind blow in and carry the distant sounds of the usual weekend parties. Leaning forward, he peered through the windshield, then glanced at me.

"Do you know him?"

"Yeah." I licked my lips, clearing away a few remaining sugar crystals from the ornate blue and green agate sugar cookies we'd had for dessert. My choice, not Dad's, but he'd had two wrapped up for me to take home, sitting warm on my lap. "I introduced you last year, when you came up for the *Tempest* production. It's my friend Alex."

"Just a friend?"

For a second time, I slicked my tongue over my lips. Too many possible answers occurred to me. Unfortunately, I took too long to answer

"Make sure he's worthy of you." Dad ran a finger down my cheek. "You deserve a hero."

"Thanks." I gave him a one-armed hug, then got out of the car.

He leaned over before I could shut the door. "Breakfast tomorrow, remember. 7:30, so don't stay up all night talking or drinking."

"I won't." Especially not the drinking, not after last week. The memory alone made me shudder, and I slammed the door in emphasis. All the same, I could feel him watching as I headed over to meet Alex.

A few steps away, I whirled around and leveled a stern look at my father.

He laughed and drove off.

Alex, when I reached him, wasn't laughing. He held the disc in front of his chest, both hands gripping the rim tight. He'd run his hands through his hair a couple of times at some point, because the strands were all awry. I kept my arms at my side, suppressing the urge to comb my hands after his and make it all straight.

"Hey, Viola."

"What's up?" A stupid response, but the first words out of my mouth nonetheless. As if this was any old Friday post-parental dinner meet-up.

"I don't know, you tell me." He tilted his head to one side and stared at me.

"I tried, but your phone went to voicemail most of the day and I didn't want to leave a message." Especially since I didn't know exactly when the spell made Evan turn to Alex.

"Why not?" He tossed the disc into the air so it traced a small arc and caught it with the other hand when it came back down. "It's not that hard, all you had to say or text was that you have a new teacher."

I blinked. That wasn't what I wanted to talk to him about. Then realization dawned: he didn't know even the half of what I'd learned yesterday. My jaw hung loose.

"My father told me." He rolled his eyes. "Did you think he wouldn't?"

"The teacher thing is settled, for now, but—"

"For now?"

"Helen's looking for another turned sorcerer to take me on." I waved a hand, the one holding the extra cookies. "She's only stepping for the interim—because of the situation between your parents . . . and you and Evan."

He stiffened, eyes going wide. As with Evan, he shaped the other's name with his mouth but didn't actually say it.

"We need to talk. So much happened yesterday." This wasn't the place, though. Students in ones, twos, and groups passed along the street laughing and joking, and at any moment more might walk out of the dorm.

"How long have you known . . . " His mouth opened and closed in a fishlike motion, but only a croak emerged.

"Evan?"

A nod.

"He's in the orchestra, as you'd have known if you'd ever come to any of our concerts." Which Alex never had, a fact that had burned me a bit in the past. Only after hearing the jibe did I put together why. He actually had been there in a way, just not as himself. "Sorry, that came out wrong. We're both musicians in the orchestra, that's how I met him."

"I guess there's more to talk about than I thought." He stayed stiff and strained. A tic twitched in one cheek, and his grip on the disc tightened. "Your room or mine?"

His house sat close enough to see the lights shining from

the first floor, suggesting his father was around. That made the decision easy.

"Mine."

For the second night in a row, I led someone to my room. Gloria was out partying with Ruth. All the same, when we arrived at my suite, I brought Alex into my room rather than staying in the common area. Just in case Gloria returned before we finished talking. Also, in the interest of not doing anything for Evan that I didn't do for Alex. Even if neither of them knew it.

Alex entered and turned around, absorbing his surroundings much as Evan had. It wasn't Alex's first time in my room. The first week back at college, before the whole sorcery thing burst open, Gloria and I had a party for our friends. Nothing much changed since then.

Save the addition of the white feather lying on my desk.

Alex noticed at once. Pinching the quill between thumb and forefinger, he held it up to the light. Stuck his nose close enough to sniff every barb. Ran it along his arm and stopped partway, where he pressed the quill against his skin. For a moment, his arm appeared to turn to a white wing and the feather one of hundreds. To this day, I don't know whether I imagined it or not.

"Where did you get this?" His voice had a gruff note. Standing three-quarters away from me, he swallowed hard.

"Regina. Your mother."

Another swallow. He turned his head to look at me, shoulders and torso still facing away. The hand holding the feather shook.

"I know about Evan, the swan, and you."

He still didn't say anything. Backing up, he dropped onto my bed. It creaked under his weight, groaning more as he shifted further until he leaned against the wall. One hand rested in his lap, feather cupped in his palm. The other formed a fist pressing into the blankets and mattress hard enough to make a dent.

I left the extra cookies on the desk, then settled higher up on the bed. Leaned against the headboard, which made us almost close enough to touch. Heat and intensity poured off his body despite the gap between us.

Leaving the feather in his lap, he crossed his arms over his chest. This time, his lips formed a straight line rather than a smile. I matched his pose, equally serious. Once again, we played a waiting game to see who would break the silence first.

But silence bred secrets, and so many lay between us that I didn't want to chance leaving more. Or wasting this time with him. Might as well get the worst over with, or so I thought at the time.

"I watched the swan land on the lake, a little over a week ago. It turned into Evan. That's when I believed in sorcery, though I didn't accept it for another day."

"That's when you turned." His head bobbed as a huff escaped his throat. He looked over at me, mouth twisted and eyes dark. "Not for me, for . . ."

Neither of us spoke the name. I planted my hands on the bed and leaned forward, shaking my head.

"It wasn't like that."

"No?" He matched my posture. Our bodies remained separated, but only an inch or two separated our heads. Every breath, every word hit me with a puff of air. "You didn't turn with me. What is this, the pity talk? The let-Alex-down-easy so we can go be musicians together . . ."

"What are you talking about?" I reared back, blinking and shaking my head.

"You chose Dad's class instead of keeping her as your teacher—well, you had to if you didn't want to drop—but that doesn't mean you chose me." He glared at me, teeth bared.

"Why do I have to choose?" I leaned forward again. Helen had said as much, but not explained. I'd let it slide among all the shocks and bared secrets—but not now. Why the insistence on choosing? "Can't I be friends with Evan and friends, or more, with you?"

"It won't work that way." A snarl escaped him.

"Why not?"

"It never has! For years, guys, friends, people I trusted knew both of us, and every one of them ended up dropping me." He pulled back. Picking up the feather, he ran it between his fingers over and over. His shoulders hunched over, stiff and tight.

A familiar posture, in a way. I'd sat so myself enough times in the past that my back ached in sympathy.

"Were they sorcerers or mundanes?"

"Sorcerers. Mostly. Some mundane friends got fed up when I could only hang around with them part of the time. Others didn't care, or didn't notice." His gaze fixed on the feather. "The sorcerers . . . even friends whose parents were friends with Dad, not her, stuck around for a while. But sooner or later, they shaved off. Some ignored me. Others played tricks. I wasn't popular in high school, even in sorcerous circles. Being a guy who's cursed made things worse."

"I can guess." I shifted over to sit next to him. Put my arm around his shoulders, stroking stiff muscles under smooth cotton. He didn't lean in, but neither did he pull away. "I hated high school."

"It wasn't as bad as it could've been, but I wouldn't go back for anything."

Another silence, but less tense. My arm dropped away as he stretched over and dropped the feather on the desk. That alone sent a chill running through the room as though a sudden breeze had snuck in. Sitting back, he grabbed my hand and held it.

"So you haven't chosen?"

"I don't see why I have to. Why anyone has to." My turn to grimace and glare at him. "Can't I be friends with both of you? You're such different people, anyway."

"I wouldn't know." He gave me a sideways glance, then turned serious. "You will have to decide, though. My father will demand it, if he ever realizes you know . . ." A wave of his free hand completed the sentence.

But I declined to let him off the hook and fill in the blank. Kept my lips zipped shut.

This time, he broke the silence.

"How are we different?"

"I never really knew Evan until I believed in sorcery. We were just both in the same orchestra." I rubbed my thumb against the back of his hand, stroking smooth skin over muscles and bones. "Before, I'd have described him as a nice guy, but hard to get to know."

"Now?"

"He's still a nice guy. Walked me home from Regina's to make sure howling wolves didn't rush through the forest and carry me off." Even though I paused, he didn't laugh. Maybe he really meant the question. Didn't know his . . . whatever Evan was to him. "Plays the violin well. You can tell he takes it seriously and practices. Smart, too. But so moody. Always brooding and staring at the lake. He's never thrown a disc to me. I don't know if he's touched one."

This time, a laugh escaped Alex. Short and sharp but real mirth nonetheless.

"You only met through orchestra?"

"Yeah."

"That doesn't start until after the first day of classes. We met before classes started." He grabbed my hands and held them fast. "You're my friend first."

"I'll always be your friend."

One of us tugged, don't remember which, and the next moment our arms wrapped around each other. I rested my cheek against his warm chest and his head became a welcome weight atop mine. We sat there, neither quite willing to risk disturbing the harmony.

Maybe he'd have kissed me, but something about our conversation disturbed me and all at once it dawned. Rolling my head to the side, I stared up at him.

"You can't even say his name, can you?"

He jerked in surprise. Eyes narrowed, shadows growing in their depths.

"Only one has a body at any given time. It's the rule. I'm me or I'm . . . not."

"But Evan said he sort of rides along with the swan."

"That's different. There's only one swan."

A faint gleam of white feathers crossed his eyes, but for less than a millisecond. So short, I wasn't sure what I'd seen.

"I ride along, too. Sometimes. A lot when I was in high school, not so much since I've been in college. Since Emilio's living with us, and we started hanging out with you. All of you." He added the last words under his breath, but I knew he meant me as much or more than the rest.

His arms tightened around me.

"Choose me."

❧   26   ❧

The wind blew me downtown. Nipped at my ankles, left bare between the top of my skimmer socks and sneakers and the bottom of my leggings. Blasted my back, sending a chill through my muscles despite three layers of clothing: tank top, crew-neck shirt, and jacket. Roared past my ears and tangled my hair no matter how many times I combed my fingers through strands and tucked them back behind my ears.

Maybe I should've worn a hat after all. Too late for that, though not too late to have second and third thoughts about where I went and why.

The wind might have blown some of the sense out of my brain, but I forged on regardless. Despite the blusteriness of the day, lots of other students and townspeople ventured out and about. More than once I dodged doors swinging open suddenly, and folk laden high with packages who didn't look about them as they walked.

My goal was the coffee shop on the corner, five blocks from campus.

The bells chimed as I swung the door open. Warmth hit

me first, even before the lovely blending of coffee, tea, and plenty of cinnamon. A locally owned spot, nearly every seat was filled from the buttery leather sofas to the bright orange beanbag chairs to the ladder-back chairs surrounding circular tables of various sizes. Only a third of people talking, though, as others nodded to unheard music or focused on laptops and tablets.

At the far end, a woman rose and nodded at me.

Regina.

I didn't recognize her until the second glance. For once, she'd dressed casually in jeans, no less, with several splotches of mud on the hem and knees. She wore a blue long-sleeved shirt, not unlike the green one I sported under my jacket. Hers had bits of greenery, broken leaves and blades of grass, clinging to her sleeves in places she might not readily see. A smudge of dirt marred her chin. Only her hair, held away from her face by two enameled blue barrettes, and her hands were completely clean.

Slipping along narrow passages between chairs and people, I skipped waiting in line and went over to her by the most direct route.

A ceramic mug half-full of tea sat on the table in front of her. Something fruity based on the smell carried by wafts of steam still rising. The table also bore a small plate with the remnants of a muffin—though there were so many bits of muffin they might have added up to nearly half of the original.

How long had she been waiting? Her food sent contradictory messages; the tea that she'd just arrived and the muffin that she'd tarried.

I'd woken to the ding of her text asking to meet me here at eleven. Spent an hour deciding to come. A minute texting back my agreement. Then two hours re-thinking.

Too late to back out now.

"I appreciate your coming." Regina smiled and held out her hand.

"No problem."

My fingers were icy compared to her warm ones, but she didn't jerk away or make any comment.

"Can I get you anything to drink?" She gestured at the coffee bar, where the line had dwindled to a single customer waiting for her order. "My treat, of course."

"No thanks, I'm good." Despite the wonderful cooking odors, I still tasted the eggs from my breakfast burrito when I licked my lips.

"Very well." After a brisk nod, she settled back into her seat.

I took off my jacket and hung it over the back of the other chair, then sat. The wood seemed solid enough, chair seat flat and firm, but one of the legs squeaked as I settled in. A brief chill ran through me as someone opened the door to leave, setting a draft through the place, but as soon as the door closed I warmed back up.

"I know Helen is taking over your teaching for now," Regina said. "I'm sure she'll do well by you."

"I have a lesson late this week. She already sent me a box of books to read first." I shaped the box with my hands to give a sense of size: short and wide and deep.

"A box? That's Helen for you." Regina laughed. "She always was an overachiever."

A grunt escaped me. The box materialized in my room at some point in the night. It wasn't there when I went to sleep, but first thing in the morning I barked my toes. The plain cardboard form slid across the bare floor while I hopped in place. A moan or two of pain might've escaped me. Yet when I finally picked it up, it wasn't as heavy as it seemed. The sides bore a couple of rounds of USPS stickers on it, plus a fresh one with the note from Helen.

As for the inside . . .

"They're picture books. Probably ones her daughter outgrew." I shook my head, not sure how to take it. As a compliment, entrusting me with works potentially passed down across generations—or as an unfortunately accurate assessment of my level of sorcerous knowledge.

My First Book of Spells. Symbols for Kids. Mommies and Daddies are Magic! None more than thirty pages long and all filled with full color illustrations. One rhymed.

"What a clever idea." Regina chuckled again, fingers rubbing along the handle of her tea cup. "You'll likely learn faster with Helen than you would have with me."

A faint pressure built in my ears. The usual coffee shop noise remained, but became more distant as though I'd moved yards away without taking a step. Tossing my head and swallowing didn't dispel the pressure or sense of distance. It reminded me of what Emilio had done a few days earlier, though not whatever Regina and Sebastian had thrown up at her house.

"Did you just cast a cone of silence?"

"Not quite. Rather, an aura of confusion." She rapped her fingernails against the porcelain muffin plate, making it chime. Not even the people sitting closest noticed. "Much more discreet for a place such as this. People will hear us talking, but anything longer than one syllable will be muffled enough that even someone paying attention won't understand. Similarly, if anyone here can lip read and should happen to try reading either of us they'll have trouble."

"It makes my ears feel like I'm thirty thousand feet up." I pressed my fingers against the base of my ears. Didn't help.

"That should wear off in a few minutes as your brain adjusts."

"Okay." I rocked back in my chair. The legs squeaked, so I returned to all four on the floor. "So, why are we meeting?"

"For me to apologize." She laid her hands flat on the table, arms tight against her chest. She lifted her chin and stared straight into my eyes. "I'm sorry I didn't immediately turn you over to Helen. Would've simplified things and not put your studies at risk. Instead, I dragged you into the mess of Evan's and my lives."

My mouth gaped open, until I realized and snapped it shut.

I beat back my first instinct, which was to protest that she hadn't done anything much. That I'd gotten myself into the mess after seeing Evan change shape and then chasing him down.

Evidently she thought she needed to apologize. Maybe she was right.

Plus, when she mentioned enemies on campus, she didn't share any names or I'd have, maybe, told her I was in Sebastian's symbols class and friends with his son, back when I still didn't know they were sorcerers. Or the deeper reasons they were at odds.

So, while she hadn't intended to complicate my life, it was partly her doing. Her fault.

And she was sorry.

"Okay." I gave a sharp nod. "Apology accepted."

"Thank you." Regina's arms relaxed and she settled against the back of her chair. "You won't hold it against Evan, will you?"

The other shoe dropped. Maybe her apology was genuine, but also ranked secondary to making sure I stayed Evan's friend.

Alex said he'd lost friends to Evan, when they were forced to choose. This might be one step in how. A rough silence stretched between us, punctuated by the distant sounds of conversation muffled through the spell, as I worked through what I could offer—promise—as a response.

"I'll stay friends with Evan—and Alex—as long as I can."

She smiled at the first half of my sentence, but faltered at the second. Her face took on a blank look, although only for a moment. Then she returned to her usual self, and nodded at me.

"He said you talked, the other night."

"Evan or Alex?"

Again, the blank look this time accompanied by rapid blinks. "Evan, of course."

"Did he tell you about what?"

"No, of course not." Regina's lips tightened. "He's a grown man. He doesn't tell me everything."

"Flying was one topic. Do you think he might ever turn into a swan and fly away?"

Her eyes closed and she shuddered. A hint of tears glittered in her lashes. Head tilting down, she picked up a piece of the broken muffin and divided it into three even smaller sections. "That's why he needs people he cares about, other than me, to root him here."

"I can't promise I'll be his roots, but . . . he worries me." I liked him, yes, but pitied him too.

"It's his father's curse. If that were only broken, all would be well." Regina hit the table with the heels of her hands. A visceral wave of energy ran through my gut from front to back. The recently split sections of muffin flattened against the plate, despite being untouched. Then she shuddered again, and gave me a rueful smile. "But that's one of the things I shouldn't talk to you about. There lies danger, and Helen coming down on my head a second time in one week."

"I'm friends with Alex, too, you know. Not just Evan."

No reaction from her other than a bland nod. "How nice, it's good to have friends."

"Doesn't he mean anything to you? Alex, that is."

"I'm not sure what you're referring to." She tilted her

head to one side, face puzzled. "Of course I love Evan. He's the best thing in my life."

"Not just Evan, Alex." I emphasized each syllable and consonant.

Her brow wrinkled and she shook her head sharply. "I'm not sure I'm hearing you right. Do you mind repeating what you said?"

"Alex. Your son. The other half of Evan."

"I still didn't get it. I'm so sorry."

No matter how close I examined her face, no sign of understanding appeared. It seemed as though two simultaneous auras of confusion existed: one between us and the world, and the other protecting her from any mention of the part of her son she denied.

Part of me wanted to shake her, make her hear what I said. I didn't have the power, knowledge, or imagination to break through and make her see. Sebastian might be just as bad about Evan. All the same, I wouldn't accept that assumption until I tested it as well.

If nothing else, the two of them certainly made me appreciate my parents all the more. Irritating as their situation was, they'd shielded us from most of their arguments rather than dividing us between them.

A flash of color out of the corner of my eye caught my attention. Twisting around, I noted Emilio in a bright lime-green jacket over jeans at the counter placing an order.

The chair legs scraped the floor as I pushed back from the table. Gazed down at Regina for once rather than across or up.

"Thanks for the apology. I'll stay Evan's friend as long as I can."

"That's all I ask." She grabbed my hand, the layer of sweat on hers made her fingers slick and slip off so she couldn't hold me back.

With a nod, I headed off. The aura of confusion popped as I passed through it, or at least my ears popped and the volume in the room increased three-fold. I dodged around other customers to intersect Emilio as he left the counter. He stepped to the side at a tall table with cream and sugar.

"Hey, fancy meeting you here."

"Ditto." He high-fived me, then popped the top on his hot chocolate.

Steam bearing the strong scent reached me and I salivated. Licked my lips, tasting the last bits of egg from breakfast which didn't go well with chocolate.

Emilio rubbed his fingers over the hot surface and bits of spice fell into the liquid. An instant later, cinnamon and cayenne pepper mixed with the chocolate aroma. "What brought you down here?"

"Just meeting someone. All done. You headed back to campus?"

"Yup, came for the chocolate. So much better than the dining halls."

"I'm sure."

Glancing back showed Regina watching us, eyes narrowed. Shoulders back, her fingers wrapped tight around the mug handle. She lifted her tea and sipped, never taking her gaze off of me.

Emilio and Alex shared a resemblance, and Alex looked like a younger version of his father. Whether or not Regina knew Emilio, she might guess him to be a relation of her ex-husband.

Something to consider another time. Not now, though I did encourage Emilio to hurry along a bit.

Only to run into Evan as we left the coffee shop. Almost literally, as Emilio pushed the door outward, bell ringing overhead, and Evan caught it. He wore only a long-sleeved shirt with his jeans and sneakers. Letting the door swing closed behind, he blocked our way.

"Hey, fancy seeing you here." Evan's head swung up-down and side-to-side as he took in Emilio and then glanced between us, eyebrows rising.

"Hi. I just was talking to your mother. Oh, this is my friend Emilio." I pointed at him, then Evan. "Emilio, this is Evan. He's a friend from orchestra."

"Nice to meet you."

"Same."

They shook hands, a brief gesture. Emilio flexed his fingers after, wrapping both hands around his chocolate and blinking rapidly.

A moment later Emilio and I headed back along the side-walk toward campus. Evan watched for several steps. I turned my head around three times before he went into the shop.

"Had you ever met him before?"

"Who?" Emilio sipped his chocolate and a blissful smile curved his lips.

"Evan." I swallowed, my throat thick.

He wriggled as though a flea had jumped into his ear. The smile dropped from his face, leaving a blank expression. "Sorry, who?"

"You just shook hands."

"No clue what you're talking about."

First Regina, now Emilio. Would the same thing happen to me someday? If choosing one meant forgetting the other.

nother day, another apology, and another blank face. More than one of the last, actually, because I put several people to the test.

First, there I was having a nice Sunday brunch with friends.

A special occasion, of sorts, because we'd all trekked across campus to the dining hall known for the best-made crepes. No place on campus smelled so good on Sunday mornings, with the intense baking aroma added to sweet or savory toppings. Very popular place, although thoroughly institutional in appearance from the black-and-white tiled floor to chrome everywhere, and long lines wrapping this way and that as though we were at an amusement park. Faculty and staff sometimes showed up here Sunday mornings instead of going to a restaurant in town. To wit: Sebastian sat over in a corner with a couple of other professors.

I wore my usual, a shirt in purple this time with black leggings and sneakers, my hair pulled back in a ponytail. Nothing out of the ordinary, but all fresh from the clean laundry pile. Gloria glared at me when we walked over together. She had the better put-together outfit: yellow top matching the new-dyed streak in her hair and glittery lemon earrings, plus a butter-yellow shoulder bag, although her leggings and sneakers matched mine.

"You're swaggering," she said, an accusation repeated by Marta when we reached the dining hall.

And maybe I was, but I'd stayed in and had an early night. On top of being well rested, I'd gotten to text last night with Bea for nearly an hour, and she was doing fine. We tried looping Rose in, but she was out on the town.

My other friends? Not so good any of them.

Emilio: hungover and bleary eyed, in blue jeans and jacket.

Gloria and Ruth sluggish and constantly leaning on each other. Didn't help that Ruth'd chosen to wear bright orange and blue after hotfooting it back to her dorm room first thing this morning—so she and Gloria sitting together made for an eye-aching sight.

Marta, also hungover, slumped on the other side of Emilio along with Lina. Both wore decidedly wrinkled T-shirts and pants.

Although a fourth hangover victim, Gordon proved more chirpy about it than Emilio.

"Shoulda been there, Alex my boy!" Gordon gave Alex a rocking pat on the back when the latter settled down between him and me. "Emilio, dude, don't you agree? Great party. Total blast."

"I'm sure I'm sorry I missed it." Alex bent his head and cut his crepe into mini-bite size pieces. If he hadn't partied the night away, maybe Evan did instead? Or went out on the pond and they took a long flight.

A dangerous line of thought, since this was in no way the place to ask. Especially with Gordon here, now the sole mundane in the circle of sorcerer-majority friends. I nudged

Alex with my shoulder and smiled at him when he glanced my way.

He put his arm around my waist and squeezed.

Ruth caught the motion and gave a thumbs up and big smile. This drew Gloria's attention, then everyone else.

"Woohoo! Was that were you were at? Nice going." Gordon threw up his hands when Gloria and Ruth directed dagger looks his way. "Both of you, I mean. Couldn't happen to a nicer pair."

Alex's hand tightened at my waist. He drew in a deep breath, probably to offer a correction—but what could he say to explain where he was if he did?

"We're not saying anything." I jumped in ahead of him. "Yet."

"Just as long as we're the first to know." Ruth pointed a finger at me, then Alex, and back and forth between us.

"No promises." Alex moved his hand up to cup my shoulder and hold me a little closer.

He smiled around the table, then his gaze lifted and his jaw worked.

I followed his line-of-sight to his father on the other side of the room. Watching us.

Sebastian raised a glass in acknowledgment, then looked away.

"What's wrong?" I leaned over and whispered for his ears only.

"Nothing much," he said, eyes flashing a warning. "He just wasn't happy earlier."

A moment later, Alex's phone dinged. Not the usual sound, but one particular to arrival of texts from his father. Jaw tight, he pulled it out his phone and read the message. His eyebrows raised and he gave a huff,

"Excuse me." He smiled down at me, then pulled his arm away so he could text.

I dug back into my crepe, still good and strawberry sweet with congealing melted butter and a hint of sugar. Managed two bites before Alex's phone dinged again.

He nudged my wrist. When I turned to look at him, he passed his phone over.

<<Ask Viola if she'll spare me a moment before you leave.>> Sebastian's text glowed at the top of the screen.

<<Why? What's up???>> Alex in blue.

<<I need to apologize.>>

"Up to you." Alex said.

"It's okay." I nodded, but the strawberry and butter turned sour in my mouth. I pushed my food around on my plate.

Alex noticed, though I don't think the rest did. Then again, he didn't finish more than half of his crepe either.

"You don't have to—" He nodded in his father's direction.

"It's not that." I twined my fingers with his, although my stomach seemed to have developed a pit at its center.

At least we would meet on neutral territory. Sebastian escorted me down to the far end of lounge area between the dining hall and adjoining dorm. Alex waited at the other end, watching us with arms crossed and chin high.

"Thank you for agreeing to speak with me." Sebastian fingered the high collar of his tunic, worn over trousers and polished dress shoes. Apart from the matter of clothes and age, he resembled Alex so closely—technically, I suppose, this was the other way around but I never could quite view it that way—that I had to keep glancing back and forth.

"No problem." I flashed a smile Alex's way. It fell off my face when I turned back toward his father. I nibbled on my lip.

"I apologize for last Thursday." He bowed his head, hands clasped together against his chest. "I overreacted and needlessly dragged you into an unpleasant situation, for which I am sorry."

"Okay." I swallowed, clearing my throat with a cough. "Apology accepted."

"Good. I appreciate your willingness to do this now, so we can start afresh on Tuesday." He offered his hand, a little more at ease.

My nerves jangled as the lean, long-fingered hand stretched toward me. My own fingers seemed numb as icicles as I took his warmer one and we shook. Withdrawing from the clasp, I linked my hands together and pressed them against my belly to keep from shaking.

"Regina isn't teaching me anymore, but I plan to stay friends with Evan."

A tic jerked a couple of times in his cheek, but his face otherwise went blank for a long moment. Then he nodded. "Yes, Helen's taking you on for now but looking for a longer-term teacher. Someone who can help coach you through your first months. I'll keep my eye out for a good match, too."

"Thanks, but what about Evan?"

Again, no expression except faint puzzlement followed by a friendly smile.

"We'll find someone."

"Right." My suspicions confirmed, I had no need to push any further.

But I did anyway, with my friends. One by one over the next few days I dropped Evan's name into conversation. Ruth had no idea who I was talking about. Ditto Lina and Marta.

Gordon proved a slightly different matter. I ran into him Monday afternoon, as I headed for home after my work-study and he went the opposite way; i.e., to work. We met near the archway. Gordon had stopped by the dining hall first. The smells of mac and cheese and bacon made my stomach grumble.

We shot the breeze for a few minutes, long enough for me to figure a way to bring up Evan. Simple enough, in the end. Gordon asked about my plans for the evening. Was I going to meet up with Alex. Wink, wink, nudge, nudge.

"Nope, I've got orchestra rehearsal." Swinging my backpack over one shoulder, I mimed playing an oboe. "Like always, with"—I named several wind and string instrument musicians—"and Evan, of course."

He blinked and tilted his head to the side, eyebrows wrinkling. "With whom?"

I repeated the list of names.

"Did you know your voice changes when you say Evan's name?"

"No." I stepped back, hitting the stone wall. "No, I didn't."

"Well it does." He shrugged. "I thought you should know. In case, you know, you talk about him with Alex."

"Alex knows I'm friends with Evan," I snapped back.

He raised his hands to either side, shoulders high. "Hey, it's your life, not mine. I just wanted to make sure you knew."

"Thanks."

Only one other person heard when I said Evan's name: Gloria.

We were back in our suite late at night, getting some relaxation in before bedtime. A forgettable detective show played on the television mounted on one wall. The living room was, as usual, fairly neat. Stuff might be piled on side tables and bookcases and occasionally a chair, but never the floor.

I laid out on the sofa. The nubbly green fabric rubbed my back through the thin fabric of my blue pajamas with every move. I had my psychology textbook face down on my stomach as I stared at the screen. And gobbled down popcorn from a big bowl on the floor right where my hand easily fell into it for another scoop.

After ceding the sofa to me with no argument, Gloria sat cross-legged on the swathe of blue and gray carpet we'd scrounged to cover the ugly gray vinyl floor. Hair down, and streak bright as always. Her long, white, lace-trimmed night-gown pooled around her, as did technological devices. Her tablet on one side, phone and a complicated calculator with way too many keys the other, and laptop straight ahead on the low table in the middle of the room. It started out on her lap, but she moved it out of reach when she kept dipping into the popcorn and didn't want to chance getting the butter on the keyboard.

I'd run out of ways to sneak Evan into conversation by then. But somehow chance, and it had to have been chance because I didn't cast any spell, resulted in an actor on screen bearing a strong resemblance to Evan.

So, in the end, all I had to do was point and say, "Hey, that looks like Evan."

"Who?" Gloria blinked.

"Evan, he plays the violin in orchestra."

"Huh." She studied the screen, then nodded. "Right, the dreamy one. We all thought he was so cute that time."

"Wait, what time?" I pinched my leg, hard, to make sure I wasn't dreaming.

"After your concert last year, the first one, remember?" She tossed a single piece of popcorn in her mouth and crunched. "You and Terri and I sat around going over all the cute musicians. The lovely harpist. That gorgeous drummer. And three violinists who really sparkled. Terri went all googly-eyed over them, especially . . . Evan, was it? Saying how cute and she wouldn't throw him out of bed for eating cookies, and it was clear you agreed even though you tried to pass it off as didn't he know he looked good, too."

At first I had no memory of this whatsoever. Then, as she talked, bits and pieces returned. Not much, but enough I blushed at recalling all the teasing Gloria and Terri had given me.

"Is he still around?" Gloria glanced over her shoulder at me.

"Of course. He's sophomore like us. Still in the orchestra, too."

"Interesting. It's a small campus, you'd think I'd see him in passing but I don't remember it. Oh well." She dug her hand into the bowl and nabbed the last pieces of popcorn.

Before I could follow up on this, Gloria's phone dinged loudly. A very particular ding, reminiscent of a tornado siren.

After over a year of living together, I recognized most of her customized phone noises—and this was unmistakable. A warning, she'd once admitted, used for certain relatives.

Besides, she turned pale whenever she heard it. Not a good look on her.

Picking up her phone, she glanced at the message and cursed.

"Help me clear the room." She grabbed her laptop and tablet and shoved then at me. I swung around and set them on the sofa next to me. With a grunt, she shoved the low table onto its side and against the far wall.

An instant later, a large crate materialized in the center of the room with a boom.

Wooden slats formed a two-foot box. Someone had taken the time to paint the sides in gaudy red and gold, and even hammer sparkly sequins into the sides.

Before I drew breath to ask anything, the top popped open on big, squeaky springs. A large clown whooshed up from the crate.

I jumped, shrieked, and scrambled onto my knees on the sofa.

Resembling a hand puppet, but built on a giant scale, wearing a bright red shirt, tall red hat, and matching red nose. Face stuck in a wide grin. Rainbow-colored confetti filled the air, covering everything with a layer of shaved paper curls. Several tangled in my hair and one sprang into my mouth until I spat it out—the horrid thing left an aftertaste of over-medicated cherry cough drops.

"Happy Homecoming!" The clown sang as it wavered back and forth. "Here's your costume."

Deflating, it lay limp across the crate. Almost as scary as when blown up. I certainly didn't want to get any closer to it.

"Oh, God." Gloria sank to the floor in a heap among the piles of confetti, head in her hands and dozens of curly twists of paper caught in her hair and the lace edging her nightgown.

"Your family sent you a costume for Homecoming?" Whatever it was, the collapsed clown covered it completely. Unless the clown was her costume?

Homecoming was a big deal at Arden. We didn't have a football team, so soccer took pride of place when it came to fall athletics. But the Friday night costume party ranked higher than any other college event save graduation. Tons of alumni came back for the party every year, and costumes were mandatory. The cleverer the better.

But getting one delivered from home by sorcery?

Which led to wondering . . . did sorcerers go for magic costumes?

I must've asked that out loud, for Gloria raised her head.

"Of course Homecoming is sorcery here. Everything's magic at Arden for those who can see it. And this"—she gestured at the confetti and limp clown—"is why I liked living with a mundane. If you'd still been one, we'd have skipped the clown and at least half the confetti. Do you know how long it takes to clean this stuff up?"

"Can't you just . . ." I waved a hand, in hopes the stuff would clean itself up. Nothing happened, other than the clown lifting one hand and waved back. Totally creepy.

"You haven't met my cousins, yet." Gloria threw her head back laughed, with an edge of resignation or desperation in her voice. "Some things must be done by hand in my family. Confetti cleanup included."

"So, what are you going as? The clown?" The collapsed fabric looked too big for her, but maybe it shrank after being donned?

"As if!" She stuck out her tongue and gagged. "No, the costume's in the crate. And you can wait until Friday to see if you can guess who I am. One thing about sorcery, it lets us truly disguise ourselves when we want to."

❧ 28 ❧

I picked pieces out of my clothes and stuff for hours. Even my hair, despite repeated washings, dripped bits of curly paper longer than it should.

Out walking with Alex nearly twenty-four hours later, an errant evening breeze zigged through the otherwise oppressively still air. Next thing, confetti crackled as a piece danged over my ear. The end scraped the collar of my windbreaker as it bounced up and down.

How could I have missed it?

"Hold still," Alex leaned over and plucked out the offending piece, tossing it aside. He ran his fingers through my hair, and several more cascaded around us. "I think I got it all."

"That's what I keep thinking, and being wrong." At least it hadn't popped out of my mouth. Memory of the horrid taste lingered. I licked my lips and only found the residue of honey from baklava after dinner. "Let's go on."

He linked his arm through mine, our lightweight jackets whispering as the fabrics rubbed against each other. Glorious colors spilled across the sky overhead, as the sun headed down. An almost full moon hovered above the eastern horizon.

We were on a mission: to find the best place to congregate with our friends during the costume party. The college changed the layout every year, to keep things interesting. New stages for music, food, and drink. Plus mazes, labyrinths, a haunted house, and ample space to dance. Even a kid-friendly area for parents with young children. The celebration took over the entire campus for one night. Last year, Homecoming made Halloween anti-climactic. I expected the same this time around, or even more so with sorcery involved.

Hired laborers had already started laying out fences, erecting gigantic tents, and setting up dance floors. Ropes dangled along walkways at least seven feet off the ground, ready for lanterns the lighting of which officially opened the party. Arrays of port-a-potties gleamed turquoise blue in several locations—we stayed well away and upwind of them.

I stopped in my tracks in front of a half-finished frame of . . . something. Scaffolding laid the framework to support an immense floor, not yet installed, but additional lumps and poles stuck out from either end and the middle.

"What is it supposed to be?"

"Something cool?" Alex scratched his head and tilted it sideways. "Maybe some kind of ship? Could be a good place to meet up."

As soon as he said ship, the lines became clearer. Sort of. The poles in the middle might become masts. All the same, it didn't resemble any kind of ship I was familiar with. "How can we make plans to meet somewhere if we can't describe it? It'd be easier to just gather at one of the buildings."

"But not so much fun. We'll just stay to meet up at the big wooden thingamajig closest to the lake bandstand." Alex pointed at the gazebo along the lakeshore, then spread his arms wide and turned in a circle on the grass. "We need space to surprise each other."

"Surprise." I wrinkled my face and stuck out my tongue. "Gloria got her costume from home, but she refused to show it to me. Said I'd have to find her that night."

"Pretty standard." Alex wrapped an arm around my shoulder.

"Last time we coordinated our costumes. We were fairies from *Midsummer Night's Dream*." The college had supplied the outfits for a small fee completely refundable if all items were returned in good condition. Small gossamer wings included. A lot of freshmen rented fairy costumes including many men, most of whom went bare-chested offering a fine array of eye candy. My costume had fit perfectly, wings fluttering in the breeze the whole night.

Probably sorcery, and I'd never known.

"First year students almost always get college costumes. How can you plan the kind of thing to wear here unless you've been at least once? But since this is our second year, more is expected of us."

Kind of him to use *our*, when this had to be his tenth or twentieth since he'd grown up here.

I made a face and stuck my tongue out at him, which he coughed at but otherwise kept a straight face.

"Unless you're part of a group with a theme, most people try to keep things secret. Remember, with magic it's a lot easier to disguise yourself. Though that's not the main point."

"Then what is?"

"Being clever. Showing off your imagination. Putting together a costume that even mundanes can enjoy whether or not they get the whole joke." His gaze grew distant, mouth curving in a wide smile. "One time when I was about seven, after I begged and begged, my father made me a spider costume with lots of extra legs, all of which I could move independently if I wanted. I really creeped out some other kids, and a bunch of adults."

Just imagining it unsettled me.

"Two years later, I was into jesters for some reason. I think we'd been doing a unit on the European Middle Ages at school and I'd learned to juggle." He pretended to toss balls in the air, well enough that illusory white objects arced from one hand to the other. "So Dad got a standard kid-size jester outfit and added some extras. I could pretend to walk on air —basically, turn on and off invisible six inch stilts—or juggle balls that appeared to burst into flame."

"Woah."

"I'll show you." He lured me over to the bandstand and had me hang over the railing as he turned the sluggish water into a scrying surface. Standing right next to me, his body brushed mine and emanated warmth.

For an instant, the lake offered a blurry reflection of us— sort of, because the water made everything fuzzy and weird.

A small, circular wave cleared a space below. A many-legged creature formed atop the waves. A long, segmented body in brown standing on stubby legs at the front, but with matched pairs of legs extending behind and around—and topped with the face of a young Alex. All of the legs worked independently, with no sign of automated controls.

Cute and creepy.

Another wave passed over, and a slightly older Alex wore parti-colored tights and tunic, but no hat. He stood several inches off the ground, juggling bright yellow tennis balls that burst into fire as they rose high. His hands glowed and flames wreathed his face.

"Cool." I closed my eyes, thinking back to last year. Then shook my head. "What did you wear last year? I don't remember seeing you, or was that the point? Since it wasn't your first and you didn't have to rent a fairy costume."

His body stilled next to me, turning cold in an instant.

"I didn't go. It wasn't my turn."

The image of jester Alex vanished, as the usual ebb and flow of the lake encroached on the scrying surface. The blurry reflection returned. I used it to reach out and locate Alex's hand, entwining our fingers, while looking away from him so he could recompose himself.

Only to realize that although the water reflected only one of me, he cast a manifold reflection. Despite the still air, something set the water rippling—a distant rowboat, perhaps, or bird or fish. The ripples didn't change my reflection, but his altered. One minute it was just him, the next his arms and hands multiplied. Three or four even five hands and arms, or rather human appendages and wing feathers. For a few moments, half of Evan's face slid out from the reflected Alex's head. The beak of the swan rose above.

Evan glared up at me.

"What's with your reflection?"I shivered and blinked, but the water kept twisting Alex's reflection same as before.

Alex looked down, cursed, and pulled me away. Retreated to the land side of the bandstand. Leaning back against one of the poles holding up the arched ceiling, he wrapped his arms around me and dropped his head into the crook between my neck and shoulder.

"I forgot."

"Forgot what?"

"Moving water reveals truth, especially when it runs deep."

The sky grew darker overhead, sun setting. A sudden breeze blew up, raising goosebumps across my skin. I burrowed in closer to the rumble in his chest as he spoke.

"There's a reason some cultures have a myth about what beings can't cross running water. The deeper it flows, the more it shows."

His words slowed, and he growled. A lovely bass note under my ear.

"So, what are you planning for your costume this year? Your sorcerous debut?"

"My what?" Pulling back far enough to see his face, his smile had a fake edge. I held him tighter as I let him change the subject.

"It'll be your first with sorcery. You have to do something memorable."

"I . . ." The fact of the matter was, I'd planned a simple mundane costume. No ambition to win one of the many awards burned in me. I just wanted to watch and enjoy and get ideas for next year. The sudden pressure to excel this time around made me gulp.

The kids' magic books from Helen had helped more than I'd expected. I now boasted experience testing a number of variations on summoning things across distances, changed the color of shirts and pants, and once managed to fetch something around a corner. Plus other little spells to straighten things, see or hear across long distances.

All the same, none of these added up to making a sorcerous costume.

"Tiya Helen will surely help, didn't you say you're having a lesson with her tomorrow?" Alex patted my back, resting his head on my shoulder again. "Don't let her pawn off one of Leonie's old costumes on you, though."

I stared up at the moon rising up through increasing cloud cover that made things delightfully spooky—but was not at all inspirational for costumes. Maybe I could crib off of him. "What are you wearing?"

He pulled back and shook his head, smiling down at me again but this time with genuine pleasure rather than faked. "Let's see if you can pick me out. I'll give you a hint, though. I'll have my feet and my waist on the earth."

"That's a hint?"

"A riddle. Will you go for one, too, to show your smarts, or be mysterious and make people figure out who you are?"

"Way to make this into work, not fun." I retreated a few steps, bracing my hands on my hips as I glared at him. "If you don't stop teasing, I'll come as myself."

"Don't worry. Whatever you wear will be fine." Alex snuck up next to me, and wrapped his arms around my waist. "No matter how you disguise yourself, I'll find you."

I leaned against him, arms moving from my hips to his. Feather-light at first, his lips settled on mine in a kiss that swiftly deepened.

At least Evan couldn't see this. Or could he?

❧ 29 ❧

riday night, I pushed the window screen up and out of my way. The sleeves of my lightweight chiton fell down to pool around my upper arms. The multitude of small buttons that kept the cloth together scraped my skin, sending shivers through me. The band around my waist rose up, settling under my breasts. I'd picked up the classical Greek chiton at a sale of discarded theatrical costumes, not realizing how many authentic details the designer had incorporated—or how close the soft, worn linen would cling to my body.

Leaning out, I arched my back and gazed up at the full moon, faint but noticeable against the slowly darkening sky. Wisps of clouds in unequal bands drifted across the blue. A warm, light wind blew: the kind that ruffled the skirts of my chiton rather than tossing them this way and that. Small weights sewn into the hem kept them hanging the right way, so I wouldn't have to worry about flashing my undergarments to the world. The air tasted of hot sugar and chocolate.

The evening fit my costume perfectly. My white half-mask and headdress lay on the bed. All I needed do was don it to become a living embodiment of the moon. I left the window open and turned to trail my fingers over the lacy veil attached to the mask.

Before I could wrap my fingers around the soft satin surface, my phone rang. My older sister's face popped up on the surface and her favorite tune blasted out.

"Rose, what's with calling me on Friday night?"

"You mean you actually have plans?" She made a rude noise. "You're growing up, little sister."

"Plans enough that I don't have time to talk."

"So it's a big night tonight, eh?"

"How'd you guess? You haven't taken to practicing magic have you?" A moment after the words escaped my mouth, I slapped my forehead with one hand. Of course she hadn't. After my time in high school, any weekend night plans meant a big night.

"Nah." She chuckled, fortunately not realizing how seriously I could've meant the words. "I just remembered you plotting your costume with Mom before you left. Is it what you wanted?"

"Oh yes."

"Send me a selfie, okay?"

"All right." I snapped a photo of myself in the full length mirror on the closet door and texted it to her.

"You look beautiful. Go have a blast and live it up. You deserve it!"

Slipping the phone into my pocket, along with my ID, I dragged in a deep breath. Took off my glasses and placed them in their case by my bed. Everything went blurry, but I located the mask and affixed it over my eyes and nose. A strap around the back of my head held it firm. The thin, silky cloth attached covered my head and fell to the middle of my back.

Donning it symbolized taking on the seeming of the moon.

Energy rippled through me, and ozone tainted the air for an instant. Although blurry, I appeared as normal as a modern woman could wearing a chiton and mask. A moment later my vision cleared, as the spells Helen helped me embed in the mask—she did almost all the work—replicated my glass prescription for this one night. Now, the folds of my chiton reflected the hills and valleys on the moon's surface. I glowed with moonlight when no clouds obscured the moon, even though the sun had yet to set. As wisps skittered in front and hid it from the earth, whether wholly or in part, I and my clothes became likewise cloaked in shadow.

Magic turned me unrecognizable.

And not just me. I left the dorm and entered a familiar world made strange.

On opening the door to the outside, sounds hit me first. The roar of a crowd somewhere not-too distant. Faint bells mixed with different strands of music, rock and rap and a fainter strain that had a fairy lilt winding in and out of heavy drumbeats.

The air carried hints of sugar and oil. Chicken frying and pies baking.

The temperature hovered on the border between warm and neutral. I might have to dive back into the dorm for a coat (or a blanket or towel in a pinch), but for the moment I enjoyed the lukewarm air on my bare arms.

All my senses shrieked delight at me except one: sight.

I expected to see wonders, but didn't get them at first or second sight. Silly, I suppose, to have my hopes up high for a visual spectacle considering the subtle sorcery in my own costume. I was going as the moon, after all.

Nevertheless, disappointment filled me. Maybe the special effects in movies and television made me blasé.

A long-haired pirate in full swagger tipped his red bandana-wrapped head at me and gave an "arr" of approval.

The blousy white shirt featured an opening down the front, which he'd arranged to show off a tan, muscled chest gleaming with sweat—or oil. A red sash bound his waist, blue trousers covered his legs, and a knee-high black boots his feet. The sword hanging from his side (peace-bound to the sword hanger with a strip of white cloth), clanged when it hit his boots.

"There she blows!" The blue and yellow parrot fastened to his shoulder bobbed its beak likewise.

A flush stained his cheeks and he pinched the parrot's beak with two fingers, his swagger losing a little flash. A woman in a bright pink dress liberally bestrewn with gilded lace grabbed his arm and gave me a glare.

Passing nearby, a horse on two legs gave a laughing neigh.

Folks in costumes streamed in from the town streets and street parking. Walking animals. Pirates. Shakespearean characters galore, of course. And many, many more.

Though, none of the costumes seemed particularly sorcerous. They could go anywhere on Halloween without anyone mundane batting an eye.

Until I looked deeper.

A gleam of white flashed in the corner of my vision. The next moment, it resolved into sharp teeth—a dozen or more filling a broad, gray mouth. An immense shark straight out of *Jaws* headed my way with, oddly enough, a pink balloon hovering above. Its long string caught around one of the shark's fins.

All this I saw out of the corner of my eye, but absorbed a surprising amount of detail. Enough to make goose bumps line my arms and legs, and my heart-beat thrum at my throat.

But when I jumped and whirled around to face the shark head on, it disappeared. Instead, Jules in a pin-striped suit sauntered along. He carried a briefcase in one hand, the other held tight to Leonie dressed in a large, pink oval outfit puffed out on the sides and front.

"Hi Viola! How do you like it?" Leonie tugged out of her father's grip and turned around in a circle, bouncing up and down on her toes. The stuffing in her costume filled the back as round as the front. No tails, no fake ears or facial makeup.

"You're a pink grape?" Her recognizing me didn't rank as a surprise, since she and her father helped Helen help me create the costume in the first place.

"No!" She stamped a foot, in matching pink Crocs. "I'm a balloon. Didn't you see me float?"

"I don't—"

"Look at us out of the corner of your eye." Jules tapped the side of his face.

I turned my head. Leonie disappeared and the pink balloon manifested instead, floating above a grinning shark. The wide mouth opened, teeth catching the moonlight, and I jumped back. Faced them, and the illusion disappeared again.

Balloon and shark. Leonie and Jules.

"See?!" Leonie tilted her head to the side, chin up.

"Wow."

"It's a sideways illusion." Jules shifted, presenting his profile. "You'll see a number tonight, though ours are some of the best if we do say so ourselves."

"And we do." Leonie gave a sharp nod. Raised her hands to high five her father.

"So you're a balloon and you're a . . . shark?"

"A lawyer straight on." He stretched his hands out to either side, briefcase dangling and the latch flickering in the light. "And a shark ready to bite when you're not looking straight at me."

"Cool."

With that, the costumes around began to take another, more sorcerous appearance. Not all, true, or even half, but enough. I wasn't due to meet my friends until full twilight, so I followed as Jules and Leonie played guide, leading me through the crowds to the main stage where Helen had gone ahead to spend some time with alumni. At first we walked side-by-side, but that meant I constantly had a shark swimming next to me. Goose bumps continued to cover me, so I dropped back where I could follow Jules instead. Much easier on the nerves.

Leonie bounced back and forth between holding her father's hand and mine. That I could handle, as having a human bopping into balloon form didn't play quite so much havoc on my nerves.

"Look there." Leonie tugged at my sleeve. "Look, look."

Another girl about her size held tight to a woman's hand. The girl wore sneakers and gray pajamas with an array of miniature animals—lions, giraffes, zebras. At first blink, nothing special. Then the animals chased each other across her arms, legs, and torso. A minute later they froze in place. Another chase. Freeze. Chase. Freeze. Then the crowd swallowed her and she vanished from sight.

"I did it last year." Leonie sniffed, nose in the air. "Copycat."

"You had dogs and cats." Jules tapped her nose.

She stuck her tongue out at him.

A man in a multi-colored suit featuring dots and lines pushed past us. The dots on his costume also moved—growing and shrinking. As he walked on, the dots and lines on his back resolved into something approximating a map of the campus with the dots perhaps representing people.

Costume after costume, magic trick after magic trick. I stopped searching for the sorcery soon enough, because it was too distracting. Flashing colors and unexpected movement made my head ache a little. Better, simpler, easier to go with the flow and let the strangeness float past. The decision alone eased the throb in my temples so I could enjoy.

The main stage, i.e. the biggest, sat at the center of the academic quad. A broad oval, it had two acts going on simultaneously, one at either end. A band filled two-thirds of the stage, playing soft rock and golden oldies to a crowd of alumni while a group of college officials—one and all dressed as Shakespeare, down to the beard—moved among them.

Whoever had laid out the stages gave a lot of thought to sound and amplification. Close to the stage, the music blasted with the crowd roaring approval on occasion, but move just far enough away and one could only hear it as though distant. Magic at work?

At the closer end of the stage, a sorcerer entertained adults and children with tricks. At least, I thought they were tricks—mundane magic. Maybe, maybe not, for the woman, dressed in white tie and tails, turned firebreather with no warning whatsoever. Leaning back, she blasted red and orange flames at least three feet high. A wave of heat radiated far enough to make me shiver and Leonie bounce on her toes. Perhaps the sorcerer had palmed a bladder of gasoline—or actually worked a spell. We didn't linger long enough to discover.

Instead, we worked our way around the crowd to where Helen stood in a small clearing with a line waiting to meet with her.

As with the others, her costume disappointed on first sight. She wore a long-sleeved black shirt and black pants. Odd socks clung to her clothes at irregular intervals, along with the occasional dollar bill and a wallet. A couple of keys glittered here and there, and she had not one, not two, but three pairs of glasses shoved atop her head.

A wooden frame surrounded her. The board across the top bore the legend: Lost and Found.

She held a burlap sack that each person in line dug into and pulled out something. The young girl with the moving zoo on her pajamas pulled out a baseball and went into raptures. Her mother extracted a cupcake covered in mint green frosting. A student I recognized, one of the orchestra percussionists dressed as a xylophone complete with ripples of soft wooden notes as he walked, retrieved a faded gray T-shirt and clutched it to his chest.

"What is she?"

"Ask her, not me." Jules chuckled.

"Mama knows all kinds of people." Leonie nodded vigorously. "She got Mimi to help with her costume so she can reach into the museum."

"Close, but you're missing some details there." Jules grabbed her hand as she tried to dart forward. "Wait your turn, honey."

Another college student, who I didn't recognize, dug in the bag for ages. It billowed and collapsed around their arm, suggesting it was empty. Nevertheless, the woman persisted and eventually succeeded in maneuvering out . . . a standard trombone. The brass flashed in the lantern lights as the sky turned pinks, reds, and dark blues. She gave a cry of delight and raised the instrument to her lips for a series of squawking notes that added to the general cacophony.

The line shrank, person by person, until finally Leonie got to rush into her mother's arms. I hung back as Helen bent to hug her balloon daughter. She straightened and kissed Jules, then smiled at me and held out the bag.

"Come, find that which was lost or forgotten and, this once, may be found again."

"What?" I blinked and threw out my hands.

Leonie hopped up and down, clearly eager for her turn but not begging. Helen would have let me go first, but I nodded for Leonie to go instead.

Helen bent back down and opened the bag for her daughter. Leonie thrust her arm in, drawing back with a much-loved stuffed animal of some kind. Nothing that existed in real life. A cross between a rabbit and a giraffe, perhaps? In purple with pink spots.

"Malapop!" Leonie hugged it close, twirling around and around.

"Good choice." Jules wrapped an arm around Helen as they watched Leonie. "She certainly cried buckets when that thing got left behind at the airport."

Another quick kiss and word, then Jules escorted a bouncing balloon away. As they moved into my peripheral vision, he again became a shark, this time swimming off into the distance.

"So, what are you?" I studied her up and down.

"A living lost and found." She opened the bag wide and extended it toward me and the line of others crowding behind me. "This one night, Mimi of the House of Memory has agreed to let those who believe in sorcery take back something loved that was lost or forgotten. Trifles only, but still . . . seek and you shall find."

A faint chill moved along my arm as I reached into the bag. Rough burlap brushed against my fingers. Nothing else. I reached deeper, until my whole arm was in it up to my shoulder. My hand stroked the loose stitches.

Pain bloomed in one finger, as something scraped it. Scratched. I jerked back. Gingerly reached for whatever it was. Thin. Glossy and slick on one side, but sharp at the corners.

Paper?

Withdrawing my arm, another flash of cold encircled my skin as I pulled out a photo. Nothing flashy or special at first glance.

Only a photo of three little girls dressed up for

Halloween. The tallest, no bigger than Leonie, as a black and white cat with a bright pink dot at the end of her long nose. The middle as a ladybug, complete with black dots on red ovals of cardboard in front and behind, black tights, and a hair band with antennae. The youngest a toddler in a lion onesie, being propped up by a large masculine hand.

Rose, me, and Bea. I'd almost forgotten that day. Staring down at the crinkled paper, memory shards blew through me. The weight of the frame holding the cardboard flats that made me a ladybug. Rose's hand in mine, both of us sweaty and slick but holding hard to each other. Dad keeping Bea from toppling, so she pressed against my side.

Mom waving and calling for us to hold still a moment as she took the photo.

And the day last summer when I looked through the photo albums and online photos and didn't find this . . . because it didn't exist anymore.

That same night, Bea stumbled and accidentally deleted the image before it got saved anywhere.

Holding the photo sent a burst of warmth through me. A feeling of family, and being loved. Mom and Dad were splitting up, but both cared for all of us.

Little though I wanted to let go, I had no place in my costume to put it. It wouldn't fit in the pocket without being folded, so Helen kindly sent it home to my dorm room.

After which I moved on rather than monopolize her time, especially given the long line behind me.

Twilight turned the world into a harsh mix of shadows and light. A cloud passed over the moon, casting me into grayness as I slipped away.

Time to find my friends.

And Alex.

The lanterns hanging from ropes tied across campus offered light, except where I actually passed. Turns out, I hadn't thought through the consequences of going as the moon. With clouds hiding the orb above, shadows wreathed me. I could see to find my way, but no one else seemed to see me!

People apologized when they bumped into me or stepped on my feet. The first couple instances I didn't mind too much, but by the fifth I pushed my way to the edge and took the long way round. My banged toes hurt. I leaned against a stone wall and took a deep breath, then forged on.

Lights flashed from small stages and dancing floors scattered across campus. Crowds roared, ever more riotous but without any signs or smells of alcohol, or weed, or anything more than a faint hint of incense here and there. Plus the occasional mustiness clinging to a costume inadequately stored.

The long way round meant I crept upon the ship stage from the lake side. It was now complete, and turned out to be an immense trireme rising from the grassy sward. Dozens of wide oars made for pathways up the sides to the wide top where many costumed revelers danced beneath red-and-white striped sails that billowed with the wind. The sails glowed, casting a soft, creamy light over the deck.

Children and teenagers swarmed up the oars, but with my toes still aching I roamed around the ship and found a gentle ramp suitable for wheelchairs and walkers and the walking wounded at the back.

A gusty whirl far above removed all but wisps of shadow from before the moon with perfect timing, just as I reached the deck. I gleamed so much I cast shadows of my own. Little flickers of light ran up and down my arms and crackled over the cloth covering my hair. A group of warriors nearby—Phoenician, Roman, and Viking—raised tankards of foaming liquid in my direction.

None appeared familiar. I gave them a curtsy, and meandered around the dancers in search of any friend. Anyone I knew whatsoever, for that matter. The music here, piped in through speakers set high on the masts, featured a heavy, strong beat and men's voices singing in chorus. Sea chanties, and other marine songs underscored with the heft of the oars slapping ocean waves. Even the air took on a briny, but not unpleasant, tinge.

The dock didn't rock or sway, but my walk loosened as I passed in and around. My head ached with the constant stimulation; new images and strangeness everywhere I looked and so little familiar. A low hum unconnected to any music buzzed in my bones, from jaw to toes.

Still no faces I knew. A raggedy patchwork woman smiled and waved at me. Irregular patches of paint or makeup covered her face and exposed skin, matching her piecemeal gown—a crazy quilt turned into bodice, skirt, and sleeves.

I waved back, studying her more closely. Nothing about her reminded me of anyone I knew.

Perhaps understandable, as she'd been waving at someone behind me.

Prickles of pain sent me leaping sideways, bumping into a gray gargoyle seated on the railing. A walking cactus inched past me, then clumped forward—crowd quickly parting around it—headed for the patchwork woman. A saguaro, complete with sharp-looking spines.

A shiver rippled through me as I sagged, leaning my side against the wooden railing.

Then warmth radiated throughout me, sinking into my bones, as someone stood directly behind me but didn't touch. The air between us heated so quick it nearly caught fire.

"I told you I'd find you." Alex's breath wafted over my shoulder.

He waited, leaving time for me to pull away. I didn't move a muscle.

His arm curved around my waist as he stepped up beside me, heavier than usual. Grayer, too, with much longer fingers than any human. A half-mask covered his face, also gray. Indeed, his whole body had turned stone gray with marks resembling limestone or some other porous stone. He wore loose trousers and simple sandals, but no shirt. Heavy wings grew on his back starting from his shoulders, and two stubby horns protruded from atop his head.

Smiling at me, he briefly lifted both hands to cup his chin. In that moment, he became a living, breathing embodiment of the bored gargoyle of Notre Dame. His body vanished below the waist, turning into a pedestal supporting his torso. Even when he brought his hands down and no longer replicated the posture, his skin seemed made of stone and every iota of his body heavier.

Alex's beautiful form shone through the illusion, the base on which it was built. He circled me with stone-strong arms.

His gaze traveled over me from top to bottom, eyes lighting in appreciation.

"O beautiful moon."

"O serious gargoyle." Though I wished to come up with a better reply, my tongue tripped on the few words. I blushed. He smiled, lifting a hand to trace the curve of my cheek with an over-long finger. The tip was rough against my skin, resembling fine sandpaper.

"Would you care to dance?"

The hard beat of the sea chanty faded and the music turned to something light and floaty. A flute carried a pensive theme, accompanied by a harp or lyre. Several sweaty dancers left the deck, descending to earth by oar or the ramp at the back, and leaving ample space for couples and the occasional threesome to sway in harmony.

I laid my head against Alex's shoulder, wrapping my arms around his waist. He held me close as we tripped lightly to the music. Closing my eyes against flashing lights, impossible costumes, and all the hullabaloo, I leaned in. Inhaled the mix of stone and sweat that clung to his chest. Let the distant hum and roar of the crowd fade to background noise for the pulse of his heart and breaths filling his lungs. Bits of energy lingered in some of my muscles, but for the most part I relaxed against him.

"How are you holding up?"

"Over-stimulated." I craned my neck to the side. Started to lean back so I could see him, but he whispered a kiss against my neck and I stayed with head pressed against his chest.

"That's not a surprise. It takes a lot that way, especially with all the sorcery floating in the air tonight." He stroked rough fingers along my arm. "You're sparking magic just breathing. Would you like to get away from it, for a while at least?"

The hesitant note in his last words did get me to draw back and study his face, or what I could see around the half-mask. He licked his lips and stood still, gazing down at me with eyes shadowed behind the elaborate facade.

"You have somewhere in mind?"

"Not my room." He shuddered, a croaking laugh escaping. "Unless you fancy hearing my tiya's voice again."

"Once was enough." I mirrored his shiver. "Somewhere else."

"There are quieter areas around. At the heart of the maze, or between the library and admin buildings . . ." He nodded his head one way, then another. "Or—"

"Or my room." My turn to lick my lips and wiggle as he stared at me for along moment.

"You want to go home?"

"If you'll escort me."

Our eyes met. He pushed his mask up to rest on his forehead. Lines along his nose and around his eyes showed where it had pressed against flesh, but now I could see his pupils. The gleaming sails reflected in them, as though a fire burned within.

"You're sure."

I nodded and held out a trembling hand.

He wrapped his fingers around mine. Pressed them. His mask slipped back onto his nose. As gargoyle and shadow-wreathed moon, we left the trireme.

Left the dance.

Left everyone behind.

We walked in silence, hand-in-hand. With every step, our sorcerous disguises faded. My gown emitted less light. He became more human and less stone. His fingers shortened within my clasp, skin no longer quite so rough to the touch. Horns shrank into nothingness, and just as well because they really didn't suit him.

But the wings stayed, though they lightened towards white.

Ripples of sorcery, power, and electricity crackled and snapped along my arms and his. Across his chest. Everywhere we bared skin other than our faces and linked hands.

Without him near, hand in mine, I might have grown cold. Instead, warmth pulsed in my veins.

When we reached the dorm, though he was clad as a gargoyle not a vampire, I said the words to invite him in.

He followed me up the stairs, breath warm and irregular on my neck and back. The distant sounds of others partying, inside and out, faded. Only our passage through the stairwell, along the hall, and into the suite mattered.

When the suite door clicked closed behind us, I removed my mask and head covering. The spell shattered and my gown lost the last bit of lunar glow to become nothing more than ripples of cotton tied at the waist with a heavy cord.

Alex doffed his mask. His wings flared out and vanished, leaving a few feathers to drift and fall to the floor. Just him before me, now, in ragged gray pants and sandals.

Bending, I scooped the gray feathers up and stepped into my bedroom to lay them aside on my desk, with the others.

Alex followed me, took my hands in his. The room abruptly seemed too small to hold the both of us, but I didn't protest or make any move to leave.

"Thank you for a lovely evening."

"No, thank you." He cupped my head with his hands, thumb rubbing over my cheek. "Best Homecoming ever?"

"Absolutely."

He kissed me once. Twice. More. Soft and deep, tangling lips and limbs. My hands stroked his chest and back. His loosed the cord about my waist, and tugged my chiton to the side to bare a shoulder.

I whispered his name as he moved to strew small, light caresses across my skin.

He said mine back to me, then added three simple, glorious, unexpected words.

"I love you."

The next instant, we jerked apart.

I bent over, pressing a hand against my belly. Red-hot pain shot through me as though a fish hook pierced my innards. Stumbling to the side, I grabbed the door frame and held on for dear life as something pulled at me.

"Argh!" Alex's body bowed, shoulders and head arching back. Every fiber of him vibrated. He bent forward and back, this way and that, as though a string growing ever more taut.

Something somewhere broke, with a twang that nearly deafened me. Dropping to crouch against the wall, I covered my ears with my hands and rocked.

I didn't close my eyes. Not more than one blink.

A strange but familiar light surrounded Alex. A silver aura. He reeled, and his body stretched and reformed. Limbs shifted, lengthening slightly. Hair darkened. Nose grew narrower. Eyes wider set.

Alex vanished, and Evan stood in his place.

He shook his head, hair flying, and grimaced. Drawing in a deep breath, he calmed.

Opened his eyes.

Saw me—for the image reflected in his eyes and on his face.

My costume in disarray.

My room, with feathers on the desk.

"You were here with him." He backed away from me, muscles tensing. "You chose him? Why?"

"I don't . . ."

"You chose wrong. He chose wrong." His mouth twisted into a snarl, but his eyes held liquid pain.

Whirling around, he leapt to the window I'd left open all evening. Hands gripped the frame, nails scratching against the wood. Casting one last glance at me, he threw himself out.

I rushed after him, my heart beating heavy in my throat. A force tugged at me, grinding my torso against the wall. My body hurt as though I'd leapt through the window instead of Evan.

He was gone.

A white swan beat the wind with its wings, soaring off into the distance. Partygoers below oohed and pointed as feathers fell to earth in its wake.

{chapter ornament} 31 {chapter ornament}

Grabbing my glasses and phone, I raced after Evan as fast as I could.

On the ground. By foot. In sandals and a half-undone costume that billowed behind me as I ran, one hand holding the skirt high enough I didn't trip. Dodged this way and that, although the crowds of revelers had started to diminish. Shivered the first while, until I got going and became suffused with warmth—on the surface. Deep inside, the new pain in my midsection kept pinging.

And all the while I dialed anyone I could think of to help. All two of them: Sebastian and Helen.

Sebastian answered first.

"What happened?" No surprise at me calling him, but rather shards of agony in his tone.

"Alex turned into Evan who turned into the swan and flew away."

That got me a sideways glance from a walking, talking, dancing bear as I skirted a dance pit. It reached out after me, but I ducked the swiping claws and sped up.

"That shouldn't be. I have Alex until tomorrow noon." He

paused to groan and cough. "He doesn't shift shape into a swan much anymore, not since starting college last year. *Where is he?*"

"He flew east." Fast as I ran, I still had to slow and circle around the stages and attractions erected for the party. The whole thing turned into a maze, as though designed solely to slow me down. Because the outer corners were where two, ten, even twenty couples had retreated to exchange kisses, caresses, and more. If I'd counted bare bottoms as I passed, I'd have had to use at least two hands.

A sheen of sweat made my costume stick to my back and legs. My glasses kept slipping down my face, no matter how many times I pushed them up. They steamed, making it hard to see. Every muscle in my legs ached.

"The lake. She's behind this."

"No, she wasn't . . . there." Too late. The phone chirped to let me know he'd ended the call.

A moment later, Helen rang me, also sounding strung out. "What happened?"

The same question deserved the same answer.

"Alex turned into Evan who turned into the swan and flew away."

A snort and some kind of muffled curse, though I didn't catch the words. Then she returned to the line, more clearly. "What happened before that?"

"He said he loved me." The plaintive plea in my voice made me cringe, but it was true and heartfelt. Whether or not I loved him back, and I did, it shouldn't have had that result.

"Damn, I was afraid of that. One or the other. Words are magic, those especially." Little surprise in her voice, but a great weariness. "Where are you?"

"Heading to Regina's. On foot." And nearly to the library and the lake front.

"Don't confront, don't challenge, don't do anything but stand witness."

I jerked, as her words sent a jolt of energy and warning through me. "Whatever."

"I'll be there as fast as I can."

Another ding, another call ended. Excellent timing. Navigating the path around the lake, dark and deep, required attention and focus not to trip. I tucked my phone in my pocket, the better to focus on the way ahead.

Instead I stumbled into a clearing and a pair of entwined lovers. I tried to dodge, but tripped instead and plowed right into the person in the cactus costume, sans head and with spines no longer glittering sharp but turned soft instead. A mercy, since it saved me from getting thoroughly scratched otherwise. I went down, rolling to the side, while the cactus pitched into the patchwork woman. Had a hand up her skirt, at the time, resulting in the patchwork woman almost flashing me as they both pitched forward into a bench.

"Viola, what the . . ." The cactus turned on me with Gloria's face drawn up in a scowl. Farther behind, the patchwork woman's features rearranged beneath the makeup into Ruth.

"No time to talk. Sorry." I got back on my feet, waved at them, and pelted off into the darkness.

My stomach burned, as though a fishing hook remained piercing my flesh and the rod began to reel me in. Or maybe it was all imagination, or guilt, or whatever—but Alex's agony and the betrayal on Evan's face, one or both, impelled me to chase after them.

"Wait up!" Ruth shouted, Gloria echoing her a beat later.

"No time!"

Their footsteps resounded behind me, helping push me forward. I had to reach Regina's house, and Evan, before they could delay me. Holding my skirts high, I lowered my head and powered through the aches in my legs, lungs, and belly. The chase stretched on forever. My breath came in pants and whining shivers when I finally reached Regina's house.

The gate lay closed again. Distant lights shone in the house.

But the moon overhead illuminated better than spotlights, highlighting each and every one of the damp feathers leading from the shore to the gate. More shone on the other side of the fence, albeit fewer and with more space between them, from gate to house.

I grabbed hold of the gate, chest heaving. The thunder of my chasers sent ripples of energy through the earth. Maybe Regina hadn't changed anything and locked me out. My fingers wrapped tight around the metal rods.

"Let me in. . . . I need to . . . . see Evan." Dragging in a deep breath hurt, and didn't stop me from panting and gasping for air.

The latch clicked and the gate swung inward silently, even as Gloria and Ruth caught up. I slipped through, but it opened farther and let them in as well.

"What are you doing?" Gloria grabbed my arm, fingers digging as I strained to move on. My sandals' flat soles gave me little traction on the stone path or grass. My costume snagged on her spines, even though they seemed to be some kind of rubber rather than metal, and not sharp.

"Breaking and entering." Ruth took hold on my other side, pinning me in place between them.

"It's Alex's mother's house."

That stopped them for all of a minute.

"He never talks about . . ." Gloria blinked, without relaxing her hold one whit.

Ruth shook her head. "I thought his mother was dead."

"Divorced. Really, really bad." I hung in their grasp,

breath coming in short gasps. "No time to explain, but I have to find Evan. See what's happened."

"Evan who?" Ruth's grip eased only a fraction.

"The hot violinist." Gloria pulled back, face puzzled. "Why do you need him? What about Alex?"

"They share the same body. Or they did." I stopped resisting their hold, fumbling for some way to explain. "Like Jekyll and Hyde, sort of, except not really."

"Say what?" Gloria asked.

"Twins?" Ruth frowned.

"No, one body between them." For the first time, I was in full sympathy with any sorcerer who'd ever tried to explain magic to a mundane. "Half the time they're Alex, half Evan. Except for when they're a swan. Until now." It sounded insane, even in sorcery terms, even to my ears.

As my captors puzzled through my description, I let them support more of my weight. Gloria slid her hands around and Ruth buckled a little. That same moment, I tore free—literally, as my gown ripped in at least two places—and raced up the path with them in hot pursuit. Reached the bottom of the stairs and grabbed the railing before they got hold of me again.

The kitchen door opened, bright lights spilling into the yard. Regina's body appeared as a dark silhouette against the light.

"Viola? And friends?"

Despite wearing red-and-white striped pajamas and nothing on her feet, she left the house and practically floated to face me, glowing with joy. She grabbed my hands, squeezing tight. This not being enough, she let go, threw her arms wide, and wrapped me in a close embrace. Gloria and Ruth's hands fell away as they moved back.

"Thank you, thank you, a thousand times thank you."

"Is Evan here? He's okay?" I craned my head around Regina to peer into the house. No sign of Evan nearby.

"Shook up, but recovering. But he's himself again, with control of his own time. Thank you."

"What about Alex?"

"Evan will be fine." She let go and moved an arm's length away, setting her hands on my shoulders. "He's mine, as he always should have been. Sebastian's hold has weakened. I don't know what you did, but I am so grateful."

As before, she failed to react or acknowledge I'd said the A word: Alex. Sibilant sounds from behind suggested Gloria and Ruth were whispering about something, but I didn't catch any of the words and didn't care.

"Can I talk to him?" My hands trembled, but I turned them into fists. My cold fingers heated only slightly pressed against my warmer palms.

An odd flicker crossed her face. Twisting, she glanced back up at the house. Specifically: at the window over the kitchen. The room lay dark, or mostly so. Only a few flecks of light shone along whatever hung across the panes.

Then the curtains twitched, or maybe it was only my imagination.

At any rate, a pleasant—but firm—smile curved Regina's lips as her eyes narrowed. "No. I'm sorry. He doesn't want to see anyone. Not now."

Before I could protest, her eyes lit with malicious pleasure.

"Ask another time. I have a visitor to attend to." A dark smile lit her face as she whirled about and stalked through the house.

I tried to follow, but the door shut behind her and wouldn't open again. Twisting the knob didn't work. Nor banging on it. Dread filled me, and a sharp pain kept tugging at my innards as though a rope were tied around me, and someone down a well at the other end. Or something like that. It impelled me against the door. I had to get to the other side, even if I couldn't go through.

"She said no." Gloria pulled me away.

"We're still sort of trespassing." Ruth huffed and helped.

I shook them off, ducked under, and dashed across the grass to the side of the house. They followed of course. Everyone should be cursed with such friends.

There were two people I knew who might visit Regina tonight, and only one likely to bring such maleficent glee to her face.

Running around the side of the house, shades of last time, I almost expected another cone of silence and fiery confrontation.

Nothing like that met my gaze. Instead, Regina filled the front stoop standing tall. Motion detection lights along the front of the house burst into light, flooding the driveway and sidewalk with harsh yellow illumination.

Sebastian stood at the side of the driveway, a good twenty feet away from the house. His body canted forward, but his feet failed to move so much as an inch farther.

Helen restrained him. Standing behind and to one side, she had a hold on his shoulder. Her fingers curved as though claws.

She cast a warning glance at me, then on to Gloria and Ruth. The latter both stopped in their tracks behind me, jaws snapping shut with audible clicks.

"Give me back my son!" Sebastian clutched at his abdomen with one fisted hand, the other raised high.

"The son you despise and ignore? My son? Never." Regina shook her head and stepped down onto the sidewalk. "Your hold is broken, old man."

Sebastian jerked backward, as though an immense wind slammed into him. His fist twisted against his belly. I doubled over, clutching my stomach as it seemed to lurch against my skin and muscles. As though I'd become part of a game of tug-of-war, but as the anchor and with no idea what pulled where.

Then Evan appeared in the doorway. First as little more than an outline in the doorway. A mass of dark gray against the warm interior light, with only a few features lit by the whiter, brighter outside bulbs. His eyes flashed white as he moved onto the stoop.

The pain in my gut throbbed, but with less force so I could rise from a hunched position.

"Go back inside. You don't have to see this, darling." Regina laid a gentle hand on his arm.

"No, him I want to see." Evan patted her shoulder and shook her hand off, moving past one slow steady step at a time. "I want him to see me."

"What's that?" Gloria blinked hard a couple of times and rubbed her eyes. "A ghost or something? He's almost transparent, as though made of smoke."

"What are you looking at?" Ruth's neck cracked as she looked this way and that, puzzlement clear on her face. "There's nothing there."

Evan paid little attention to Ruth and Gloria, giving them no more than a quick glance. I received a longer look, and flinch so slight I'd have missed it if not for watching close. Helen, likewise, got a look although in her case his mouth tightened.

"Here I am. Can you see me now?" Evan's shoes crunched fallen leaves as he strode forward. He stretched his hands out to either side, body canting forward.

Sebastian trembled. His hands clenched as sweat poured off his forehead.

"There's no one here but me unless I let them out." More steps. More broken leaves.

Gloria's breath whistled next to my ear. I risked only a moment glancing to where she watched Evan's progress, her eyes wide.

The ache in my midsection increased, as though white-hot claws dug deep. I wrapped my arms around myself, trying to stay vertical.

Sebastian started to sway, gray tainting his skin.

"This isn't wise." Helen's hands no longer held him back, but propped him up.

"Neither was your spell." Evan's face resembled a mask of tragedy, features exaggerated and mouth cast down in a snarl. "We were happy as a swan. Then all of you had to spoil that. I want him to see me, know me."

Step, step.

Crunch, crunch.

He kept walking forward . . .

Right through Sebastian, as though they didn't exist in the same world and so could occupy the same space.

Sebastian jerked in agony and staggered to the side.

Evan crumpled, tears pouring down his face.

Regina raced to Evan's side. Wrapped her arms around his shoulders and helped him up. His tears left traces of silver on her. When he stood, a pool of white feathers remained against the dark concrete.

Unsteady step by unsteady step, in marked contrast to his earlier pace, she helped him up into the house—glaring at any who moved toward her. In the doorway, back facing out, she turned her head.

"This is my property. I want you gone." She waved a hand.

A thrum of power swept us down to the end of the driveway and into the street in the blink of an eye.

❧ 32 ❧

"What happened?"

Between them, Gloria and Ruth asked the question ten or twelve or twenty times. Everything blurred enough all the details mixed up together. I wasn't sure how we all wound up in Helen's kitchen. Probably her doing. She seemed almost as wrecked as me—though not so much as Sebastian. A ghastly gray-green tinged his complexion as he sat hunched over at the table sipping slowly from a steaming mug.

I didn't hunch, but my teeth chattered and fingers still had a residual tremble despite being wrapped around a warm mug of hot chocolate that might have been laced with something else. The merest sip had a citrusy kick, and the fumes made me a little dizzy. Or maybe they made the dizziness less present? My backside held a residual ache from dropping heavily onto the chair earlier—although my belly hurt more. Every time I thought the pain gone and tried to straighten fully, little prickles made me wince.

Helen sat in a third chair, wavering. Jules, next to her,

watched her and Sebastian closely. He'd brewed up whatever it was we drank.

Gloria and Ruth twittered around us, sometimes leaning against the back of the sofa and the rest of the time wandering aimlessly around. I lost track of how many times they circled the table.

Likewise, I couldn't recall how many times and ways Helen explained to them the complicated relationship between Evan and Alex and the swan.

What stuck in my head was her answer as to why Alex's declaration of love turned him into Evan.

"Words are symbols." She patted my hand, her fingers trembling as much as mine. "They work to cast spells—or accidental magic. When Alex said . . "

"That he loved me." Tears slipped down my cheeks.

"A declaration of love establishes a bond between two people. Specifically, in Western culture a man leaves his parents and cleaves to his wife. Declarations of love form a part of that transition."

"But it's not like he asked me to marry him." I wrapped my arms across my chest and rocked back and forth.

"That doesn't matter. His words reflected your elevated importance to him . . . and changed his bond with his father." Helen glanced over at Sebastian. "In a better world, this wouldn't make a difference. But we live in this one. The spell I crafted balancing Alex and Evan was predicated upon their connections to their respective primary parents being and remaining equal. Alex loving you destabilized that."

Such irony, that Alex pulled back from loving me when I retreated from believing in sorcery—but he'd have been safer then. If I hadn't accepted sorcery, he might even have stayed himself more as an unknowing me plus his father could have outweighed Evan's bond with Regina.

Too late now for regrets.

Sitting there, at the kitchen table, all I wanted was to get him back. He shouldn't lose his life, freedom, control over his body at least a minimum amount of time just because he loved me.

"We have to get Alex back."

"Yes!" Sebastian slammed a fist against the table, setting the china rattling. All other conversation ceased.

"Hold on, man." Jules laid a hand on Sebastian's shoulder, cast a glance toward the hall leading to the bedrooms, then flicked his fingers. The spell insulating Leonie's bedroom from the noise in the kitchen flickered with light as it grew stronger. Helen sent him a quick smile.

"Agreed." Ruth planted both hands on the table. Next to her, Gloria jerked her chin in agreement. "But how?"

"That's the one-billion-dollar question. Easier said than done." Helen rubbed her temples, a shudder rippling through her body. "For starters, what do you mean get Alex back? To live as he did before, sharing his life and body with Evan and the swan? Or give Alex the control that Evan has, mostly, now? Or split them in two, whether they like it or not?"

"Points worth considering." Jules nodded, patting Sebastian's hand—and gripping tight when he made to shove back from the table. "For more than fifteen years, they've shared a body. Anytime they could have split into two separate people, but they didn't."

"Because the spell only lets them have one or two bodies, not three." I swallowed hard, muscles raw and hurting to begin with, apart from the onslaught of guilt at revealing that information even though Evan hadn't told me I couldn't.

"What?" Helen startled, shoulders stiffening. Jules, Ruth, and Gloria also showed surprise, but not Sebastian who rocked back and forth in his chair with his hands pressed against his abdomen.

"That's what Evan told me." The spots of pain in my

innards deepened, and I rubbed my stomach even knowing it wouldn't help much.

"His words exactly?" Jules asked.

"Close enough."

"Or perhaps the problem is one of division. If they separate into two bodies, as the spell allows, it needs to be equal. Balanced." Helen squeezed her eyes shut for a long moment, then let out a hissing breath and shook her head. "Or maybe not. It was a long time ago. I worked the spell in the heat of the moment, and . . . evidently something went wrong."

"So how do we free my son?" Sebastian wrapped both hands around his mug, knuckles whitening.

"Rebalance the spell? Force the split?" Helen threw up her hands.

"Whatever, so long as it frees Alex." Shivers racked him, and his face had aged in the few hours. Every sign pointed to him starting to fall apart no matter how he tried to hold it together.

Not that I was doing very much better.

But someone had to clarify the issue Helen had raised, about Alex versus Evan or Alex and Evan. Since I started the get Alex back theme, I amended it. "Free Alex, but without sacrificing Evan."

As before, Sebastian showed no sign of hearing or understanding me. Ruth gave a head shake as though a dog with a flea in her ear. Gloria frowned and wrinkled her brow.

"That would be just as bad as this." Jules got up and removed a quilted cozy from over the steaming chocolate pot. Walking around, he refilled our mugs then rubbed Helen's shoulders. "Same problem, with a slightly different cast of interested parties."

Sebastian hunched, arms wrapped across his torso. "He keeps pulling, trying to reach me. I'm holding on, but the rope slips through my fingers."

Helen and Jules exchanged glances.

"Let's break into groups and brainstorm plans." Jules encouraged Sebastian to join him in the living room as one group—although they wound up going down the hall instead last I saw.

"Why doesn't Sebastian even recognize Evan's name?" I asked. "Or Regina Alex's, or . . ." A glance Ruth's way showed her bent over her phone, texting away.

"Yeah, I barely saw Evan tonight. And Ruth didn't see him at all." Gloria frowned, fingers rapping against the table top.

Still no reaction other than a quick sideways look from Ruth.

Helen, on the other hand, gave a laugh that turned into hiccups. Her chest heaved, tears starting in her eyes. Still hiccuping, she grabbed a glass of water. At length, her body subsided though drops still trickled down her cheeks.

"Why?" She gave a coughing laugh, then quickly downed water to avoid another bout of hiccups. "Because one of the most pernicious things about the nest of spells Regina and Sebastian wove themselves into is that the sorcery requires people knowing—believing in—Evan *or* Alex. Any crack, any explicit acknowledgment of the other risks the whole wall crumbling."

"That's really twisted, even for magic." Gloria blinked and shuddered. "My family's bad for tricks, but not so much for torment."

"Even Alex and Evan won't name each other outright, although I suspect each knows the other exists." Helen sat back down next to me, eyes narrowing perhaps to hold back more tears.

Tilting my head back, I raced through memories of the last encounters I'd had with them. They'd chosen their words with care, but I found myself nodding agreement. Fingers a bit shaky, I nudged Helen with a hand and she grabbed hold tight.

"I tried to build into the spell the means for them both to exist, but it's still one or the other. Never both. Sooner or later, almost everyone has to choose. Most do it without even knowing what they've done. I don't know of one member of Sebastian's family who realizes Evan exists. Out of Regina's relations, Jules and Leonie and I are the only ones who see and recognize Alex." Helen pointed at Ruth, blithely ignoring us. "If people know one well, they usually rewrite their memories to exclude any interactions with the other, even by chance. It's a miracle of sorts that you"— she nodded at me— "believe in them both. Most likely because you began as a mundane with no reason not to consider them completely separate individuals. Which may have carried over to Gloria, as roommates."

I hunched over my chocolate. Drank slowly, as my head started to nod. Innards kept aching, the more so as the liquid, mug, and I turned cold.

Helen threw a blanket over my shoulders, then grasped my chin with firm fingers and tilted my head up. Made clucking sounds. "You're dropping. Get her home to bed."

Gloria and Ruth grabbed me more gently than they had earlier, the latter tucking away her phone.

"Sebastian's taking a snooze in the spare bedroom." Jules returned, dusting his hands. "He collapsed from fatigue. I didn't have to do anything more than take off his shoes."

Everything whirled for a while after that, leaving me unsure what happened next. Then somehow I was getting stripped and put to bed. My bed, though, in my dorm room. My blankets and sheets, although a faint avian musk hung in the air—perhaps emanating from the feathers scattered on the floor.

Helen tucked the blanket about me and turned to leave.

I grabbed hold of her.

"Have to save Alex."

"A delay won't hurt." She patted my shoulder. "He's not going anywhere."

"Evan might turn into the swan and fly away."

"Not yet."

"Can we save both of them?" I asked.

She didn't answer.

❀ 33 ❀

B y the time I woke up, the Save Alex campaign was well underway.

Though it would've been too late to stop anything anyway, I wouldn't have noticed if I'd known.

A disgusting taste filled my mouth. Merely raising my head to reach for the water bottle always kept by my bed made me groggy. I lay back, panting, and counted to four or five, I forget which, before untwisting the top. I hadn't refilled it the night before so it had only three mouthfuls, hardly enough to freshen me. My belly ached, but I welcomed the pain as a form of connection to Alex—twisted though the thought was.

Shivers racked my arms and torso, and my teeth chattered. My ripped costume still covered me, sort of, but the flimsy fabric offered no warmth. Nor were the sheets and thin blanket up to the task, since the window remained open—screen up at the top, leaving an opening wide enough for a man to leap through

Or a swan.

Or both. A memory flashed before my eyes: Evan with his hands braced around the frame, ready to jump.

Then a second image: Alex's torment as he turned into Evan.

Alex and Evan.

Alex or Evan.

Rather than continue that line of thought, I leapt from my bed. Had to clench my teeth against the cold of the floor. Swayed a little. Grabbed hold of the bedside table, and inched over to the window. I wrapped my fingers around the frame and pulled. Much as I wanted to slam it shut, I lacked the strength and settled for shutting it period.

Only to stand with my nose pressed against the glass, holding on to the frame as I stared out at the familiar campus scene. Almost every evidence of last night's party had vanished. People . . . litter . . . tables and chairs. Only tents here and there remained as evidence that something had happened here the night before.

My phone, lying on the table next to the bed, vibrated. A sound so familiar I'd barely noticed it until now. I whirled around and took three faltering steps before I dove under the covers. Stretched out an arm to grab the phone and bring it under with me. Now that the window had closed, the blanket gave a modicum of warmth.

Enough to clear my head.

Until I checked my messages. The text function had gone bonkers. I must've slept through dozens, even hundreds, of vibrations as message after message came through.

Scrolling through, I didn't really note the contents at first, just the senders. I'd been added to some group list with Gloria, Ruth, Emilio, Lina, Marta . . . and Sebastian. And others whose names I didn't recognize.

I didn't see Helen or Jules's names anywhere.

For once, I skipped over the messages from Rose and Bea

asking about last night. What could I tell them? That I was fine? No, because I wasn't and I didn't want to outright lie to them. How about *'sleeping late, hangover, talk to you later?'* Better even if far from the truth. They might even believe it, though they knew I didn't drink much or often. All the same, I put off contacting them until later.

Better to deal with the group text first. Bit by bit I scrolled back until I found the beginning.

<<Alex's been kidnapped!>> Ruth, explaining her view of what had happened and enlisting help.

<<Kidnapper: his estranged mother no less.>>

<<Big, bad divorce from Prof Noches.>>

<<Hates Alex b/c chose to live with father.>>

<<HAVE TO GET HIM BACK!!!! HIM AND VI SO CUTE LAST NIGHT!!!>> The last complete with a snapshot I hadn't noticed her taking of Alex dancing with me, both of us having eyes for no one but each other. Almost made me blush just looking at it.

Within minutes after Ruth started the thread, Emilio jumped in.

<<Omigod!>> He chimed in. <<Say it ain't so!>>

<<Regina's one bad dudette.>>

<<Cursed Alex.>>

<<Turns him inside out so no one can see, hear, or touch him.>>

<<Help free him!>>

And on and on they both went. Neither made any reference to Evan whatsoever. The closest they came was when Emilio suggested I might have some small immunity to Regina's spell because Alex cared for me.

The long and short of the burgeoning message thread: it was time to rustle up every bit of magical knowledge in existence to find a way to free Alex!

What about Evan? Helen wasn't sure we could keep both.

A shiver rippled through me, and I went back to scrolling through the texts.

I must've spent a quarter of an hour at least, as the texts got more and more tangled. If it weren't for the knock on the door, and a rumbling in my stomach, I might've stayed there half the day dazedly reading over.

"Hey, I heard sounds." The thin wood door muffled Gloria's voice, but her meaning came through. "You up and decent?"

"Yeah." I emerged from under the covers and dropped my phone back on the table, then yanked the covers up around my neck.

Gloria opened the door, tidy and bright-eyed as though she hadn't been up as late as me last night. All dressed for a cool morning, too, in a jeans jacket over a green Arden T-shirt, leggings, and cute blue shoes with heels higher than I ever managed in daytime. Marvel of marvels, she bore a tray of waffles still steaming with a side of fruit and a glass of orange juice. All fresh from our favorite dining hall, kept warm by sorcery.

"Eat up." She settled the tray on my lap. "You're going to need it."

"This is wonderful." I slurped a third of the orange juice first, savoring the citrus bite as it went down my sore throat. "But it does beg the question: why?"

She ducked her head and pulled on the blue streak in her hair, then dropped into a heap at the bottom of my bed. "Call it guilty conscience."

"Oh?" I set the tray aside and leapt out of bed long enough to grab the nearest sweater from my dresser—wool dyed a bloody pink. Back under the covers, I dug into the waffles, since she went to all this effort. After the first bite hit my sore—and empty—stomach, I made sure to chew and eat slow.

"Ruth's bound and determined to save Alex. I tried to slow her down, but didn't manage."

"I saw." I jerked my chin at my phone. "What gives with that?"

That she'd help, I assumed from the get-go, but I hadn't expected her to lead the charge.

"You do know how long she's been shipping you and him, right?" Gloria rolled her eyes.

I swallowed early, nearly choking on a lump of half-chewed waffle. "Say what?"

"She's watched him watching you for ages." A snorting laugh escaped her. "They were in some class together last year and she kept telling me how cute it was seeing him leave class looking for you to bump into while pretending it was acci-dent. She likes the idea of playing matchmaker, and I swear she'd have turned you herself to help the two of you get together if she could've."

Memories flickered across my eyes: of Ruth encouraging me to sit next to Alex when we ate together in study hall, and sending photos of him my way. I'd known she liked us together, but not how much. Then again, considering every-thing I'd missed about sorcery I shouldn't be surprised to have my past constantly getting rewritten.

"All the same, that doesn't explain why she's made this a big deal." I waved a hand at my phone. I'd made the mistake of turning the ringer back on when setting it aside, and it kept dinging with more texts as Ruth, Emilio, and others suggested ways to frame a rescue spell.

"She understands that Alex became vulnerable when he said he loved you, so she feels guilty at having helped contrive, at least in her mind, the circumstances." Gloria picked at a fraying edge of her jacket. "That's my expert opin-ion, at least, though you're the psychologist-to-be. I'm just a folklorist."

So much I'd missed.

"Ruth doesn't hear when I say the name Evan. I've texted about him and no one else responds, or they act as though I wrote Alex's name instead." Pulling out her own phone from a pocket, Gloria tilted her head down and rubbed her thumb over the texts scrolling across the screen.

"I'm not surprised." I shook my head, swallowing a last bit of strawberry and then setting the tray aside only half-eaten. The food I'd consumed weighed heavy in my belly. "I asked her and Emilio and Marta and Lina, and even Gordon, about Evan and none of them recognized his name."

"I barely saw him last night. He was little more than a shadow, and I had to squint to see that much. But he was there." She watched me from the corner of her eyes. "You saw him. You know him."

I drew in a deep breath and let out a sigh, then nodded. "He turned me. At least, I saw a swan turn into him—"

"Seriously? That's what turned you—a swan turning into a man?" A curse escaped her as her head snapped up. "I'm the folklorist, but you're living in a fairy tale. The Swan Princess, sort of."

"Then who's the wicked witch? Or wizard?"

"You'd know better than me."

I opened my mouth to answer, then shut it with a click. Two or three times, at least, before I answered. Gloria waited, picking at her hem while not saying a word.

"I don't think Regina or Sebastian are doing this deliberately. Though that doesn't mean they're not villains." I ran a hand through my tangled hair, hitting a couple of knots and pulling strands loose. "But . . . they each love their son, even though they deny the existence of the other's. I guess they're all victims of one kind or another, though Alex and Evan have it worst."

Mouth tight, Gloria gave a short nod.

Neither of us said anything for a couple of moments, though the room hardly remained quiet with both our phones dinging away. She stayed bent over her phone. I grabbed mine and skimmed over the recent texts. Sebastian had joined the discussion, making suggestions of ways to save Alex. Plus Emilio added distant family members too, his parents and other relatives in the US and Philippines, who all chimed in.

All bound and determined to save Alex.

"Do you want Alex back?" Gloria tucked her phone in a pocket.

"*Yes!*" I stiffened, back straight against the cool wall. My belly hurt with the continued connection, as though he were pulling on me. Trying to get back. How could she doubt me?

"What about Evan?" She tilted her head to the side and gave an inquiring glance.

"I want Alex free, but . . . without sacrificing Evan. They both deserve to live." Although neither admitted to the other's existence, both showed care for the swan, at least.

"Can we save Alex without hurting Evan?"

"I don't know. Helen might, though she wasn't sure." I hunched my shoulders, pulling my blanket high as I wrapped my arms across my chest. "I don't think anyone's getting out of this without getting hurt. Question is, can we make it so they both live?"

"And if we can't, who will you pick?"

My fingers twisted around the blanket until it pulled tight.

Our phones kept dinging.

❁ 34 ❁

At orchestra rehearsal, we practiced a piece with plenty of action for oboes. My eyes followed the line of music on the sheet propped on the stand. Sweat beaded across my forehead and made my blue blouse cling to the small of my back. Leggings kept the backs of my thighs from sticking to the chair. My fingers ranged up and down the keys as I played. A light minty flavor filled my mouth from the mouthwash I'd dipped the reed in after last sterilizing it.

All the action was wonderful, because it meant I had too much to do to watch Evan. So I didn't. Not at all.

Except maybe one or two glances during breaks. Plus when the conductor gave notes, as the horns had a bad night collectively and came in for extra attention. And also a couple of times when my belly turned sore with residual prickles from the hooks or whatever it was that had stuck in my midsection after Alex lost his shape.

Evan seemed okay, overall. Though, really, how would I know? He looked the same as always, in a "Nothing beats violin" T-shirt and jeans. Hair smooth and parted on the side.

Face calm. Fingers light on the bow.

This time, he didn't notably slow down when packing up his instrument after. Not that he rushed, either, but he should've been well away by the time I left the building.

No such luck—or misfortune. I wasn't sure which.

A long, lean figure trudged along, hands empty, of course, headed toward the lake. Unmistakable, nevertheless, given his stance and stride—not to mention the invisible strings tying me to him or his other half. Third.

He headed one way and I another. Tracking after him was the wrong way to go. It meant a significant detour with no real reward other than more misery. The more so since a cool breeze had kicked up, more than a match for the light windbreaker I'd pulled on over my shirt. My fingers already chilled around my instrument case handle.

Which I could send home.

Or could I?

Drawing a deep breath, I clapped my hand against the side of my case. The spell took a moment to work, leaving me on the knife's edge wondering whether I'd wasted the power or sent something else somewhere else. Then my case vanished. A thrill went through me, head to toe, although my nerves kept a residual shiver after. Since it was my first try, I might have sent it to the wrong place.

Then, with a hop skip and jump—and a mental curse—I caught up with Evan.

He must've meant me to do so, for he hadn't moved far, only enough that he could see the glimmer of moonlight on the lake. Which meant I basked in the rippling path of light as well, standing next to him.

Something planged deep within me. I still hadn't figured out what connected me to Alex—and Evan—since it was invisible and intangible except for when it made me ache and turned me off of eating. But sparks of power danced within me, in part due to his proximity.

Evan didn't say anything or glance my way as we waited. An evening breeze swirled around us, carrying the scent of moldering leaves and smoke from some not-too distant fireplace.

"What are you doing here, looking for someone else?" he asked.

"You looked a little lost. Like you needed a friend." I inched close enough for the warmth pouring off his body to seep into my right hand, at least.

"You don't count." Flat. Unyielding.

On the other hand, he didn't move away.

"I still think of myself as your friend." I stayed put, hardly daring to breathe during the long pause that followed.

"Even after . . ." He turned his head and lifted an eyebrow, a supercilious look ill-suited for his face, though I wouldn't presume to tell him as much.

"Yeah."

"You chose wrong." Waving a hand my way, as though I were no more nuisance than a gnat or fly, he moved on.

"I didn't make a choice. He did." I stayed put, but dropped my voice and fisted my hands. Willing the words to reach him whether he wanted to listen or not.

Evan stopped in place. Took another step, then stood hanging one foot forward and the other back. No real physical resemblance, of course, but he reminded me of a squirrel in the middle of the road with a car barreling towards it and unable to decide whether to cross or not.

Mouth shut so as to offer no incentive either way, I watched. Shivered, too, tucking my hands under my arms to keep my fingers warm.

After two minutes and thirteen seconds—I counted—

Evan returned and faced me at arm's length with his back to the lake.

"What do you mean?"

"Tell me your side first. What you think happened that night." The last thing I wanted was to make a choice between them, other than Evan as a friend who could've maybe been something more—if he weren't so moody—and Alex who already was. But if I might have to, I wanted as much background as I could get.

Besides, he might let something slip that could help. Who knew?

"Why, so you can trim your tale to fit mine?" He mirrored my stance, arms crossed over his chest but with his head held high.

"I promise I won't lie. Surely there's some kind of truth spell you can use, if you don't believe me."

He grunted and tilted his head back, then blew out a long breath.

"Truth for truth?"

"Bargain."

A shimmer of electricity passed between us as we shook on the deal. The breeze around us carried off a few sparks from where our fingers met. The bright orange flecks quickly faded to yellow and then nothingness.

"You first." I dared him. Would have broken fast enough if he'd resisted, but he didn't.

"I don't know how time passes." Evan looked down. Probably no more than a trick of the light that the top of his head briefly appeared a silvery white before resolving into brown hair and a thin part line. "It's sort of like floating on a lake, looking upward. I'm not alone. We just are, as we float. Sometimes glimpses come through. Sometimes more. Sounds. Sights. Smells. As though the lake turns into a theater, of sorts."

A brief flash of heat soothed the sore spots on my belly. Might be an indication Alex watched this moment, or not. Believing in sorcery opened a lot of doors I hadn't realized existed—but it certainly hadn't made life any easier or simpler.

"I got some of the night. You were dressed as the moon. We followed you for a while. Then you danced with . . . you smiled. Eyes light."

"You recognized me?"

"It came through, knowing it was you. Maybe by choice, maybe not." He snapped his jaw shut, shoulders hunched up near his ears. With a violent shrug, he stuck his hands in his pockets and affected a casual air belied by the tension in his muscles. "Anyway, that was one bit."

Evan stared off into the distance. I barely breathed, drawing in air through my nose as quiet and shallow as I could to avoid making noise and disturbing his recount. My phone vibrated in my pocket, a low buzz muffled, I hoped, by my pants. He showed no evidence of hearing it.

"And then, the waters rocked. I spilled out, into being me, and you were there. No mask. No belt." Evan pointed a long finger at me. "In your room where I didn't belong. What else was I to think? I've had friends choose against me before. Not often, but a couple. They never recognized me afterward." A frown wrinkled his forehead, and a few more words slipped out, so low-voiced I almost didn't hear them. "I don't see why you do."

"You turned me."

"An accident."

"Maybe. Maybe not." I threw my hands out to either side, before tucking them back under my arms. "I almost turned last summer, after watching your mother march through Alex. I managed to forget that, but not you."

"Lucky me." He laughed, harsh and explosive.

"Unlucky you." I shook my head. "Your parents are loving, well-meaning monsters."

"Well, we can't have everything."

"No." Drawing in a deep breath, I let out a huff as harsh as his. Then gave him truth for truth. "I danced with Alex, and invited him back to my room, because I've known him since the start of school, and . . . you don't need all the details, but I love him. That doesn't mean I don't also care for you."

"You chose him."

"It doesn't have to be that way. One or the other." I withdrew one hand from warmth and rubbed at my aching midsection. "What if we could help you separate into your own selves? You could keep the swan. Still be able to fly when you want to."

"It won't work. Don't you think we've tried?" He slapped a hand against a thigh.

"It's worth trying again now, especially since things have changed."

His lips curved in a cynical smile. "You just want to trade me for him."

"No, that's what I'm trying to prevent." I stretched out my other hand, fingers trembling in midair. "But I need your help."

"Forget it. You loved Alex and helped him, that's the last kind of thing I need."

Whirling, he ran off toward the lake. His footsteps resounded, hard soles meeting the pavement, for several seconds before they died away. He didn't throw off his clothes, that I saw, or turn into a swan as I watched. All the same, a few minutes after he disappeared from sight around a bend in the path, a white bird raced across the lake and up into the air.

Leaving me shivering behind.

35

With perfect timing, my phone vibrated in my pants pocket. Again. I'd ignored the repeated buzzing ever since making the mistake of turning the silencer off after rehearsal. An automatic move.

Turning around, I headed back to the dorm. Took all of five steps before I dug out the phone to check texts even if that meant reading more entries in the long screeds about ways to save Alex.

Instead, worse, several texts from Bea waited in between all the others. Tapping on her name brought up the full list of her—many—texts to me in the last hour.

<<What's wrong?>>

The words glowed on my phone.

I hadn't answered any of queries she'd sent in the past day. Yesterday I'd managed to hedge things. Send a couple of light, "busy-busy, chat later" messages, but today she wasn't buying. At least not this evening.

<<Write to me.>> *Sent about the time rehearsal ended.*

<<Talk to me, even.>> *A few minutes later, as I finished putting away my oboe.*

<<You're worrying me.>> *I'd been headed out the door.*

<<You do know you can tell me anything, right? Well you can.>> *Following Evan, convincing him to talk to me.*

<<So do it!>> *Mid-conversation.*

<<Seriously WHAT'S WRONG?>> *Still in conversation.*

<<Call!>> *About when Evan turned into a swan and flew away.*

Even making the offer constituted a major escalation on her part, since she preferred texts.

In this case, so did I. She might read too much into my voice.

<<All's well enough.>> I texted back, too tired to come up with a story that could explain anything of the strangeness that was my life. She didn't need that laid down on her, after all. Had enough to deal with in her own life. <<Busy, busy, busy.>>

Then she took the bull by the horns and called me.

Feet shuffling along the path as I neared my dorm, I tried not picking up and letting it go over into voice mail. Couldn't quite bring myself to press the button that would send her right there. Had to torment myself listening to the tune ring out her call tone, so sunny and breezy.

Once around. Twice.

She'd be okay. She'd leave a message, griping at me. I'd text that everything was fine, stop worrying, let me study, and that would be that.

Instead of waiting and leaving voicemail, she gave me all of a five-minute break. Long enough to climb the stairs, get into my room, and throw myself down on my bed.

Then out pealed the bright, cheerful, irritating ring tone she'd chosen. Why had I ever allowed that?

Rubbing chilly fingers against my aching forehead, I broke and answered the call.

"Hey, sis."

"D-do not hang-up or p-pretend you have t-to g-go some-where soon. T-talk to me. What's g-going on?"

Her voice had a sharp edge that hit me where it hurt—the more so since she used a lot of words starting with hard consonants, sounds she usually tried to avoid. Made more worse by the note of injury in her tone, something that usually had me ready to leap up to arms to defend her; except when I was the cause.

I toed off my shoes and socks, and tried to soft pedal things.

"Why would you think something's wrong?"

"Uh, you're not checking in on me constantly." She grunted. "That's what you always do, monitor things, so when you're not it means something's up with you. Your turn to share."

"It's not easy to explain." Catching my fingers in the wool blanket folded at the foot of my bed, I dragged it up around my shoulders and arms.

"Who cares? Share." Another grunt, and I could just imagine her rolling her eyes at me and tapping one foot against the floor in a syncopated beat.

"I mean it!" I blew out air in a huff. "Everything's well enough, just complicated. Okay?"

I cringed, hearing the lie in my voice and hoping, fruit-lessly, she'd miss it.

"Would you accept me saying that?"

"No, but I'm older—"

"One year, eight months, t-twenty-three days." Bea ran the words together almost into a single word, having calcu-lated the difference in our ages once a decade ago and never forgotten since. "G-give over."

"You want the truth?" I rubbed my temples again, but my mind was a blank. Maybe a little of the truth spell Evan and I shared earlier still clung to me too, justifying what escaped my mouth next. "How about this: a guy I like said he loved me, and a moment later turned into someone else who changed into a swan and flew away and now I have to figure out a way to save him from a series of bad spells gone wrong without sacrificing the guy he turned into."

A long pause, so much so my ears attuned to the crackle of air between us, dead other than the faint huffing of our breaths.

"That sounds like sorcery," she said, so soft I barely heard her.

"It is, gone wrong." My fingers tightened around the phone. The case creaked, and I eased off a bit so as not to miss her response.

"You're now a sorcerer?"

"Yes." I'd thought I knew everyone in my life who turned out to have a hidden predilection for sorcery—until those words. Yet I didn't fall into shock this time. Perhaps my earlier discoveries had inured me or, more likely, I had no shocks left to give at that moment and would react at a later date.

"Why didn't you t-tell me?"

"How would I know to tell you?" I rolled over onto my side, grabbing for the almost-empty water bottle. "I didn't know you would believe me. Is Rose . . ."

"No, Rose hasn't as far as I know." A giddy little chuckle. "Won't she be p-pissed if she ever t-turns and realizes we both went first?"

"That'll be a slap all right." A few mouthfuls of water, stale but still drinkable, and I lay back down on the bed. One hand kept the phone propped near my ear. "How did you turn anyway?"

"I went years ago. Mikey's moms are both sorcerers, so I sort of caught on while hanging with her."

"And you didn't tell me."

"I didn't think you'd believe me." She managed to repeat my words and phrasing back at me, then ruined it with a snort. "Do you mind, me knowing first?"

"No. I do wish you'd been able to tell me, though I'm starting to understand why you wouldn't." I rubbed a hand over my stomach, pressing to try and relieve the unpredictable growing and ebbing aches.

"Good. So, what's the sorcerous mare's nest you're in? Maybe I can help."

"It's a fairy tale gone wrong." I gave her the overview, and she kept quiet for the most part. Maybe a wise choice, because I kept on talking and talking until I realized I'd been babbling for well over ten minutes. Told her practically everything, including my fears we'd fail because I didn't want to choose who lived. Force Alex and Evan to split apart and have them hate me because the swan died.

"Well, that's sorcery for you." A long sigh resounded in my ear. "As Mikey's main mom always tells me, sorcery tends to create two problems for every one it solves. The tricky thing is to find a solution whose problems you're willing to live with."

"That's not exactly helpful." I pushed up from the bed. Nearly tripped over one of my discarded shoes, then kicked it and its match out of my way. One rolled over and the other flew to thud against the wall. Padding over to the window, I scanned the dark night sky wondering if a swan flew somewhere in the distance or if Evan had returned home.

"It wasn't meant to be." This time she gave a huff in emphasis.

Neither of us spoke for a while. Leaning my head against the glass cooled my brow.

"You really like Alex, don't you?"

"I love him." It got easier to say with every repetition.

"Sure? Seems a bit quick, since you were only friends the last time we talked."

The teasing note in her voice didn't demand an answer, but I gave one anyway.

"We've been friends for over a year, but there was always that possibility of something else there." I drew aimless circles on the window with my free hand. "He just didn't want to tangle up someone who didn't believe in sorcery."

"Got it." A pause. "And Evan?"

"A friend. Someone I'm sorry for, because he's gotten a raw deal. As bad as Alex, I just don't want to trade Alex for him." White flashed in the corner of my eye, but on the wrong side of the glass. Inside not outside. The small pile of feathers on my desk gave off a pale luminescence. Rather moonlike. "But, maybe, that's a choice I'll have to make."

"I don't have any advice you can't think up for yourself, or g-get from someone else who's there, except . . ."

"Yes?" I crossed to my desk. Pulled out the drawer, wood scraping as it opened, and swept the feathers into it. The wood stuck when I tried to slam it, then creaked as I eased it closed.

"You haven't asked about my stutter. Why it still happens, sometimes, even if I know sorcery."

"Ah . . . no . . ." Of course I hadn't. Ever since Bea stopped doing speech therapy at the end of middle school, Rose and I had an unwritten rule that neither of us would ever raise the subject with her, but always let her choose if and when she wanted to discuss it.

Plus, as a sorcerous neophyte—no matter the hard lessons I kept having to learn—I was still figuring out what sorcery really could do. Apparently, I didn't think big or broad enough.

"So, is there no spell to take the stutter away?" Even though she'd opened the door, asking seemed wrong.

"I don't know yet," she said. "I'm still learning, too. And while it might not have occurred to *you*, it sure did me as soon as I b-believed. When I asked Mikey's main mom, she said that the more personal a spell, I mean the more it t-touches who you are as a person, the more important you b-be involved in any changing of it. She refuses to cast any spell on me to stop me stuttering. P-promises if I find one—think it up or d-discover it in a spell book somewhere—and still want it cast after t-talking through it with her, she'll help me do it."

"Okay." It took a while to parse through that, but I followed her. Sat back down on my bed, head aching. "I take it you haven't found any spell?"

"Oh, I've found several only none where the cure is worth the side effects. I'll g-get there sooner or later." Her cheery tone dropped away for the last words. "You're missing the p-point."

"Which is?"

"You're afraid you'll have to choose Alex or Evan. B-but if you're the one choosing"—I could almost see her shaking her head—"you may lose b-both."

36

The rescue effort launched the next night.

I didn't dress for war or combat. Put on nothing more special than my usual jeans, jacket, and sneakers. Under the jacket, I wore the same worn, green Arden T-shirt I'd worn when I turned sorcerer—and before that, on the long-ago day when I'd first met Alex. Pulled back my hair in a pony tail, tucking straggling strands behind my ears. Settled my glasses firmly on my nose.

A calm sky met my eyes when I stood at the window. A few breezes, but only enough to kick up the occasional leaf to flutter along the ground. The sky tinged toward dark, but several of the gathering crew held flashlights at the ready—in addition to smart phones.

Quite a crowd there below. Several familiar figures, from Sebastian in a blue polo shirt and slacks to Gloria and Ruth in matching knee-length tunics and leggings to Emilio in a T-shirt and ripped jeans.

Marta and Lina, with a couple of other students whose names and faces were little more than a blur to me this night.

Jules with Leonie's smaller form jumping up and down beside him.

And an older couple I didn't recognize, but presumed were Emilio's parents who'd flown in specifically to help.

We'd chosen Wednesday night to make our move because it was time Alex would've spent as himself if the spell weren't unbalanced. According to Sebastian—and Helen—Alex usually had Wednesday afternoon to Thursday noon, little though I'd ever noticed.

I didn't understand all of the parts of the spell they planned on casting, another thing to blame on my neophyte status. Nevertheless, they all seemed to think we had a good chance. Even Helen, who'd gone on ahead to carry out her part of the plan.

Ruth waved at me to come down and join them.

As I turned around, knees knocking just a bit, my phone buzzed.

<<I'll be thinking of you.>> Bea texted.

<<Wish me luck.>>

<<Always.>>

If only I were half so confident. Gritting my teeth, I walked down the stairs. Wrinkled my nose against the stench of stale weed from someone's old joint. Then summoned up determination. Grit. Courage.

When I hit the door to the outside, though, my reflection just gazed back at me with a shell-shocked look. Not a good sign.

Outside, Emilio made introductions all around. His mother's voice sounded exactly the same as when her spell had warned Alex not to get too active kissing me way back when.

"So you're the person Alex let himself get close to." She tilted her head to the side and gave a short, sharp nod. The glint in her eye suggested the spell might've fed some info back to her as well as made us jump apart at that moment. Pity, in a way, it hadn't kept us further apart.

"The most complicated part is getting hold of Alex when most of us can't see, hear, or feel him—and doing it without *her* at hand." Sebastian slapped his hands against his legs, body twitching. "Helen has headed over to Regina's, to distract her."

We—read I—were to somehow lure Evan out and off her property onto the path. Me because I was the only one guaranteed to be able to see Alex even when no one else could. Helen might, or possibly Jules or Leonie, but I was the focal point of the spell.

The plan was to pull an adapted Tam Lin. The idea being to cast Regina as the fairy queen holding Alex against his will. I'd grab him—Evan, whom they considered the disguised, invisible Alex—and hold onto him no matter what happened and what he might transform into.

"Regina will probably turn him into a swan, at least, if not more things, trying to get him away, but if you hold on . . ." Sebastian frowned at me, eyes dark and desperate for hope.

All I had to do was hold on, as the others poured strength into me.

And win Alex back.

I understood that much. Then Emilio took a turn, explaining additional details about anchors and ways to protect me from injury should Regina turn Evan into fire or a ravening beast or some such. They were really going to town with the Alex/Tam Lin and Regina/fairy queen theme.

My concern was what this would do for Evan and the swan. Though I had hidden allies.

Helen and Gloria, with Jules and Leonie's assistance, planned to braid an additional spell into the mix to split Evan and Alex in two, possibly swan to make three. They weren't sure the spell could stretch to that, though, because at that point the only way for both to live would be to make the decision for them.

All very well and good, but I had a bad feeling. My stomach pained me from whatever residual spell connected me to Alex, or Bea's warning, or because I hadn't slept well any night since Alex turned to Evan.

If we got this wrong, maybe Evan would turn into the swan and the swan fly away, never to return.

I became the advance guard, leading the way. The rest followed. Far enough behind that they wouldn't be connected to me, which meant I couldn't see or hear them even though I knew they were there.

This last time, I retraced the same path I'd traversed before. The first time running away. Then chasing Evan. Walking with him as escort. Going to lesson with Regina. So many times.

Cooler now. Wind picking up a bit, though the sky remained mostly clear as it darkened. The smells of autumn predominated: moldering leaves, smoke in the distance. Leaves and twigs crunched under my feet.

No sound from behind, not a crunch or stray word or any flash of color or flesh—though I only turned back twice to look. One of the sorcerers following must have worked a spell to keep them concealed to all senses.

And all the while, I wondered how we'd find Evan. Get him out, so I could grab hold.

In the end, that proved the simplest thing of all.

$\maltese$ 37 $\maltese$

Evan stood in the middle of the path, legs apart and hands clasped behind his back. Dressed, at least partially: jeans and a thin, white T-shirt but with bare feet. The gate lay open behind him. He faced the lake, staring out at the water and reflected moonlight.

I didn't hide my approach. Couldn't, for there were too many fallen leaves on the path to completely avoid. Anyone with ears to hear would recognize the approaching crunches.

"What do you want this time?" He glanced my way, then turned back to the lake.

"What do *you* want?" I asked from a few feet away.

"I asked you first." He fixed his gaze on the water, though his hands shook.

"You won't like the answer." Step by step, I drew closer. My breath caught in my lungs, the air seeming abruptly colder. I locked my own fingers together, in front, to keep from trembling.

"So what else is new."Evan lifted an eyebrow and grimaced. "Who're you really here to talk to, anyway?"

"Why wouldn't I want to talk to you?" Two more steps. "You're in control, now. Don't you like it?"

"Control isn't how I'd describe it."

"Then how do you?" Another step. The warmth radiating from his body warmed even my chilly fingers.

"Fewer restrictions." He looked down, neck curving and nape exposed. "But not none. I'm earth-bound. I can fly, but still have to come back whether or not I want to."

I slid an arm around his shoulder. He didn't resist, even leaned into me. "I'm sorry."

"Why? It's not your fault." This time, when he met my eyes his face was so close I could have kissed him.

"No, but this is." I grabbed hold. Wrapped my other arm around his waist. Both hands twisted, fingers taking hold of flesh as well as cloth.

He startled, but not much. Wasn't wary yet, though the movement made him slip a little within my embrace. I slid my hand down from his shoulder so I could entwine my fingers in an oval around him. Evan's body was warm against mine—similar to Alex's, but not completely familiar. Longer, a bit narrower at the waist, and just as well since that's what I ended up holding onto.

My whole body ached, belly but also arms and legs, torso and head. As though little electrical shocks flooded through me. And him.

Then, as the first installment of sorcerers materialized on the path behind me—Sebastian, Emilio, and Emilio's parents —crackles filled the air.

Sparks manifested, in varying shades of white and blue, as Ruth and other friends followed.

Then flecks of red and green surrounded Evan and myself, along with sizzling sounds as though we'd been tossed from a frying pan into the fire, as Gloria, Jules, and Leonie appeared.

Evan no longer looked at me. His gaze was directed

beyond, at Sebastian. When he spoke, however, I was probably the only one to hear his words above the snaps, crackles, and sizzles. "Stuff me back inside, will you?"

"We want to help, let you separate and live." I squeezed as he began to writhe within my grasp. "All three of you."

"Three?"

A high, piercing scream overrode anything else he might say. With a shimmering blaze of light, Regina raced down the yard. Helen followed, but far behind.

The air shimmered with Regina's fury, making my eyes water. Steam covered my glasses. I couldn't risk losing hold long enough to wipe them clear. Relying on sound and other senses told me little more than that a great clash was underway. Primal elements come into direct contact and clashing.

Grunts.

Yells.

Moans.

Then the sudden shock of cold water surrounding my feet. Soaking through my shoes. Evan had made his move, either able to see or from long familiarity with the shoreline. Determined to make it into the lake, he was dragging me with him.

I held on. Couldn't do much more, although my glasses started to clear as we left the shore.

A faint moldering smell—algae or something—made me wince. Lily pads and weeds brushed my pant legs, their long stems twining around me until my unwitting forward motion ripped them from the mucky bottom. Even through the soles of my sneakers, the slurp of the rotting vegetation covering the lake sucked at me.

Water soaked my pants to the knees, then the thighs.

The cold made breathing deep, even thinking, difficult. Nevertheless, I dragged in a gulping breath and dug my feet into the muck to slow Evan's progress.

"Hold on!" A dozen voices shouted different variants on the words, but the meaning came through clear enough. This was what they'd expected.

I shifted my grip to wrap my hands around my wrists.

He wiggled within my grasp. Squirmed. Struggled. Doing a good job of it, too, slick as a greased eel, even with me wrapped around his waist. His hips didn't fit through or his shoulders and arms. Given time, he might break loose. I had my head down, and hunched my arms and shoulders to cling closer. Every bone in my body ached, even my teeth.

Evan stilled, lungs heaving. The occasional cough escaped him, and a faint groan.

My head rested against his hip, near the water. My glasses cleared, and our reflections shone true in the water around us.

Reflections.

The water made an almost perfect mirror, revealing a much better picture than reality. The lake became the kind of surface Alex had said showed truth.

Loops of sorcery filled the air around us in a myriad of colors. Lassos of some kind? All attached to the people on shore, and in the midst was me holding onto a mass of barbed wire or a whirlwind or one of those old games where dice sit in the center of a wire octagon, turning this way and that without ever leaving.

The whirling force had hands and wings . . . and faces peering out. Several of them.

First, the swan battling within the whirlwind and occasionally getting feathers in my mouth or along my skin.

Then Alex, writhing as he tried to grasp the loops of sorcery cast by his family and our friends.

And the strongest, the figure of Evan holding desperately onto the thick loop of magic linked to Regina, which knocked other lines out of the way.

Plus . . . someone else. Small, a little boy no more than three or four, hiding alternately behind Evan and Alex but peeping out at me.

A flash of Sebastian and Regina in his face, for he was the same little boy I'd seen in Helen's scrying bowl days or weeks ago. The child who crawled into the lake to escape his battling parents and became a swan, but never quite became himself again after.

A very thin, faint line connected him to Helen.

Oh. Of course.

He was why Alex and Evan never split. They'd protected him all along, as much or more than the swan. Evan as good as told me the problem with Helen's spell was that it assumed they'd need two bodies and didn't allow for more. Not three, but four. Because she'd unknowingly held onto the memory of the little boy all these years.

Cold crept up my body, into my chest and arms. My lungs seized, refusing anything more than shallow breaths. My arms shook with holding on, helped by my fingers turning cold as icicles so they locked against my wrists.

Everyone's yelling

"There's four of them." I tried to yell, but failed.

No one listened anyway, except Evan—and Alex—in the reflection.

Mustering a burst of sorcery, I filled a whisper with desperation to carry my words to the shore.

"There's four of them, not three! The boy they were before lives."

Helen heard. Froze, shock clear on her face despite the distance. Her sorcery or whatever spells she cast shifted. The thread connecting her to the little boy strengthened, but not much. Such a flimsy little thing, it remained at risk of being severed by one of the many spells soaring about.

Evan changed within my arms. Harder to hold. His T-shirt ripped at the hem. Jeans slipped away. Slick, wet human skin turned to firm feathers and down over wide, muscled wings.

That slow-forming beak had a sharp cast, when I dared glance up at it. I ducked my head right back down to watch our reflection. Pried my fingers loose, and wrapped my arms tight around the swan's neck. My hold wouldn't last for long. Once the shape change completed, all the swan had to do was duck out of my arms.

Before the shift was done, the swan began battling for freedom. To cast me off. I held on, teeth banging together as a wing tip clopped my jaw. Couldn't see or hear anything above the splashing water covering me and my glasses.

"Give up. Let go." Someone's words reached me, as though from a great distance. Helen or Gloria or Jules or whoever. I don't remember.

Give up?

No, no way, I'd promised not to. Alex deserved it, and so did Evan. The boy they both once were. Even the swan, formed of desire to escape—but only so far as a better family.

But let go . . .

That I could do. And maybe more.

Let go of all of them.

Really let go. Strip away everything else with me.

After all, everyone else made decisions for them all along. Not listening. Not letting them decide. At least, not enough.

I stripped every vestige of Helen's spell off in the process, hoping that in some way freed them from their parents' unwitting spells as well.

Abandoned any expectations this would help Alex or Evan or the boy.

Accepted I might never see them again, or only as a swan.

Really let go.

Let them go.

The swan trembled in my arms, thrashing without ever bringing its beak into play.

Power. Belief. Intent. Desire.

I opened my arms and fell back into the water. Swallowed some as I went under, and threw it right back up as I fought to the surface.

Symbol. All the ingredients for sorcery.

The swan glowed as strong as a full moon.

Flicked its wings as shrieks rang out from land for me to grab it again. The threat alone was enough to set it in motion. Settling its wings against its side, powerful legs propelled it out toward the center of the lake.

On shore, only two remained standing. Rebounding sorcery had blasted them all off their feet. Regina and Sebastian held themselves up by sheer will and hands wrapped around the rods of the fence.

I slogged my way out of the lake. Gloria and Jules helped me clamber over wet rocks and dry off. Probably using the same spell Alex had, way back when.

Gritting my teeth against parents shrieking for their sons to return, I wobbled on my feet. Fought back tears.

Turned around in time to watch the swan power across water. Build up speed. Wings spread wide, flapping as it began to lift from the surface.

At least they made the choice this time.

Then, as the swan cleared the lakeshore, it faltered. Wings twisted, slanting in the air. An unearthly shriek rang out, then the white form vanished and a loud thump resounded. The impact sent ripples through the ground as a mini-quake, knocking us all off our feet.

Scrambling up, scraping hands against rocks, I pelted down the path to the bushes around the corner. Had the lead, but soon others' breath heated my neck.

Only to stop and kneel next to a brace of soft-leaved

bushes bearing a dazed human figure. A man shorter than Evan, taller than Alex. Hair of deep brown, not black, and matching eyes. A face melding the features of Alex and Evan.

I reached for him, and his fingers twined with mine.

By his choice.

Or, rather, theirs.

❦ 38 ❦

There will be a happy ending, though not necessarily the one you're expecting.

Because it's not happy ever after for us, at least not the way the books and movies and television shows portray with the fade out at the end. We're not at the end, though we're happy enough, and together. Might make it together all the way to the end of after, at least we plan to. There are always bumps and bruises along the way.

His legal name is Alan now. That's what's on all his official documentation and what people call him most of the time. Evan grumbles about the name, but even he admits that Alan is preferable to Evex or something completely unrelated. Alex rarely mentions the matter.

I use all three names. They all survive, in one body with one head, brain, and heart. Alan dominates these days, likely making up for the years he could only watch. But Alex and Evan are both alive and well, and regularly make appearances. Others may not notice, but I recognize the signs as do those for whom it matters.

Family reunions are never easy. Regina and Sebastian

might have done better if Alex and Evan had split, for then they could go their merry ways without truly acknowledging the damage left behind. We don't have them over together very often, but there are certain occasions on which they are requested to be polite or leave, and so far they've always chosen politeness. As have their respective sides of the family and Helen and most of our friends.

The same is not true of so many other sorcerers. Too many intrude where they are not wanted. Ask impolite questions. Demand answers. Decline to believe those answers we are willing to give, and refuse to go away.

That's why I've written this story in the first place.

This book.

This spell.

For all the sorcerers who refuse to take no for an answer and rival paparazzi for persistence and annoyance.

You cannot unread what is contained here. This is all you'll ever know.

Remember, words are symbols.

From here on, any sorcerer—anyone—who is so much as aware of the existence of this book cannot ask any individual mentioned in it so much as a single question about the events . . . unless said individual gives explicit and knowing consent to be asked. Even then, that permission extends only to them and no one else.

In short, leave us alone. If we want to share information, that's up to us. You cannot pester us anymore. That's our happy ever after.

And so, finally, we may walk out in the evening without being accosted or forced to go to great lengths to avoid invasion of our privacy. Perhaps we will mosey along the lake shore, not the one near Arden, but where we live nowadays. Alan and Alex and Evan—whoever controls their shared body at that time—may strip, if they desire, and send their clothes back home to wait. I do not need to, for we take different routes to the same goal.

If you pass by the lake, you will not see us. Only two swans swimming in the water—or flying in the sky. Free to be whomever and whatever we choose.

THE END.

ORDINARY SORCERY

Adventure runs in the family when Viola's sister Bea's gets a job in *The Museum of All Things Lost and Forgotten*

Bea detests snap decisions. Better to take time, examine options, and make informed choices. Order above chaos, always: in life and magic.

Her new job in a magical museum suits her to a T. Lead tours through the public displays? Easy peasy. Run mapping sweeps to keep abreast of the ever-changing back rooms? The best kind of adventure.

Until she stumbles across an unattended child lost in a long-forgotten forest. Restoring the child to her parent begins an adventure requiring Bea move fast— or risk catastrophe.

Enter the spellbinding and richly imaginative world of *The Museum of All Things Lost & Forgotten*.

Read on for a taste . . .
A text message from the future arrived on my phone around noon.

My sneakers' rubber soles squeaked against the slick, polychrome marble floor, mostly muffling the arrival ding. The elaborately decorated stairway before me used to be a bit slick, but otherwise a piece of cake. No more. A layer of dust blurred the intricate figures inlaid in the marble—circles, diamonds, and suns. More flecks drifted in the air, collecting on my uniform shirt and shorts and graying the dark green. The grime coated my tongue, tasting disgusting and making me sneeze.

Rather than pulling my phone out, I grabbed the gilded wood railing tight to keep from slipping and falling. Although steady, no guarantee it would support my weight. Better to use it for balance. I inched forward. Broke into a sweat when my feet slid to the side. My hair stuck to the sides of my head.

Bell-shaped earrings pealed with every shallow breath— not a good sign. The other times I'd climbed or descended the stairway, water chimed in the fountain at the very center, but it had ceased to flow. The vaulted glass ceiling overhead clouded over, filling the hall with a gray gloom.

Everything had an aura of dullness and dilapidation, from the floor to the frescoes and intricate trompe l'oeil tapestries lining the walls of the upper level, to the bust of Louis XIV of France positioned directly above the fountain. Even the gilt bronze dolphins supporting the red marble fountain basin seemed to spit dust.

The last time I'd passed this way, the chamber gleamed with newness and the fragrant scent of cleaning oils rubbed into the marble to make it gleam. What a difference a week made!

The railing creaked and swayed. I loosened my hold and scooted until I reached the flight of steps. Step by step I descended to the fountain's landing. Instead of taking the wide array of steps leading to the ground floor and the vestibule beyond, I ascended the matching flight up the far side.

The Grand Escalier of Versailles, also known as the Ambassador's Staircase, had existed for less than a hundred years, between the Sun King and his successor, Louis XV. It manifested as part of the D.C.-based Museum of All Things Lost and Forgotten a month or so ago, and based on its increasing decrepitude wouldn't last much longer before it returned to storage in the virtual vaults or wherever lost and forgotten places and things went when they weren't readily accessible from the museum. They shuffled around, some staying in one place for a long time and others appearing then disappearing.

Some other chamber would manifest here instead. Perhaps the replacement would be less dangerous.

I questioned my decision to take the year-long internship at least once a week, sometimes as often as three. Then I'd turn a corner and find a treasure long lost to war or modernity.

Chichen-Itza when new-built.

Nebuchadnezzar II and Amytis's Hanging Gardens in full flower.

The Buddhas of Bamiyan.

Employees regularly witnessed such sights. Few other people saw them. Then again, most visitors came in through the front doors of the museum and never made it past the superficial display rooms, cafe, or shop.

I'd shared a photo of the staircase with my sisters and friends when it first showed up, fresh and beautiful.

The sorcerers among them believed it a magical shadow of the real thing.

The mundanes asked about the museum's finances and how it survived since it kept making expensive replicas of famous lost places. When I replied that the museum ran on lost and forgotten monies, they laughed and assumed I jested.

Not true, but not worth convincing them otherwise either.

Before going through the wide door into another hall, I sneezed on a fresh mouthful of dust. Then pulled out my phone and turned to take a photo of the decaying version.

The newest text flashed onto the screen—listed as being sent by Beatrice Portia Williams aka Bea aka me with a send-date one week into the future. The text message came from me—or rather, I'd send it to myself in about a week.

Messages from the future constituted the magical equivalent of mundane fortune tellers and fortune cookies. The Webmasters of Fate offered the service for people requesting advice from a future self. The notes arrived without anything to indicate whether the advice came from a future self who wanted the future she lived in to become real or hated it and sought to ward it off.

At least this was simple and direct.

<<Run>>

Not on this slippery floor I wasn't.

Unlocking my phone, I deleted the message. Turned off notifications for texts. Then snapped a photo of the stairway in all its faded glory.

The big ornate doors stuck in place. Bits of gold leaf and enamel flaked off as I pushed the handle. Tucking the phone back in my pocket, I threw myself into the task.

The doors swung open, hinges creaking as they rotated.

I hustled through before the doors shut, glancing ahead only to check whether the surface on the other side required stepping up or down.

And wound up under a full moon. Fallen leaves and twigs crunched beneath my shoes. Tall trees soared to either side, the source of a fresh, crisp scent. Branches and full foliage arched and obliterated the sky except for small, scattered patches of midnight blue and the stark white of the moon.

A forest?

Wavering, I leaned against the nearest tree. My fingers dug into scaly bark and thick branches covered in long needles. The moon turned the world into harsh contrasts of shadow and light.

Lost again! Not my fault this time.

Everything in the museum moved but followed certain rules. One of the most reliable specified all interior doors— i.e. any door that, back when it existed in the outside world aka mundane reality, had not opened to the outside—would only open onto interior spaces. The same wasn't true of exterior doors. They opened anywhere.

If I'd left the Grande Escalier by the doors on the lower level, where ambassadors once entered, I might wind up anywhere.

But I'd stayed on the upper floor. The door *should* have led to another inside space or one of the halls in the very real building connecting the museum to the mundane world.

My phone still registered eastern daylight time, showing early afternoon despite the dark night surrounding me. Perhaps I'd leapt across far distances and arrived in a land-scape tied to one of the museum's other outposts—Beijing or Sydney.

Or someone had gone awry and I unknowingly retraced their steps.

Goose bumps covered my forearms no matter how I rubbed them with my cooling hands. A chill wind blew through the branches, carrying a hint of snow mixed with the stench of fresh droppings.

A pile of dark scat lay only inches away. Damp mud preserved a couple of paw prints. Bits of bone protruded from the droppings. It probably wasn't human bone.

Opening the mapping app on my phone, I noted the deteriorating condition of the Grande Escalier and documented the shift from hall to forest, and day to night.

Anyone else who passed this way would be forewarned—as long as they checked the map first. We had to keep sweeping through the halls, chambers, and natural environments closest to the museum proper because they changed on an irregular and unpredictable schedule.

The doors I'd passed through vanished. No matter. One of the highly recommended suggestions—in other words an unofficial rule—involved never retracing one's steps. Circling back worked, as long as one took a different way and always moved forward or sideways.

I just had to figure out a convenient exit point.

Then a loud sniff broke the silence.

No sign of any creature or being, but a sob followed the sniff.

"Hello? Is anyone there?" I stepped over the scat.

"Papa?" A child's voice rang out, high-pitched with an edge of hysteria. "Papa!"

Hoofing over damp ground, I nearly slipped more than once on muddy spots covered with damp leaves. Stray branches brushed my shorts, leaving bits of bracken behind. A couple minutes run, then I stumbled to a halt.

A *young* child stood in the clearing—four or five years old at best. They wore dark sneakers with red flashing lights around the heels, knee-length light-colored shorts, and a short-sleeve shirt. Both shirt and shorts had mud stains, as did one of the child's hands. Their fine black hair was short, no longer than the tips of their ears. A bracelet of big, plastic beads encircled one wrist in bright primary colors against light-brown skin. Tears trickled down round cheeks.

No parents or other adults anywhere. Trees in view

aplenty, but no humans. Not even shoe marks or footprints in the mud or on the fallen leaves.

Nimur, the spirit of memory to whom everything in the museum—the House of Memory—belonged, had a hard and fast rule about no unattended minors allowed whether they came through one of the front doors or the back ways. If they said it once they said it a hundred thousand times: *"Children do not belong among the Lost and Forgotten."*

So much worse than the Grande Escalier leading to a forest.

Find out what happens next in The Museum of All Things Lost and Forgotten!

৩৵৩

Be among the first to learn of new releases: sign-up for her newsletter at https://BookHip.com/PCSWMCK. Book recommendations, updates on stories, and snippets from works-in-progress—plus a free Dancing Princesses story for signing up!

ABOUT THE AUTHOR

Alea Henle writes non-fiction by day and fiction by night. Contemporary and historical fantasy, fantasy romance—and more! Check out her website www.aleahenle.com.